THE CAT VANISHES

ALSO BY LOUISE CARSON

NOVELS

In Which: Book One of The Chronicles of Deasil Widdy

The Cat Among Us

Executor

NOVELLAS

Mermaid Road

POETRY

A Clearing

Rope: A Tale Told in Prose and Verse

THE CAT VANISHES

A MURDER AT THE MAPLES MYSTERY

LOUISE CARSON

DOUG WHITEWAY, EDITOR

Signature
EDITIONS

Cover design by Doowah Design.
Cover icons courtesy of Noun Project.

This book was printed on Ancient Forest Friendly paper.
Printed and bound in Canada by Marquis Book Printing Inc.

We acknowledge the support of the Canada Council for the Arts and the Manitoba Arts Council for our publishing program.

Library and Archives Canada Cataloguing in Publication

Carson, Louise, 1957-, author
    The cat vanishes / Louise Carson.

Issued in print and electronic formats.
ISBN 978-1-77324-028-2 (softcover). — ISBN 978-1-77324-029-9 (EPUB)

    I. Title.

PS8605.A7775C39 2018   C813'.6   C2018-905154-X
                                                C2018-905155-8

Signature Editions
P.O. Box 206, RPO Corydon, Winnipeg, Manitoba, R3M 3S7
www.signature-editions.com

For Gray and Pumpkin,
who didn't make it

CONTENTS

*D*aylight entered the basement from one cobwebbed window where a few empty pots, some hand tools and a bag of soil on a dirty bench indicated a gardener had once been, and maybe still was, in residence, but that any gardening was for the time being in abeyance.

The only other light that broke the gloom came through cracks in the stone foundation where ancient mortar had crumbled and fallen away; where, doubtless in summer, spiders and beetles, earwigs and ants crept through.

Now that insect life was, like the garden, temporarily stilled, the cracks admitted only thin slivers of white light and cold drafts.

The ancient furnace crashed on. As it heated, warm air began to blow out of vents all over the house.

Water ran down some of the basement walls, oozed up through cracks in the floor, puddled. In one corner, a sump pump wheezed on, pumped half-heartedly for a few seconds before switching itself off.

Old furniture, covered in fine green mould, waited for someone to rescue it. A pile of lumber against a wall bloomed with mushrooms. A few crates of wine rested on a metal rack near the foot of the stairs.

Daddy longlegs, year-round residents, spun extravagant filmy creations, undisturbed. And, in one damp recess, something moved.

PART 1

OLD BONES

1

Wasn't Christmas supposed to be all feasting and merrymaking? Getting together with friends and family? Especially the latter? Gerry Coneybear shivered, thinking of her fractured family: her parents dead for years; Aunt Maggie murdered last spring; Uncle Geoff a recent suicide; Cousin Margaret committed to a mental hospital after her "breakdown"; and the rest of the family not speaking to Gerry.

Well, that wasn't entirely true. Sometimes Cousin Andrew, who lived across the street, waved as he got into or out of his car. He was busy closing down the furniture business he'd shared with his father, Geoff. There had been a Petherbridge's furniture store in Lovering for at least three generations that Gerry knew of. And Andrew had his newly widowed mother, Gerry's Aunt Mary, to worry about. Her house was up for sale, as she'd never be able to maintain it — financially or practically — without Uncle Geoff.

The only other member of Gerry's family who was giving her any attention was Prudence Crick, her second cousin, still coming to clean The Maples three times a week. Not that Gerry was a messy person. Well, she was, a bit, in her bedroom and maybe in the bathroom. No, Prudence came so frequently because of the cats.

How many were there now? There had been the original twenty. Then Stupid — er, Graymalkin, as Gerry's neighbour Mr. Parminter had renamed him — had migrated next door to live with Mr. Parminter, and Marigold, the leader of the pride, had died. So, eighteen. But then Mother, a kindly feline, who couldn't resist a sad story, brought home five black and white kittens, their eyes barely open, a few weeks ago. So, twenty-three.

Gerry looked down at her feet, where the large banana box she'd gotten from the grocery store housed the kittens, all fast asleep against Mother's vast marmalade-and-cream striped side. Gerry could hear Mother's purr: steady, contented. How old did kittens have to be before you could give them away? She'd enjoyed feeding the little things warm milk from an eyedropper, but was thankful they'd graduated to tinned cat food. No more getting up twice in the night to top them up.

She shivered again in the drafty room, this time from cold. Time to get more wood. She reminded herself that when she sold the painting by Paul-Émile Borduas that had been hanging innocuously on a wall of her Aunt Maggie's house, she'd be able to afford all the insulation she needed.

She put her empty coffee cup on the mantelpiece above the fireplace and walked from the living room into the large formal dining room where a few cats dozed on towel-covered chairs, then through the foyer and turned left, towards the back of the house. She yanked on the door that led to the screened-in porch. The door tended to stick where snow blew into the frame, melted by day, then froze at night. She stepped out onto the porch.

A delightful, vine-covered paradise in the other three seasons, in winter the porch had little to recommend it. Snow sifted through the screens and made small windswept drifts across the grey-painted wooden floor. Though it was morning, the sky was overcast. More snow, Gerry thought glumly, as she reached down for an armload of wood.

Six trips later and she'd finished transporting the pile of wood from the porch. She made up the fire, carefully placed the screen in front of it, and gently pulled the banana box a little further away from the hearth. Such was Mother's trust in Gerry that she barely opened her eyes.

When Gerry went into the kitchen, some of the cats that had been keeping her and Mother company by the fire followed, crowding around the shallow tub of kibble under the room's tiny table.

Gerry looked at the top of the fridge, where she still half-expected to see Marigold majestically eating her chopped chicken, far above the plebeian throng. A lump came into her throat. Well, the little cat had been sixteen. She'd had a good life, even if she was…a bit intense.

Putting her coat on over her robe and pajamas, Gerry went out into the kitchen porch for her boots. Only Bob, of all the cats, followed her outside.

He walked on the cleared surface of the driveway, then lurked under Gerry's little red car as she removed the padlock from the shed and slid the massive door aside.

Thin grey light tried to enter through two small windows at either side of the long building. Gerry switched on the lights, bare bulbs in the ceiling. "Better than nothing," she mumbled, stooping for wood.

A large rectangular piece of plywood was hidden behind the pile. Gerry's family tree was painted on it and only the original couple's names were visible at the moment, at the top of the tree: John Coneybear and Sybil Muxworthy, Gerry's great-great-grandfather and -mother. "A lot of good you guys did me," she muttered. "Gave me a family only so I could piss them all off."

Bob had noiselessly entered and sprung up onto the woodpile. Six cords, stacked and ready. She'd already used up half of one of the cords and it was only December.

Bob's fur bristled. As he was a shorthaired tuxedo cat, he looked pretty funny; only the fur along his spine and tail actually increasing in volume. "Oh, Bob, do you fluff up like that to keep warm?" A piece of wood fell off the row farthest from Gerry.

"I guess I'll get that piece in spring, eh?" But she spoke to the air, for Bob had dashed out of the shed.

She took her armload of wood and walked along the shovelled path behind the house. It led to the screened porch, inside which a blue tarp had been laid that autumn, so dropping logs wouldn't chip the paint.

That had been Prudence's suggestion. She knew all the ins and outs of the centuries-old house Gerry had inherited less than a year ago. Sure, Gerry had visited the house and her Aunt Maggie when she was a child, but that hadn't prepared her to own and maintain it. She sighed. My, she felt blue.

After traipsing back and forth about twenty times, Gerry made sure Bob wasn't in either the shed or the back porch and closed the doors. Bob was bounding like the Arctic fox hunting mice Gerry had seen on a recent TV nature show. Straight up in the air, then nose and front paws buried in snow. "Bob, are you coming in? Bob?" Gerry made the classic cat-calling sucking noise with her lips. No response. "Fine! I'll see you later."

She entered the side porch, dropping her boots, mitts, hat and coat there, and went to make another coffee in the kitchen. "Now, where's my mug?" She wandered back in front of the warmth of the fire. She clutched her head with both hands. "Agh! What's happening? I'm only twenty-five and I'm wandering around in my robe and slippers looking for things! Right!" She decided against the coffee, ran upstairs, washed and dressed.

Coming back downstairs, she ducked into the toilet where six cat boxes were lined up. Tuesday wasn't one of Prudence's days. Gerry removed the night's evidence and flung the plastic bag out onto the back porch. It could go into the garbage later. She had to get out of the house!

She grabbed her keys and wallet and started her car. Not yet cold enough that it had to be plugged in at night; that would be in January and February, she'd been told. As the defroster blasted cold air onto the front and rear windshields, she thought longingly of warm beaches, tropical breezes, water the perfect temperature. She got out and scraped ice off the windows. She was in a hurry. But where could she go?

She decided on Lovering — downtown Lovering. Technically, she lived in Lovering, but along a quiet residential road that followed the contour of the Ottawa River as it wended its way from somewhere in Ontario down to the St. Lawrence River.

Population 5,000, Lovering consisted of all the people that lived either side of the river road, or on a few side roads that led to tentative developments in erstwhile farmland, or in Lovering proper, which boasted some restaurants and cafés, lots of gift and antique shops, a convenience and a grocery store. Oh, and a library and five churches.

She passed St. Anne's Church and its little graveyard on her way to the village. Too many of us buried there, she thought gloomily. As she accelerated up a slight hill and around the curve, her tires slid alarmingly.

She decreased speed for the next curve, and the next. The houses of Lovering, many built close to the road, looked charming edged with snow and decorated for Christmas. Gerry's artist's eye took over and her mood had somewhat improved by the time she arrived at her destination: the Two Sisters' Teahouse. The coffee was excellent and a bottomless cup. She parked in front and sighed. If only she had a friend to meet with. Never mind. The teahouse had hired a window artist to spray white stars and snowflakes on its front windows. I suppose they use stencils, thought Gerry.

She took a small sketchpad and some pencils out of the glove compartment. She'd doodle some ideas for her cartoon strip — *Mug the Bug* — which ran in several newspapers and provided her with a major portion of her income.

"Coffee, please, Jane," she requested of one of the sisters who owned the teahouse. "And—" She looked hungrily at the contents inside the display case. "Is that cheesecake?"

"Lemon," said Jane, a short, pleasant-looking woman with cropped brown hair and glasses. "Made it last night."

Gerry nodded. "Mm." She walked to the shelves and chose a cup and saucer — white bone china with yellow roses — and left it near the coffee station. That was the deal at the Two Sisters': you had to choose your own cup.

Gerry sat at a table facing the front windows. She gazed blankly at the few flakes falling from a cheerless sky. Jane brought the coffee and cheesecake and Gerry absently ate her breakfast.

Winter had never affected her this way when she'd lived in Toronto. She'd had her father to be with for Christmas Day and any number of friends to hang out with over the holidays. After her father died, she'd had a few Christmases where she felt a bit depressed, but again, friends had been there to buoy her up.

Of course, her father had died of natural causes, not been murdered in his bed at home as had been Aunt Maggie. And Uncle Geoff had shot himself in the woods. And Margaret had — well, lost it. It was all very sad.

That must be it, Gerry mused. Geoff's funeral made everyone forget about Andrew's birthday, which should have been an excuse for a party, and now all of Gerry's friends were away for the holidays and—

"You all ready for Christmas?" Jane's cheery voice broke into Gerry's mood. "One day to go!"

"Huh? Oh. Yeah. You?" As Jane rattled on about having so much baking left to do and cleaning the house at the last minute before the hordes of relations descended on her for the feast, Gerry thought of the little pile of gifts hidden in her own cupboard.

One for Prudence, of course, as well as some cash stuffed in a card. One for Andrew. One for Doug, a distant cousin on her Gramma Ellie's side and Margaret's ex-husband. One for one of their sons — the friendly one, David. Gerry was no hypocrite. Doug and Margaret's eldest sons — James and Geoff Junior — had either ignored or been rude to Gerry since she'd inherited Aunt Maggie's house. She'd be damned if she'd give *them* gifts.

Neither was there anything for Aunt Mary, Gerry's father's last sister remaining alive. Gerry believed Mary was most of the reason why Margaret had become what she was. There was no love lost on either side.

As she'd predicted, it had begun snowing. She looked down at her empty plate in surprise. Had she even tasted the cheesecake?

Jane refilled her cup. "Delicious," Gerry complimented her as she cleared the plate. Jane smiled and Gerry began doodling.

Her cartoon creation *Mug* was an infinitesimally small speck on the page. He was having his own struggles with winter. Gerry had him on an adventure in the far north, dealing with a dog team, polar bears, ice floes. It felt a bit flat to her and she gave up, resting her chin in her palm

Of all her local friends, and they weren't many — after all, she'd only lived in the area for seven months — only Prudence had stayed in Lovering for Christmas.

Cece Muxworthy, Gerry's lawyer, had surprised his wife Bea with a trip to Jamaica. When they left the week before, Gerry had given them their presents: a bottle of fine red wine and a miniature painting of one of Bea's orchids. Bea had given Gerry a container of frozen stew and a cream scarf with matching hat and gloves, and the promise of "something fabulous" from Jamaica.

Gerry's aged neighbour, Mr. Parminter, had been picked up by a relative and, complete with Graymalkin in a cat basket, had been driven off to spend Christmas in Montreal.

In a way, Gerry envied him more than Bea and Cece. To be in a big city, all lights and music for the holidays; to be part of the crowd busily shopping, dining. To visit museums and galleries. To be able to buzz out with friends, have a few drinks, and then buzz home by cab, without worrying about the weather and the condition of the roads.

But perhaps the defection of her friend Cathy Stribling, owner of Fieldcrest, the local B&B (and a most excellent chef), with her basset blend Prince Charles, to Arizona of all places! hit Gerry the hardest. It turned out Cathy had a sister there. And bookings at the B&B had been steadily dropping as fall turned to winter. So Cathy gave Charles a tranquilizer, popped him into a crate, and hopped on a plane, taking a tranquilizer herself. "Because, my dear, I worry so much about Charles down in the baggage compartment: if he's cold or hungry or has to pee. I just go off to sleep and when I wake up we're there."

With Fieldcrest empty and Cathy away, there would be no delicious shared suppers, no snoring Prince Charles flumped by the fire, no cozy chats about Lovering and its inhabitants, past and present. Gerry sighed and drank her coffee. She really ought to —

The bell over the entrance tinkled as someone pushed on the door. Gerry looked up and inwardly cringed. Actually, she wasn't sure she hadn't outwardly cringed as well. Of all the people —

Aunt Mary, looking cool and self-possessed, hesitated, then ignored Gerry and proceeded to the counter. She pointed at a few items, which Jane popped into a box. Gerry relaxed — a little — and unabashedly eavesdropped. Well, it was impossible not to.

"Just a very quiet Christmas, of course," Mary was saying to a sympathetic-looking Jane, "but one has to do something for the boys and Andrew." Jane said a few words in a low voice. "What? Oh. Yes. It's for sale. But I'm told that houses rarely move in the winter, so I might be there till spring. Or summer." She paid but didn't leave, put out a hand, as if to steady herself on the counter.

"Well, I wish you a very Merry Christmas, in spite of all your troubles," Jane said in a firm tone.

Why, thought Gerry, Aunt Mary's lonely! Of course! She's lost her husband and Margaret, not just her daughter, but probably her only friend. She has only herself to blame for that friendlessness, a little voice said inside Gerry's head. "Aunt Mary," she began, but Mary seemed not to hear, turned and left the store.

Jane and Gerry's eyes locked briefly in mutual embarrassment. Jane cleared her throat. "I was just saying to your — to Mrs. Petherbridge — that today is the last day we're open until after New Year's, so everything is half price. If you want a few things to tide you over."

Gerry's heart sank. Prudence had warned her of this; that businesses tended to shut down over the holidays, some even not reopening until spring! "Well, thank you, Jane, I believe I will take a few things. Can I have the scones? And will you sell me some of the delicious clotted cream that goes with them? I have jam at home."

Jane made up a box for Gerry, similar to the one Aunt Mary had left with. Lonely women, Gerry thought drearily as she left, but at least Mary has her son and her three grandsons. What have I got?

"Oh, my gosh!" she exclaimed, as she brushed snow off her car. "Bob's outside!"

2

When she got home, she scanned the yard for her missing cat. Then she checked the back porch. Then she looked up. "There you are," she said with relief. Bob, looking every inch the panther, yawned and stretched, high up in one of the backyard maples. "Come down!" Gerry urged.

He seemed to think that a good idea and, like a lumberjack, clasped the trunk of the tree and made his way, tail first, back to earth.

He let Gerry pick him up and she cuddled him as she walked back to the house.

He was her favourite, she had to admit it. How could he not be? Playful, yet careful to sheathe his claws with her, full of *joie de vivre* and energy. Friendly, yet his own man.

She opened the side porch door, kicked off her boots and dropped Bob inside. He made for the tub of kibble. It wasn't feeding time, but Gerry walked around the house checking who was where and making sure everyone was accounted for. She herself was still full of cheesecake. She returned to the kitchen and looked at the calendar on the fridge. Something…

"Oh, I've got to check Cathy's. Oh well. Got my coat on. May as well get it over with." She let herself out again and walked through the semi-circular driveway in front of her house. Prudence had been right to press her to hire the Hudsons to remove her snow. It was worth the money as they'd already had quite a few dramatic snowfalls.

"And three or four months to go," she grumbled. She straightened her shoulders as she began walking along the side of the road, facing traffic, as she'd been taught. "Forget about it. Enjoy it. No mosquitoes."

She passed Mr. Parminter's. She'd asked him if he wanted her to check his house but he'd declined. "You know," he'd said, "since I had the house reinsulated, I'm not afraid of pipes freezing anymore. I'll only be gone a few days. No, you needn't bother."

She was almost at Fieldcrest when she crossed the road. Cathy's driveway was so long, she *had* to pay someone to plow it. "I used to have a snow blower when I was younger," her friend had mentioned, "but it's too much for me now. It's so nice to hear the Hudsons removing the snow early in the morning and then turn over in bed and go back to sleep."

Cathy's house had not been recently insulated, a fact Gerry was fully aware of when she let herself in the wide front door. Brrr. She kept her coat on.

She knew Cathy left one upstairs bathroom faucet running a little all winter, with a notice affixed to the wall, begging her guests not to turn it off. But, inevitably, one did, and Cathy had to open the cupboard where she'd removed a section of drywall to insert a handheld hair dryer and let it blow. That faucet was one of the things Gerry had to check.

Her footsteps echoed off the creaky wooden floors in the empty house. She peered into the beautiful, if shabby, living room, then crossed the hall to check the dining room. She felt a bit funny, examining the house, but, after all, Cathy had asked her to keep an eye on the place, checking it every couple of days.

It sure wasn't homey with Cathy and Prince Charles away. No B&B guests. No happy humming and wonderful smells coming from the kitchen. No canine toenails clicking on the flooring as Charles wended his weary way from one comfy sleeping area to another.

The red kitchen clock ticked sedately; the fridge went on with a click and a whir. Gerry tested the back door. Locked.

She looked doubtfully at the door leading into the basement. Should she check down there as well? From below she heard the familiar bang as Cathy's furnace switched on. Her eyes came to rest on a red tin on the kitchen counter; a tiny yellow Post-it note, stuck onto its lid, read "Dear Gerry, Eat! Thanks. C." The tin was crammed with crescent-shaped cookies, dusted with icing sugar. Gerry bit into one. It snapped crisply. Bliss! It tasted of ground walnuts, or were they almonds?

She put the lid back on the tin and, retracing her steps, placed the tin on the bench by the front door. No fear of forgetting those!

Still crunching, she went upstairs to check the bedrooms. The steps complained audibly. Why hadn't she turned on the antique wall sconce halfway up the dark staircase at the downstairs switch? Because your hands were full of cookies, she admitted silently. She licked, then wiped her sugary fingers on her pants leg, and grasped the handrail.

When she got to the top, she flicked the upstairs switch. No response. Huh? Quickly she entered the nearest bedroom and pressed the wall switch.

The room flooded with soft light. She increased the dimmer to maximum, sighing with relief. Probably not a burnt-out fuse; just a bulb. No need to venture into Cathy's basement, try to investigate the house's electric box. It could wait for Cathy's return.

This was the room where Gerry had slept when she'd come for Aunt Maggie's funeral last spring. She walked to the window. The light outside was fading. Through frosted windows and leafless trees she saw the frozen lake, the dark pines on the other shore. She shivered, an all-over-her-body kind of shiver. She hurriedly peeked into the other bedrooms, ran down the stairs, picked up the red tin and bolted for home.

Now it was cat feeding time and Gerry coffee time. She made up the fire and subsided into her rocker with a cat on her lap and a good book.

The alarm switched on and Christmas music softly played. Gerry made a little sound in her throat and turned to face the window. She opened one reluctant eye. The blind was white cloth and though it preserved her privacy, it still admitted light; in this instance, the dull white light of another sunless day. It might even be snowing.

Bob, at the head of her bed, attacked her through the pale green coverlet. She sat up and they had a quick game of bite-the-hand-that's-poking-you before she swung her feet onto the bedside rug. Lightning, the emotionally and physically damaged calico cat with whom Gerry had a love-hate relationship, was long gone from her place at Gerry's feet.

The alarm had been set because it was a Prudence day and Gerry refused to let her walk to work along the narrow river road in winter. Prudence had never learned to drive, but now, thanks to the legacy left her from Aunt Maggie, she hoped to buy a car and Gerry had become her driving instructor. She quickly dressed, fed the cats, and started the car, before coming back inside to make an instant coffee in her travel mug. Lots of brown sugar, lots of cream. "Ahhh," she said after the first sip.

Bob bounded outside as she closed the door. She caught him and thrust him back inside. "No, Bob. Maybe later, when I can supervise you." She slowly backed the car out onto the road and, sipping her coffee, made the short trip to Prudence's, past Fieldcrest, past the tennis club, past the Parsley Inn (scene of many delicious lunches and suppers), up the big hill with the view across the lake, and down the other side, then turned right before the ferry, and rumbled over the railway tracks.

The little white cottage with its single gable and lacy wooden trim was modestly decorated for Christmas with pine branches and cones stuck into the window boxes either side of the porch and, on the door, a homemade wreath made of grapevine, to which Prudence had affixed little bells hung with red ribbon. The whole concoction tinkled charmingly when she opened her door.

"Let's get this show on the road," she said rather grimly into Gerry's open window. Gerry slid over into the passenger seat as Prudence got behind the wheel.

"Okay," said Gerry, "remember to slowly trade positions with your feet. Brake pedal down. Clutch pedal down. Brake up and a little gas while lifting the clutch foot —"

The car juddered once and stalled, and Gerry regretted once again purchasing the standard option for her little red Mini. Just because she'd learned on a manual shift, and enjoyed the zip of changing gears, didn't mean it was for everyone.

"Okay. That's okay. We'll just start her up again." This time they jerked halfway onto the street before they stalled. "The trick is to not fully take your foot off the clutch, Prudence. It's called riding the clutch and is supposed to be bad, but really, it's the only way to back up with any control. Just let them go around us."

As it was so close to the holiday, there were fewer cars than normal, but enough people still had work or errands that cars had backed up in both directions as Prudence advanced and retreated, trying to back out of her driveway. The other drivers glared as they inched around the little red car. "You know, of course," Prudence said sarcastically, "that I'll be looking for a car with a shift. Just. Like. This. One." With each word, she hit the shift's leather covered knob with her open hand.

"Now, now. I'll tell you what my father told me. 'If you learn how to drive shift you'll be able to drive anything — even a truck.'" Gerry sipped her coffee as Prudence managed to get the car into first. "Shift into second right away, Prudence. First is just for parking."

Prudence shifted into fourth and stalled.

"It's okay. It's okay." Gerry had seen a delivery van in her side view mirror, rolled down her window and waved him on. "Look at the stick. Memorize where the numbers are. Press down on the clutch and practise shifting the different positions. Okay. Turn her back on." She patted the dash. "Good little car, good little car. You're doing well too, Prudence."

They lurched to the foot of Prudence's street. "Oh, no, the stop sign!" said Prudence.

"It's all right if you stall, just stop. Stop!" Gerry put out a hand to steady herself as the car slid halfway into the intersection. "All righty then," a by-now-grim Gerry said between clenched teeth. "We're halfway there."

Once they got going again, they were at Gerry's in a couple of minutes. Both women climbed out rather shakily. Prudence took her purse and a plastic bag out of the back seat.

"What's in there?" Gerry asked. "We're not baking today, are we?"

"Why not? We always bake on Wednesdays."

They walked around to the side entrance, where Gerry fumbled with the key. "But the students aren't coming. Why do we —"

"Gerry, look." Gerry turned. Prudence was looking across the snowy backyard and across the lake — icy at its edges, still grey water at its heart — to the dense pine forest on the far shore.

It was snowing, thick wet clumps of flakes that stood out on their dark coats. No cars passed on the road and the stillness was intense. "It's Christmas Eve," Prudence whispered.

Gerry felt a twinge of delight. She unlocked the door. "Hello, cats!" More cheerfully than she had in weeks, she thought, let the day begin.

Gerry worked at the big table in the formal dining room, which had become her winter studio, the poorly insulated bamboo room she preferred having to be abandoned in late November. She was aware of Prudence passing to and fro as she washed cat dishes, cleaned litter boxes, put fresh towels on any upholstered surface, did laundry, vacuumed, and brought in wood for the fire.

Gerry tried to keep at least two weeks ahead of schedule with her comic strip. That way, if she needed a break or got sick, it wasn't the end of the world. She was only a week ahead, so was pleased to finish two instalments that morning. *Mug the Bug* managed to win the dogsled race, though he'd almost drowned when a talking snowflake landed on him and melted. Then he somehow found himself wrapped inside a Christmas gift that was lost for a week in the mail.

The strip was very silly, but kids and some adults enjoyed it enough that several North American newspapers ran it daily. It paid the bills, or almost paid them, Gerry reflected ruefully. The private art class she taught at the house was in temporary abeyance. The three older women students — Christine, Doris and Gladys — were all going south for different periods of time while the sole male member, Ben Lymbery, though he didn't migrate, confessed to fearing winter driving so much, he tended to go out as little as possible.

The other student, Judith Parsley, a young girl just out of school, was around, as she worked at the *Lovering Herald* with her father, Bill. Gerry wondered if she should advertise in late February, see if she couldn't get a few more students. Maybe enough for another class. "Thursdays. I'd teach them on Thursdays. No. Maybe Tuesdays."

"What?" asked a frazzled Prudence, dragging the vacuum cleaner through the room.

"Oh, nothing. I was just thinking of teaching two art classes a week. If I can get enough students. Come March."

"You should let the art department at the local college know you're around. Maybe you could be a substitute teacher or something."

"What a good idea, Prudence. Do you think they'd hire someone as young as me?"

"Twenty-five isn't that young, you know." Some of the cats had fled at the sight of the vacuum, but others were curiously sniffing around it, now it was silent, while one, young Ronald, barely out of kittenhood, attacked the hose. "No, Ronald! You'll puncture it!" Prudence cried.

"And then you'll just add some more duct tape, won't you?" said Gerry, removing the skinny white cat with the thin black moustache from the battle-worn hose.

"I suppose so," said Prudence grumpily.

"What's eating you? Come on. It's lunchtime, anyway. Tell me about it."

Prudence retrieved from the fridge the pickle and peanut butter sandwich she'd brought with her while Gerry made herself ham and cheese, and they sat at the living room table facing the lake, the freshly built-up fire at their backs.

"It's the driving school. It costs a fortune, you only get about one lesson per month and they keep showing these films during class where people with dash-cams scream just before they die. It's frightening and depressing. Sometimes I feel sick after watching them."

Gerry swallowed, thinking. "I guess they're trying to scare you into being careful. Are you the only — ah — mature person in the class?"

"The only one with grey hairs, you mean? Yes. The others are teenagers."

"That's *why*, Prudence. Those kids think they're immortal. You know you're not. Anyway, I didn't learn to drive at driving school either. My dad taught me. Like I'm teaching you."

"I'll never get it," Prudence said despairingly.

"Of course you will. You just have to practise. If you drive my car six times a week times four — that's twenty-four little lessons per month! I guarantee, you'll be a good driver by spring."

"If my nerves hold up," Prudence muttered.

"*Your* nerves!" Gerry teased.

Prudence laughed. "You're very patient. Thank you. Now, let's bake a cake."

In the kitchen she laid out the ingredients. "So, it's like the dark fruitcake we made in November but this is a white or golden fruitcake. It's nice to serve some of either on a plate."

"Who am I serving cake to again, Prudence? All my friends, the students — everybody's away."

"They'll be back," Prudence said calmly. "And fruitcake keeps. You have all winter to eat it. We'll double the recipe. It also makes a nice gift."

"That reminds me." Gerry offered the red tin from Cathy's house. "Do you make these?"

Prudence took one. "Viennese crescents. Yes. But mine are different. Not ground nuts but toasted breadcrumbs. Poor person's version."

Gerry studied the fruitcake recipe. "Oh. I get it. Golden raisins, chopped apricots, and dried pineapple instead of the brown raisins, currants, dates and cherries we put in the dark fruitcake. And white sugar instead of brown sugar and molasses. White fruitcake."

"You get cracking. I'm going to dust upstairs."

Gerry happily cracked the eggs, softened the butter in the top of a double boiler, and added in the sugar. Then she sifted the flour and other dry ingredients, remembering to set a half cup aside to toss with the dried fruits and nuts, Prudence's trick so the heavy ingredients didn't all migrate to the bottom as the cake baked. Gerry sliced the blanched Brazil nuts and crushed the blanched almonds. Then, instead of brandy to moisten the mix, it called for fruit juice. She added in orange juice and mixed. And mixed. The batter was so stiff it supported the wooden spoon standing straight up in the middle of the bowl.

Prudence returned and took a look. "Is this right?" Gerry asked. When Prudence nodded, they buttered four loaf pans, lined them with brown paper, buttered that too, then added the batter, smoothing it into the corners of the pans with knives. Gerry knew the cake would bake for a long time in a low oven. She set the timer and sighed with satisfaction. "Tea or coffee?"

"Coffee, I think. I need a pick-me-up." They took their coffees and Cathy's tin of cookies to the rocking chairs by the fire. Cats appeared to wait for crumbs. Bob jumped on Gerry while Ronald took possession of Prudence's lap. Both women exhaled at the same time, then laughed.

"Christmas is *hard*," Gerry complained. Prudence nodded as Gerry continued. "I mean — when did we start? Early November?"

Prudence said, "Mm," and sipped her coffee.

"We made dark fruitcake, wrapped it in brandy-soaked cheesecloth and left it to age. We made wreaths. We decorated our houses, inside and out. We — I — tromped up into the woods and cut a tree." Gerry looked fondly at the tree, set well away from the fire, in front of the street-side window.

It wasn't big so she'd put it up on a wooden crate that she'd covered with wrapping paper. Prudence had told her that that was where Aunt Maggie had always put her tree, and that the cats, most of them, were pretty respectful of it. And they were. There was no tinsel, of course, as that could be lethal to the feline digestive system (or at least embarrassing) if ingested, but Aunt Maggie's old ornaments twinkled faintly and Gerry had added some carved wooden snowflakes she'd bought at one of the local craft fairs as well as her mother's beeswax angels.

"Then we went to all the craft fairs," she continued. Running from early November to early December, every Saturday and some Sundays were given to attending multiple annual Christmas events at local schools, community centres and churches. Gerry had bought most of her gifts at these, and quite a few nice things for herself. One woman made catnip mice in assorted gay colours and Gerry had splurged, buying one for each of her adult cats.

She'd purchased a red coat for Cathy's dog from the same lady and was looking forward to giving it to Prince Charles upon his return.

"Then we went to the carol services." Hosted by amateur groups, there were several of these. Most were fundraisers. One offered sherry and biscuits, another mulled wine and fruitcake. Dutifully, Gerry and Prudence had trudged through snow and slush to attend.

"And now it's Christmas Eve," she concluded softly, her complaining forgotten.

"Yes," her friend agreed, and burst into tears.

3

"Prudence! Whatever is the matter?" Gerry jumped up, dumping Bob, who twisted in mid-air so he landed only on the sleeping Mother and not the kittens. Mother gave him a clout on the head, then rearranged herself.

Gerry returned with a handful of tissues. Prudence wiped her eyes. "It's just — I miss her — Maggie. Every time I come here, I think, just for a moment, maybe it's all a horrible dream. Maybe she's upstairs, asleep." She blew her nose. "I'm sorry."

"No. *I'm* sorry. I should have thought about that. They say holidays make people feel their losses more keenly. And you have to keep returning to the one place where this terrible thing happened. Poor Prudence." She awkwardly patted Prudence's shoulder. "Want your Christmas present now? I was going to make you take it home to open tomorrow, but —"

"Yes. I would like it now, thank you. And I have yours in my purse." Both women got up. Gerry fetched an envelope from the mantel. Prudence brought her purse. "You go first," Prudence said politely.

"At the same time, maybe?" Gerry countered. "One, two, three — open!"

Prudence slit the envelope while Gerry ripped wrapping paper. "Oh, Prudence! Perfect!"

Prudence was silent, looking at the ticket. "You shouldn't have," she said faintly.

"You've earned it. Whose idea was it to give art classes? And even today: suggesting I apply to teach at the college? We — the cats and I — couldn't get along without you. And once I sell the Borduas, I'll have plenty of money. Is St. Lucia all right? Bea recommended it. She's been there and so has my student Christine. It's supposed to be lovely and quiet and warm."

Prudence leaned over and kissed Gerry's cheek. "Thank you. I can't wait. Do you like yours?"

Gerry looked at the collection of recipes. Prudence had typed them and cleverly photocopied them onto lovely old-looking stiff gold paper that she'd folded and then sewn together with thick brown wool to make a little booklet. In it were all the desserts she and Gerry had made that past fall: brownies and sandies; fruit and pumpkin pies; cakes and cookies. "I'll treasure it forever," she said solemnly.

Prudence was going to church with Gerry that evening, so they fed the cats and ate an early supper of meat pie with some of Prudence's homemade tomato chutney, carrots and baked potatoes. Leaving four golden fruitcakes cooling on the counter, they walked over to St. Anne's around a quarter to seven.

Strong gusts of wind blew in their faces as they covered the short distance. The small church huddled on its small plot of land — the little graveyard to one side — looking for all the world as if it felt the cold temperature, the rising wind. The trees at the side and back of the graveyard creaked and moaned, their branches clashing, bits of brittle sticks landing on the snow-covered graves.

"We'll be lucky if trees don't come down in this gale," shouted Prudence.

Yet inside, the church was serene. Simple arrangements of evergreen boughs and large white candles in glass jars adorned each window recess while white poinsettias decorated the altar. The lights were low and the organ played gently as Prudence and Gerry entered.

It was a service of carols and readings, and non-religious Gerry enjoyed the singing of old favourites as well as the special ambiance of the 150-year-old church.

When the service was over and handshakes had been exchanged with neighbours and the smiling minister at the door, they walked out into a storm.

Freezing rain and ice pellets drove into their faces. The women tried to walk on the slippery surface and almost fell. "Back to the church," Prudence yelled into Gerry's ear.

In the church porch, Prudence whispered, "Are you wearing socks?" When a stupefied Gerry nodded, she added, "Are they long ones?" At Gerry's second affirmation, Prudence hissed, "Take them off."

As other members of the congregation watched, the two slipped off their boots and socks (in Prudence's case, knee-high support hose). "Tie them around your boots at the toes." Gerry did as she was told.

This time, when they stepped onto the path, toes first, the bands of cloth caught and prevented them slipping. "Prudence, you're a genius," murmured Gerry, as, arm in arm, they hobbled safely home.

Ice pellets had formed stiff drifts on the road and in Gerry's driveway. With feelings of relief, they let themselves into the darkened house, only the little fluorescent light that lit up the stovetop illuminating the kitchen.

"Prudence, I don't want to drive. The car is caked solid with ice. I think you should sleep over tonight. We'll both be safer inside."

Prudence agreed. "I'll make some cocoa."

"Put some brandy in it," called Gerry, going to clean out the cat boxes and do the nightly count. All twenty-three little bodies were present. When she returned to the fire, Prudence was making it up, while two mugs steamed on the mantelpiece.

Gerry sat down. "I've got to check Cathy's tomorrow. I said I'd do it every two or three days. Something about her insurance." Prudence said nothing. Gerry, afraid her friend was depressed again, tried to distract her. "I don't want to gossip, but what do you know about Cathy? For example, the first I heard she had a sister was when she told me about this trip."

Prudence stirred herself. "I didn't know about the sister. I knew she had a brother." She added dreamily, "He disappeared."

"Disappeared! People don't disappear. What happened?"

Prudence sipped her cocoa. "They moved here when they were teenagers. The Stribling family. Maybe the sister had already left home. Cathy's brother was a beautiful boy. In my class. I'm a little older than Cathy. The family must have been wealthy. They bought Fieldcrest and put a lot of money into it. Hard to believe that was forty years ago.

"I think Cathy's father was the last Stribling. Besides her brother. Stribling is a local name. There are a few of them in the big cemetery in Lovering." She paused. "And the boy was his parents' pride and joy. Good at sports and school, handsome."

"How handsome?" Gerry asked. "Prudence, did you have a crush on Cathy's brother?"

Prudence was too old to blush. She replied with a simple, "Yes. For three years. I was happy if I just got to look at him. He didn't have a lot of girlfriends, but when he did, they were the cutest girls. Like you."

"Huh. Fat lot of good it's doing me. I thought Doug —" Gerry interrupted herself. "But it's not me we're talking about, Prudence. What happened next?"

"Well, we all graduated and a few went to college. He was one. He was going to be an engineer. I got a job at the grocery store — cashier. He came home on holidays but I rarely saw him. And then he just disappeared. No one saw him anymore. His parents and Cathy didn't speak of him, and the whole family seemed sad. I didn't know what to think." Prudence sighed. "Cathy never married. Her father retired and died. Her mother died. And she opened the B&B."

"She seems happy now," said Gerry, absently, as she crossed the room to peer out at the lake. "Gosh, it's hard to see out there."

"She found her niche, I guess," said Prudence, joining her. Both women flinched as a large bough off the willow tree way down the lawn by the pool cracked and hung, dangling.

"Good grief!" Gerry exclaimed.

"Let's hope that's the only one," Prudence responded.

The old house complained in its bones, groaning and creaking as they climbed the stairs to bed. Maple boughs in the front yard slapped it with their branches. And once they were upstairs, they could hear the patter of ice pellets rattling on the metal roof.

"You take my bed, Prudence, and I'll sleep in Maggie's."

"Thank you," said Prudence in a shaky voice. "I don't think I could sleep in there. Goodnight."

"Goodnight."

Gerry settled down with the four cats she'd dubbed Aunt Maggie's "Honour Guard." Blackie, Whitey, Mouse and Runt blinked slowly in the light cast by the faux glass hurricane lamp by the bedside. No one had slept in this room since the night Maggie died. Someone scratched at the door. Gerry opened it and Bob shot in. She left the door open a crack. Perhaps, in the night, Lightning would jump lightly up to join the throng. Bob briefly kneaded Gerry's pillow and was asleep before she'd climbed back in.

When she dreamed it was not of Cathy's handsome young brother tossing a football or laughing with his friends, but of a different man, a little older, dressed in overalls, white shirt and a round, broad-brimmed farmer's hat, who kept shaking his head, holding his hands in front of his body, palms out, as if to shield himself.

"Merry Christmas!" A quiet knock at her door and Gerry's eyes jerked open. Who? She remembered Prudence had slept over.

"Come in," she croaked, and sat up. "Merry — oh, Prudence! You shouldn't have!"

Prudence entered with a tray that contained two small glasses of eggnog, a plate of dark fruitcake, and two cups of tea. "The eggnog has rum in it. You're going to need it," she announced grimly. "Cheers." She swigged her eggnog and Gerry did likewise.

"Why?" She was already out of bed, a piece of fruitcake, redolent of brandy, in her hand. She put on her Winnie-the-Pooh robe and SpongeBob slippers. "What do you mean 'I'm going to need it'? And what are you grinning at?"

Prudence stifled a smile at the sight of Gerry's attire. "Oh, you know. A few trees came down, or bits of them. And — uh — just never saw you in your — uh — in these clothes before."

Gerry pirouetted. "Am I not gorgeous? Which trees and where?"

"Uh, very nice. You'll have to see for yourself."

As they were in Aunt Maggie's room at the back of the house, Gerry peered out the window, or tried to. "Drat, I can't see a thing, it's so frosted. I'm going downstairs." Prudence followed with the tray.

A few of the cats were still munching their breakfasts in the kitchen. "Is the house all right?" Gerry asked anxiously.

"I think so. I was waiting for you to go outside." Prudence gestured out one of the kitchen windows. "But look."

Gerry rushed to the front window. "Oh, my gosh!"

One of the giant old maples, taller than the house, had split. Half had fallen across the driveway, taking out the electrical line that ran to the shed. The other half teetered precariously. If it came down, it would block the road.

Gerry quickly checked the stove light. On. "Well, at least the house still has power." Prudence motioned her to look out the window that faced the side driveway and shed. Gerry bleated "Not my —"

Another giant maple had dropped an enormous limb on Gerry's car and the roof of the shed. "It's not so bad, I think," Prudence was saying as Gerry rushed outside.

True enough, the higher shed roof had taken the brunt of the fallen bough's weight. All the car windows were intact, as was the hood; only the roof was a bit dented. Gerry tried a door. "Prudence!" From inside the porch, Prudence tossed Gerry the car keys. Gerry yanked open both doors and inspected the roof's interior. She gave Prudence a thumbs up.

Bob dashed out the open doorway, took one look at the devastation, and dashed back in. Both women laughed. "Come back in," Prudence beckoned. "We'll have a proper breakfast and think what we should do. Come on."

They made bacon and eggs, then luxuriated in front of the fire with French vanilla coffee.

"This is nice," Gerry said, peering in the banana box at the playful kittens. "I'm glad you're here."

"Glad to be here. I'm just going to phone my neighbour and see if my house is okay."

Gerry lifted one of the kittens onto her lap. "Hello, Jay. Or are you Cee?" She'd named the kittens for her five art students, just their first-name initials. Gee, Dee and Bee completed the quintet. Mother stirred restlessly as Gerry replaced the kitten and picked up another. "All right, Mother. They have to get used to people handling them for when we give them away." Mother gave Gerry another look. "I said you could keep one and I meant it. Then we'll be nineteen again. So, which one?"

Mother began licking the one Gerry was pretty sure was Jay. There was a black toe on one of the white hind feet. "Jay? Shall we keep Jay?"

Prudence came in with a funny look on her face. "My next-door neighbour's birch tree came down on my house. On my bedroom. In my bedroom, actually. If I hadn't slept here…"

"Oh, Prudence, we've got to get you home. But no, I guess you can't sleep there. Oh, how dreadful. The cold will get in and the pipes will freeze."

"You're learning," Prudence said grimly. "I always leave a key with my neighbours across the street and Charlie already went in and turned off the water. There's no electricity on the whole street. Thank God I don't have a basement, just a crawl space."

"Why?"

"Because the sump pump — and everybody in Lovering with a basement has one — would be off with the electricity. No, it'll be days before I can even call the insurance company. Christmas Day, Boxing Day, and then the weekend."

"Well, obviously, you'll stay here. And not work the whole time. In fact, I want you to sit down with another coffee while I clean the cat boxes. Leave the dishes. I'll get dressed and we'll think what we have to do."

While Gerry was getting dressed, she heard the welcome sound of the snowplow. Imagine those guys, she thought, working on Christmas Day! By the time she'd finished her chores, the Hudsons could be heard cleaning first Cathy's, then Mr. Parminter's, Andrew's, and finally, Gerry's driveways, or driveway rather, this time, as only the front circular drive was accessible.

Gerry stepped out the front door. The younger Hudson scratched his head at the tree blocking the side driveway. "Just do in front of the house," Gerry shouted, indicating the semi-circle in front of her.

"I'll be back later," shouted young Hudson. "Bring a saw." Gerry clasped her hands over her head in a victory salute. He grinned as he backed his tractor onto the street and drove to the next house's driveway.

"It's all right, Prudence," Gerry shouted as she walked towards the sitting room. "The Hudsons are on the job. Prudence?" The draft coming from the kitchen told her Prudence must have gone out the side entrance. "Probably for wood," said Gerry, pouring herself a quick refill of coffee. "Drat the woman. Can't make her rest for a second." Then, remembering that the rear of the shed, where the door was, was crushed under half a tree, Gerry paused. "We can't get wood," she mused, stirring her coffee, "unless…"

She peered out the side window just as Prudence stumbled out of the tiny door at the front of the shed, where a potting bench and a stool marked the site of some of Aunt Maggie's past horticultural activities.

Prudence must have pushed on the interior door that led from this annex to the main space of the shed — where the firewood was.

"But there's furniture in the way!" Gerry exclaimed.

Prudence staggered through the door to the porch. Her teeth were chattering as she cried, "There's someone in there!"

4

"What do you mean, 'There's someone in there!'?" Prudence gasped. "I pushed—"

"Yes, yes. You're a clever woman. You pushed the door and some furniture slid inward and you slipped through the door to get some wood." Prudence was still breathing deeply and quickly, so Gerry, rather alarmed, quipped, "It's a good thing you've kept your girlish figure."

Prudence made a face and took a deep breath. "I worked my way through all your *junk* to the woodpile. I was just reaching for a piece of wood when I—when someone tapped me on the shoulder. I turned. But there was no one there!"

"It was probably Bob," Gerry reassured her. "He loves it in there. Must smell of mice." Prudence walked into the living room and pointed. Gerry followed her to see Bob in the banana box playing with the kittens. "Not Bob, then," Gerry admitted.

"I have to tell Mrs. Smith about this. I have to ask Mother—not you, dear." She reassured the cat who stirred at the sound of her name. "*My* mother—if she knows what's going on. Gerry, someone was there."

Gerry tried to look nonchalant. She knew Prudence paid regular visits to a medium—Mrs. Smith—and that she believed she contacted her dead mother's spirit through the woman. "Well, not today. Today is Christmas. We relax. We eat. I have to check Cathy's."

"I'm not staying here alone! I'll come with you."

"Fine. *We'll* check Cathy's house. I wonder if she has a sump pump. I know she has a basement."

After Gerry brought in more wood from the shed — no one tapped *her* shoulder — and they ate leftover meat pie for lunch, they bundled up and walked over to Cathy's.

On the way, Gerry noted Andrew's car was not in his driveway. He must have slept at his mother's. Neither his nor Mr. Parminter's houses seemed to have come to any harm, except for small boughs and twigs strewn everywhere.

As they mounted the wide steps to Fieldcrest's broad veranda, Gerry said, "Just walk around the left side, Prudence, and check the windows and roof. I'll go to the right, then meet you back here."

Gerry picked up a few twigs that had blown on to the veranda and rattled the windows. All locked. She walked back to the front door and opened it, Prudence coming close behind.

"Let's go upstairs first and check the ceilings for water damage." Automatically, to relieve the gloom, Gerry's hand reached for the light switch. Light illuminated the stairs. "That's funny. It wasn't working last time I was here."

Prudence paused halfway up the stairs and reached inside the fixture. "Bulb was loose. I've tightened it. Should be fine now."

They each took one side of the long hallway, peering into the bedrooms, looking at ceilings for signs of dampness.

"Okay?" Gerry queried when they met back at the head of the stairs.

Prudence nodded. "But that light's out again."

Gerry flicked the upstairs switch a few times, then shrugged. "Maybe a loose connection in the lamp. I'll leave a note for Cathy."

They checked the main floor and the kitchen. Gerry opened the basement door. "You don't have to come down here if you don't want to," she said over her shoulder. "Cathy said it's pretty bad."

"You're not leaving me up here," Prudence indignantly replied.

Gerry flicked the switch at the top of the stairs and a bare light bulb went on in the basement and illuminated their descent. "The wine cellar, I presume." She gestured at a half-full rack.

They heard a steady trickle of water and followed it to a sump pit. In a thankful voice, Gerry said, "God, I'm glad I don't have a basement. If the power goes off, the whole place must flood."

There was a dusty, mouldy smell that tickled her nostrils. She sneezed.

"Come on," urged Prudence. "It's not healthy. We've checked enough."

They were standing next to the large old furnace, a metal box with many ducts leading out of it in different directions, when they heard a scrabbling sound.

"What's that?" Prudence clutched Gerry's arm.

"A squirrel that's got in? A mouse?" Gerry suggested.

The scrabbling was coming from below the workbench that stood under the basement's one window. For no particular reason, Gerry grasped a hoe that was leaning against the wall among other yard and garden tools.

More like an old armoire or bureau, perhaps made by a farmer years ago, the bench sported a drawer with two cupboard doors beneath, one of which was slowly opening *from the inside!*

Gerry felt the hairs on the back of her neck slowly extend and was fairly certain she had stopped breathing. Beside her, Prudence made not a sound.

Bob's clever face, ears and whiskers festooned with cobwebs, peeked out of the armoire. "Bob? What?" Gerry relaxed and replaced the hoe.

Prudence burst out with, "How on earth did he get here? He never followed us! Through the snow? No!" She got on her hands and knees, and, pushing the cat to one side, stuck her head in the cupboard space. She backed up hastily, hitting her head. "Ow. It doesn't go anywhere."

Gerry picked up Bob and dangled him in front of her eyes. "Now Bob, do tell us of your travels." She laughed.

For some reason, Prudence chose to be offended. "It isn't *funny*. It feels *odd*. Something's going *on*."

Gerry lowered Bob and gave him a cuddle. "Okay, okay. I was just trying for some comic relief." When Prudence still looked troubled, Gerry added, "You're going to ask Mrs. Smith and, er, your mother, right? They'll help. Not that Bob in a cupboard has anything to do with your, er, man in the shed. I think. I mean, I do not think. Prudence, this is turning out to be a very confusing Christmas. Let's go home, relax, read a book or something."

A somewhat exasperated Gerry and thoughtful Prudence crunched their way home, Bob tucked inside Gerry's jacket. Gerry retreated to Aunt Maggie's bedroom with several cats and her book — *Fairacre Festival* by Miss Read, set in a tiny English village in the 1960s, in which its quaint villagers raised money to repair the church roof, crushed by a tree during a storm.

Apropos, thought Gerry. I wonder how many people will be talking of that very thing today — finding the money to repair damaged houses and cars. To be comfortable she changed into pajamas and dozed.

Around five o'clock she went downstairs to see about supper. As she popped a frozen quiche in the oven, peeled some potatoes and made a simple salad, she thought of all the families sitting down to feast together. Prudence being here for Christmas dinner was a surprise. There hadn't seemed much point in buying and cooking a turkey with all the trimmings for just herself. At six o'clock she tapped at the door of Prudence's room. "Prudence, supper." The sound of snoring was the only response. She decided to let her sleep. Who knew how poorly she'd slept the night before?

Gerry poured a glass of wine and ate her meal. A yawning Prudence joined her around an hour later. "I hope I'm not awake all night," she moaned, filling her own plate and glass.

"You'll be fine. It was an unusual night and day."

A knock at the front door interrupted any further discussion. "We're in our *robes*," a horrified Prudence whispered.

Gerry giggled and went to peek out from behind a curtain. Tall, male—her cousin Andrew! She threw the door open. "Andrew! Merry Christmas! Have you come for a visit?"

Homely but nice was Gerry's personal description of Andrew. He smiled, stepped into the foyer and hugged her. I'd forgotten how different it feels to hug a man, Gerry thought.

"Hello, you," he said. "Hello, cats," to the few who'd braved the cold draft of air to see who it was. "Prudence!" His voice held a note of surprise.

Gerry explained and asked if he'd eaten. "I was hoping you'd ask," he said. "I spent yesterday and today at my mother's. Doug brought the boys over today. You'd think I'd be full with all that feasting, but I've been working so hard shovelling around Mother's and then my house, that I've got my appetite back. Well, you're very cozy in here."

His gaze took in the Christmas tree, the fire, the rocking chairs and the remains of their dinner, as well as the two women in robes and slippers. While he knelt to admire the kittens, Gerry put some food to reheat and gave him a glass of wine.

"How are the boys doing?" asked Prudence.

Andrew joined them at the table. "To be honest, I think they miss their grandfather more than their mother."

Gerry and Prudence exchanged a glance. It was no secret Margaret had neglected her husband Doug (now her ex-) and her three boys because of her strange obsession with her mother, Mary. Only Gerry and Prudence and almost certainly Mary knew the truth of Aunt Maggie's death, though sometimes Gerry thought Andrew suspected.

She asked, "And they're getting used to having Doug full-time back at the house again?"

Andrew spoke slowly. "I think so. It's hard to tell. They're so solitary and secretive at that age. Anyway, what have you been up to?"

As Gerry brought his meal from the kitchen, she was surprised to hear Prudence describing the incident in the woodshed. "Tapped me on the shoulder, the way you do when you're trying to get someone's attention, but there was no one there."

Well, why shouldn't Prudence confide in Andrew? She'd known him all his life. Gerry kept forgetting that *she* was the relative newcomer to Lovering.

Prudence rose. "I'll do the dishes. You keep Andrew company, Gerry."

Gerry lowered her voice, although Prudence was making a lot of noise in the kitchen. "What do you think of her story, Andrew? Do you believe in ghosts?"

"These old houses have seen a lot of human drama. I wouldn't be surprised if some people are sensitive to the energy. Whether it actually manifests itself, who can say?"

Remembering how Andrew's father Geoff took his life earlier in the year, Gerry laid her hand briefly on the hand he wasn't using to shovel in his food. "I've thought about you, Andrew; your terrible loss; what you must be going through. I didn't like to intrude."

He swallowed a mouthful. "Gerry, I —"

"Oh!" She jumped up, went to the tree and deposited a medium-sized package in front of him. "Your present. And it's still Christmas!"

He picked it up and shook it. "Hmm. Will I be surprised?"

"No. Yes. Maybe. You don't have anything like it."

He ripped off the paper and opened the lid of a square box, then unwrapped the object from its nest of tissue paper. "Oh! It's lovely. Thank you, Gerry." He held the china foal, brown with cream ankles and blaze, delicately poised on long legs as though it had just been born, and leaned over to kiss her. Then he reached into his pocket and extracted a small box.

Gerry opened it quickly. Inside was a little gold key.

Andrew explained. "Aunt Maggie gave it to me when I was young. She said it would unlock my heart's desire. I didn't understand what she meant for a long time. Now I want you to have it. Maybe you'll find what you desire." He rose. "And now I should go. We're all tired, I'm sure."

Gerry stammered her thanks for the gift before returning it to its box and putting it on the mantel. Andrew gave both women a peck on the cheek and let himself out.

"And that's Christmas," said Prudence with a sigh, as they wearily went up to bed.

Burrr. Bur, bur, bur, burr. Whack! Burrrrrrrrrrr. Gerry stirred, a buzzing in her ear, and looked at the clock. Eight. The dent on her pillow and a few calico hairs showed where Lightning had been and gone. Bob snuggled at her belly. The familiar lumps of the Honour Guard pressed around her feet.

She turned toward the window. As usual, it was too frosted to make out details, but she saw something large and yellow high in the willow tree. The yellow thing descended, much as Bob would have, by clinging on to the tree's main trunk with arms and legs. "Hudsons!" She put on yesterday's clothes and went downstairs. "Cats, coffee," she muttered, but Prudence had beaten her to it, even already having cleaned the litter boxes.

A shopping list had been started. Cat litter — lots, headed the list. Gerry groaned. Prudence must be planning the monthly mammoth task of emptying, scrubbing and refilling the six boxes that serviced the fur brigade. She poured a coffee, shrugged on her coat, slipped into her boots and stepped outside.

The Hudsons had already removed the tree that had blocked the driveway and threatened the road, and Prudence was picking up the small boughs and sticks left over from their task. "Kindling," she said.

Gerry grunted and turned to look over by the pool. Having downed the dangling willow bough, the Hudsons were cutting it into a few smaller sections so it could be moved. When they'd done that they approached the car-and-shed problem.

"Drag her?" Young Hudson asked his elder.

"Lift her a bit, then pull down there. Or push." The father nodded at Gerry. "Might need your help, Miss."

The Hudsons tied two ropes, one at either end, to the tree that lay across the car and shed roofs. Gerry took hold of one rope, the one closest to the house, while Prudence took the other on the far side of the shed, almost in the thicket that separated Gerry's property from next door's ramshackle, abandoned house.

Young Hudson stood between the car and the shed with his saw, slicing boughs off. His father drove the tractor near his son, engaged the shovel under the tree and slowly raised it. Gerry understood that she and Prudence were to hold the tree steady as it lifted, preventing it from swinging towards the house or Young Hudson.

When the tree was high enough, Old Hudson inched forward until the tree hovered clear of the driveway, car and shed. Young Hudson shouted, "Okay, when I give the signal, let go." Gerry nodded. Prudence nodded. The tree swung ominously. Prudence slipped and the rope flew out of her hands. Old Hudson drove forward and dropped the tree as Young Hudson screamed at Gerry, "Let go! Let go!"

Then Gerry was stumbling across snow and tree to Prudence, who lay, gasping, in the thicket. Gerry helped her up. "Are you all right?"

"It happened again, Gerry. Only this time it was a hand on the rope, someone helping me."

Young Hudson was already cutting the tree into six-foot lengths. "We'll be back sometime to turn all this into firewood," his father assured them, before both Hudsons drove away, one in the slow-moving tractor, the other in the beat-up red pickup truck.

Over breakfast Prudence declared, "I can't stay here any longer, Gerry. I've spoken to my neighbour and he'll take me." When Gerry raised her eyebrows, Prudence added, "He and his wife will take me. And I want to supervise the tree removal from my bedroom."

"Gosh, Prudence, I forgot you haven't even seen the damage yet. It's going to be a shock."

"What? Another one?" Prudence replied with an attempt at humour. "I was thinking, Gerry. Will you come with me when I consult Mrs. Smith? She might pick up something through you. It's your house, your shed."

Gerry nodded. "Sure. I must confess I'm curious. I've never been to a séance. Now, I'll run you home."

When Gerry dropped Prudence off, the neighbours across the street from her house took over, and after she took one disbelieving look at her cottage, ushered her into their home. Gerry drove past her own house to Lovering to shop.

She'd loved having Prudence stay but breathed a sigh of relief when she let herself back into her house alone, laden with groceries. Something to do with being an only child, I suppose, she thought. She unloaded the six boxes of cat litter and the Mini's suspension relaxed.

She made herself a treat for lunch: ham and cheese on a croissant and, as she had no plans to drive that afternoon, enjoyed a glass of white wine with it.

She flipped through last Saturday's newspaper as she ate, found herself idly humming, "On the first day of Christmas —" She stopped. Christmas had been yesterday. Wasn't that the first day of Christmas? So, today was the second. "Two turtle doves," sang Gerry, and got up to look at Andrew's present.

The gold key, less than an inch long, glittered in the light of the fire. What did it open? A jewellery box? A music box? I wonder, she thought, and went upstairs looking for some little trinket of Aunt Maggie's that might need a key.

When her search proved fruitless, she pocketed the key and drifted into the office. It was coming up to month's end. She better have a look at the bills.

She sat down at the desk and switched on the room's electric heater. Surprisingly, she was already caught up with the banking. She looked at the boxes of family papers Aunt Maggie had stored. Why not?

Dragging the nearest one over, Gerry emptied it onto her tidy desk. Old bills going back to Gerry's grandparents' times. She should probably toss them. Packets of letters, each tied with string or ribbon. Those might be fun to read in bed or by the fire. Set aside. Deeds for property which ran along the lake, the other side of the main road, and up into the fields and woods beyond Cathy's house. These will be a nightmare to sort, thought Gerry. Oh well, I'll give it an hour.

Three hours later, it was dark outside. At some point, Gerry must have switched on the desk lamp. The deeds had indeed been difficult to sort, but once she figured out to make a short description of each one on a separate piece of paper, the task became easier. And once she had them in order, she realized she had part of her family's history in her hand, the earliest part, but couldn't yet put the pieces together.

She yawned. "Coffee. I need coffee. And cats need to be fed." She switched off light and heater and, taking the deeds with her and leaving a packet of old letters on her bedside table for later, she went downstairs.

When the beasts were busy munching, and after Gerry had emptied and scrubbed out two cat boxes and tipped them on their sides in front of a roaring fire, she sat at the table looking at the deeds, a steaming bowl of *café au lait* and two of the Two Sisters' Teahouse's scones nearby.

Here was the record of the land granted her great-great-grandfather John Conybear (the name was misspelled) in 1845 when he was — Gerry rummaged among the papers for her copy of the family tree — when he was about thirty-five years old. Family lore had it that he'd left Devon and run away to sea when he was about ten years old, emigrated while still a teen, and eventually owned his own boat, or at least a share in one.

From ship owner to trader to storekeeper and landowner had seemed to be the progression, and by 1845 he was ready to settle down in Lovering.

He extended the original house, took up farming and, in 1854, married — Gerry made another check of the tree — Sybil Muxworthy, aged seventeen! And John was forty-four!

The cat boxes were dry. Gerry lugged them into the bathroom and dragged out two more. She yawned. Maybe not. She slid the boxes back into the bathroom. Prudence always took on this nasty monthly task, and Gerry wanted to surprise her by having them all done when she came back to work. She'd carry on tomorrow.

She heated some canned soup and another scone. It had been a long day. "Oh, no!" she exclaimed, then relaxed. "Geez, so much has been happening. I thought I'd missed a day. We checked Cathy's yesterday. It'll keep till tomorrow." She smiled at the furry faces quietly keeping her company. "I guess I can always say I'm talking to the cats."

5

Gerry was too tired to read letters that night, but next morning, after her regular chores, and with two more clean cat boxes drying out in front of the fire, and over her second cup of coffee, she selected one bundle, sat in a rocker by the fire and undid the string.

The letters were all addressed to one or the other of the same two people: Matthew Coneybear, Gerry's father's father; and Ellie Catford, his soon-to-be wife. They had both been dead before Gerry had been born and she touched the envelopes with respect, wondering what she would read inside them.

A quick glance at the family tree confirmed Matthew had been fourteen years Ellie's senior. Yet he'd died only two years before his wife. What did Gerry know about Matthew? Only that he'd died on the commuter train coming home to Lovering after a hard day in Montreal doing business.

Gerry did as she'd done the day before. She took all the letters out of their envelopes, carefully paper-clipping them together so they didn't get mixed up. Then she put them in order so she'd have the sequence correct, dated them on a piece of paper, and left a space after each entry in which to describe the letter's content.

She'd expected serious, formal letters, but again she was surprised. They all seemed to be from 1933, when the couple became engaged, to 1935, when they married. So Ellie was around twenty while Matthew was in his early thirties. Yet the letters were playful. They had nicknames for each other. They gushed. It was quite touching.

The absences had been caused by Matthew being away for work — business took him to Toronto, New York. And Ellie was a young girl living with her parents in Lovering, a few miles from The Maples.

Surprised again, Gerry noted on the tree that Ellie had been the child of first cousins, Henry and Louise, both Catfords by birth. Before she got bogged down in how many of her friends and acquaintances her grandmother had been related to (many), she went back to the letters.

Not much mention of other people in those. These two were interested only in each other. Gerry laid aside the letters with a sigh, tenderly returned each to its envelope and retied the bundle with its ancient piece of string. Maybe my children will read them someday, she thought.

The freshly scrubbed cat boxes were dry. "I'm on a roll, cats." She filled the boxes with fresh litter and tackled the last two boxes. She was eating a sandwich when the phone rang. "Helloooo," she said in a comic voice.

"Gerry? Is that you?" The quavering tones told her at once to whom she was speaking.

Contrite, she responded, "Yes, Mr. Parminter, it's me. I was just being silly. Are you home? Is everything all right?"

"Gerry, would you have supper here tonight? My nephew and his wife insisted I bring home some leftovers from the delicious meal they made yesterday. No, two days ago. I must say, I'm glad to be home. Travelling is too exhausting at my age."

"I would love to come, Mr. Parminter. What time?"

"Seven too late for you?"

"Not at all. May I bring dessert?"

"Lovely. Goodbye."

"Goodbye, Mr. Parminter."

Gerry went to her Christmas tree and found and transferred two small parcels from there to the kitchen counter where she kept her wallet and keys. Which reminded her... She went in search of catnip mice.

When, on Boxing Day, she'd remembered to distribute the little oval parcels among her pets, she'd expected a feeding frenzy, but only a few cats had been excited enough to rip off the wrapping paper, and now, a day later, the mice she could find lay in corners where their "users" had left them.

"Huh. Well, that was a bust." She pulled out a reference book about herbs. "Catnip, catnip. Not all cats...may prefer fresh... aha! I wonder if you guys have some in the garden I don't know about. If you don't, I'll get some plants in the spring and we'll see. We'll see, eh, Bob?" With her toe she poked gently in Bob's direction, where, as if to prove her wrong, he was rolling from side to side, a plaid catnip mouse on his belly, alternately clutching or mouthing it, before he dashed up onto the bench where Gerry sat, back down to the floor, and crossed the room to sit, tail thrashing, under the table.

"I might have known that you'd be the one most affected," mused Gerry. "Well, let's do a bit of cleaning in here."

House vacuumed, cat boxes clean, laundry done, and herself fresh from a hot bath, it was a contented Gerry that walked to Mr. Parminter's. Doing housework always made her feel virtuous.

She tapped on the door and let herself in. "It's me, Mr. Parminter." She slipped on the little ballerina slippers she wore when visiting — SpongeBob was surely best left at home! — and followed her nose into the kitchen.

A lovely smell of roast beef and garlic greeted her. Mr. Parminter was slowly setting the table. "I thought we could eat in here tonight. So cozy."

"Let me do that." She kissed his cheek as he settled into a padded chair that swivelled, his lookout post for watching the birds in his back yard.

As she served the supper, he chatted about his family, the visit, how they'd driven up onto Mount Royal and parked to look at the Christmas lights of Montreal; how they'd taken him to visit the graves of his parents in a crypt also on the mountain; how lucky he was to have his house and cat. "Thank you again for letting me have Graymalkin, Gerry." As if on cue, Graymalkin (who Gerry could not stop calling Stupid, at least to herself) entered the room and jumped on his owner's lap. He blinked lazily at Gerry. "Work, slave," he seemed to be saying.

"Don't chop up any beef for him," Mr. Parminter was saying. "He doesn't like the garlic."

Gerry opened a tin of fishy cat food and dumped half in a saucer. "I guess it's too strong. Here you go Stu — Graymalkin. Merry Christmas. You know, only about half of my cats went for the catnip mice I bought them. So I looked it up and it's a fake cat-hormone that fools the susceptible ones. I brought him one."

Mr. Parminter took a glass of red wine from her and toasted, "To St. Stephen. Oh no. That was yesterday. To St. John."

A confused Gerry replied, "To St. Stephen and St. John. Hip-hip," and drank. She sat down and they dug in. "How do you know so much about saints, Mr. Parminter?"

"I'm a lapsed Catholic. For reasons I won't go into, I stopped attending as a young man and eventually drifted over to the Anglicans. But I still remember the saints and their days, especially around Christmas. St. Stephen, St. John, the Holy Innocents —"

"Who were they?"

"The children murdered by Herod's soldiers because he knew a troublemaker had been recently born. He had a dream or consulted a soothsayer or something. I should be able to remember."

He toyed with his food, appeared suddenly tired. Gerry was concerned. "Shall I clear? Why don't you put your feet up in your chair while I do the dishes? Then we'll have dessert and I'll go. Tell me about the storm in Montreal."

Mr. Parminter quietly chatted, stroking the cat on his lap, and Gerry only half-listened to his pleasant voice as she scrubbed and rinsed at the sink. "But I can tell you're distracted, my dear." His words penetrated her reverie. "What is it?"

She sliced some of the golden fruitcake she'd brought and offered it to him, then plugged in the kettle. "Prudence felt... an emanation in my woodshed. And Bob turned up in Cathy's *basement* of all places, when we were checking her house. Oops! I meant to do that today but time got away from me." Mr. Parminter waited. "It just feels like something is *happening*. Oh, I don't know."

He looked sympathetically at her. "Have you been very lonely?"

Tears came into her eyes. She nodded.

"I thought so. I remember, after my dearest Michael died—" He fumbled for a tissue. Gerry, who knew Mr. Parminter had really loved only the one, mourning him deeply, made sympathetic noises. He cleared his throat. "Well. For one thing, Bob is a nut." Bob was Graymalkin's archenemy. Gerry knew Mr. Parminter wasn't very fond of him. "He followed you and Prudence into Cathy's house as a joke. That cat has a questionable sense of humour."

Gerry, who'd many a time seen Bob stalking an unsuspecting Graymalkin before the pounce and ensuing kerfuffle, nodded. "He does."

Mr. Parminter continued. "Or he got into the basement somehow ahead of you."

"We checked all the windows," Gerry began doubtfully.

Mr. Parminter shook his head. "These old houses. There might be a coal chute, or an opening for chucking down firewood, or a cupboard for keeping milk cool...a...what's it called? — a cold room.

"As for Prudence, well, I respect that woman, so I don't know what to tell you. What exactly happened?"

"Oh, I just remembered. It happened twice. The first time she was inside the shed, getting wood, and she said someone tapped her shoulder. I blamed Bob but he was inside. Then outside the shed at the back, she was holding a rope while the Hudsons cleared a tree off my car —"

"Good God! Is it all right?"

"Oh yes, just a dent in the roof. It still goes, which is the main thing I require from a car. Where was I? Oh, yes, she says it felt like someone helped her pull on the rope. She was so startled, she slipped and fell."

"Well," Mr. Parminter smiled, "you have had an exciting few days. Not so lonely now, eh?"

Gerry jumped up. "I have a present for you. First Stup — Graymalkin's mouse." Mr. Parminter opened it for the cat, who sniffed the toy. Mr. Parminter dropped it to the floor.

"Oh," said a disappointed Gerry. "He doesn't like it." But she spoke too soon. Graymalkin also dropped to the floor and put out a tentative paw.

"He's a serious cat," Mr. Parminter was beginning to say, when Graymalkin pounced, salivating heavily. They laughed.

"Whoa!" said Gerry. "Success!" She offered Mr. Parminter the other small parcel. "Now, before you say anything, I didn't spend any money. I found it in with Aunt Maggie's books."

Mr. Parminter blinked as he read the title, in faded gold embossed on the little volume's cover. "*The Poetical Works of William Cowper, Excelsior Series.* You notice I pronounce it Coper, not Cooper or Cowper, although all are nowadays considered correct." He cleared his throat and read, 'To my dear Maggie. May your days be ever filled with the lily and the rose. Christmas 1960.' Funny how they didn't include the date of printing in old books, but I think you'll find —" He rustled through the first few pages. "What does that say?"

She peered at the tiny print. "'St. Catherine's, Bear Wood.'" She looked up with smile. "What a lovely name for a place. And then there's a date: October 9 — I can't make out the last digit. Is that 1850 or 1856?"

"It's one of my father's books. He loved poetry. I gave it to Maggie long ago. So long ago." He paused. "There's a poem — 'The Lily and the Rose.' Could you read it to me?"

Gerry read, "'Within the garden's peaceful scene / Appeared two lovely foes, / Aspiring to the rank of queen,'" and Mr. Parminter joined in with, "'The lily and the rose.'"

After Gerry had read the rest of the poem aloud, she exclaimed, "Why, Mr. Parminter! This is about Aunt Maggie and Aunt Mary, isn't it?"

"I'd just moved in here. They were teenagers. No, wait." He did some mental math. "Mary was a teenager — seventeen. Maggie was only twelve. Oh, how they struggled with each other! Mary was beautiful, you know, and Maggie — Maggie was not. But she was the lovelier person. A few moments with them soon settled that. So, I thought if she saw herself as the lily with 'the statelier mien,' she might learn patience. And she did. But it took time."

"That's a lovely story, Mr. Parminter. I'm so glad I found the book."

"Your house is full of such treasures, Gerry. You must guard it, and them. Now. One old book deserves another." He walked slowly into another room, returning with a slim paperback with a faded purple cover that he handed Gerry.

"*Old Habits* by Blaise Parminter. I look forward to reading it. Thank you very much."

He sank back down into his chair. Graymalkin leapt lightly into his lap. "I'm very tired," he said abruptly. "Thank you for the book and your company."

She let herself out. He was already asleep in his chair.

When she was in bed, draped with cats, her eyes closing, Gerry promised herself to check Cathy's house the next day.

In the morning when she rolled out of bed, she stepped on something hard and painful. "Is this one of your toys, Bob?" she said, yawning, with her eyes barely open as she bent to pick it up. She flung it from her with a shriek. It rattled into the black grate of the disused fireplace where it gleamed palely: a small white bone.

*S*omething moved in a damp corner, stole slowly along the cement floor. It encountered wetness, stopped, shuddering.

It was hard to see in the darkness down there. Snow had built up around the foundation and against the one window. Anyway, it was a moonless night and starlight didn't reach that far.

The thing crept slowly along the floor to the bottom of the basement stairs. Was there any point trying to mount them? No one had come before. It waited, considering.

It must have slept, for it woke with a start, wondering where it was, then, remembering, uttered one dreadful cry.

What had it done to deserve this?

It eyed the metal shelves of the wine rack. How good it would be to drink. Water would do. If it could only reach —

The rack fell over with a crash, narrowly missing the creature on the floor. Glass, flying in all directions, and wine, red and white, splattered the recumbent form.

Carefully, it dragged itself away from the mess of broken shards and sharp-smelling liquid. There must be water somewhere in this basement. It could be heard drip, dripping.

The thing found a wet corner and, losing strength, lapped directly from the floor. The last thing it felt was cool water going down its throat.

PART 2

AND NEW

6

Prudence will have a fit, was Gerry's first thought, followed by, it's probably just from a chicken, or maybe it's an old spare rib. She approached the object and picked it up with a tissue. "Definitely a chicken," she said. "Bob?" Bob rolled on her bed, displaying the three attached white triangles that made his belly so enticing to scratch. Gerry pounced with the bone and Bob's four paws and his mouth closed gently on Gerry's hand. "You are a nut," she said affectionately, "just as Mr. Parminter said." The Honour Guard gravely watched these shenanigans from the foot of the bed. "Who's hungry?" she asked.

Downstairs, she dropped the bone into the kitchen garbage.

Chores done and coffee dripping, she brought in four armloads of wood from the back porch. The pile there was almost depleted. "After church," she promised herself. As she stacked the last load by the cold ashes of yesterday's fire, she sang dramatically to the cats. "On the fourth day of Christmas, someone gave to me, four loads of firewood, three of Jane's scones, two ham and cheese, and my car crushed under a treeeee! Stay tuned for further instalments!" Snickering to herself at her cleverness, she bundled up and set off for church.

As she walked the short distance, she saw what had improved her mood. The sun! The sun! she chanted to herself. I really am a pagan at heart. The temperature had dropped, but that didn't seem to matter as long as the sun shone. She stamped her feet in the church porch and went in.

Red poinsettias had now joined the white ones decking the altar. The hymns were old favourites and Gerry enjoyed singing them. She let her mind wander during the sermon and reread the brass plaques screwed into the church walls.

Her family and several others were well represented. Her gaze lingered on the first Coneybear couples' names: John, Sybil, and a long list of children, most dead in infancy; and then at Sybil's death date, coinciding with that of her youngest child's birth — 1865. What must it have been like for little Albert, growing up without a mother? His sister, Margaret, was ten years older. Probably she and the servants had cared for the infant.

People were standing to sing "It came upon a midnight clear" and Gerry scrambled to her feet. A few more prayers, then "Good King Wenceslas looked out" saw the minister and the minuscule choir down the aisle.

Outside, Gerry looked at the drifts of snow between her and her parents' plaques on the wall of remembrance at the rear of the graveyard and regretfully turned away. She saw Betty Parsley, wife of Phil Parsley, owner of the Parsley Inn. A tall man with flaming red hair stood talking to her. The man said something, and Betty looked away, somewhat angrily, Gerry thought, and saw Gerry watching them. As Gerry turned to leave, Betty caught up with her.

"Miss Coneybear. Gerry. We're having a little party at the inn tonight — a buffet with drinks — if you'd like to come. It must be lonely in that big old house by yourself."

She knew the woman meant to be kind, but a certain cold watchfulness in her eyes made Gerry feel defensive. "Oh, I have the cats to keep me company. But thank you very much. I'd love to come to your party."

As she walked home, she fumed. Not everyone is meant to be paired off like the animals entering the Ark two by two. I *do* have the cats. And my friends. When they're around, she finished rather dolefully. Cathy's house. Got to get over there this afternoon.

She made a nice big brunch with scrambled eggs, the last of the ham and the last croissant. Maybe I should get some groceries this aft, she thought. She made up the fire and went outside to replenish the stockpile of fuel on the back porch. She let Bob accompany her.

Automatically, she headed for the rear of the shed, where the large blue tarp the Hudsons had spread over the hole in the roof stopped her. "Right," she said under her breath, and let herself in the little lean-to at the other end of the building.

She squeezed through the inner door Prudence had managed to push ajar. Remembering her friend's encounter, Gerry felt a bit nervous, but Bob slithered between her legs and ahead of her and jumped up on the woodpile, his tail twitching. "My supervisor," she quipped.

He watched her remove the first few armfuls, but by her third trip, had disappeared. "Watch out, mice," Gerry called, and continued her work.

She decided to transfer the rest of one long row of logs and settled into a rhythm. By the time she'd almost finished, she was thirsty. "Cup of tea, Bob?" No answer. She made the last few trips and then began seriously to look for her cat.

"Bob! Where are you?" Nothing. She edged around the wood to the back wall of the shed where the blue tarp sagged. She frowned. Something had happened to the woodpile. It had collapsed. "Now what?" she muttered. She looked down into a hole full of firewood. "Cripes! The tree hit the roof, went through, and hit the woodpile, which went through the floor."

"Meow!" came from the hole.

"Bob? I can't see you."

Bob appeared, dragging something.

"What is it, Bob? The rest of that chicken?" Gerry teased.

But this bone was too large for Bob to lift. Gerry got down on her knees, then had to shift to her belly. "Have you got a dead ox down there, Bob?" Her fingers closed on the bone and she raised it towards her face. She knew this one had come from no farmyard animal.

After the police had left, taking as many of the bones as they could find and forbidding Gerry to go near the hole — why would she want to? she gloomily wondered — she made her usual afternoon coffee.

She felt a bit sick. It was all very well for Prudence to experience whatever it was she'd experienced, but actual *bones* in the ground on Gerry's property — well, that wasn't even a bit entertaining.

She sat in front of the fire, clutching her mug. "At least I took out lots of wood before, before — where is Bob now?" She'd totally forgotten him in the dizzying flurry of activity that had followed their grisly discovery.

She'd phoned 911 but had been clear this was no emergency, so had been given another number to call, had called it, had mumbled a few words about finding old bones under her shed floor, and waited.

It must have been a slow day because someone came rather soon, took a look and phoned someone else. The someone else came with a few people and collected the bones. "Not to worry, miss," one of them said, "we can tell they're old."

"Prehistoric?" Gerry asked hopefully.

The woman laughed. "Not that old. But old enough that we know we're not looking at a fresh crime."

Nevertheless, thought Gerry, absently fondling the kittens in their box, this house has been in my family for over 150 years. Someone must have known who was buried or laid there. Someone must have known.

"The bone!" She rushed to the kitchen garbage and rummaged until her fingers closed around the bone Bob had brought to her bedroom. "I should give that to the police." She put it on the mantel.

She ran a hot bath and soaked, which usually helped when she felt upset, then changed into her trusty black dress, black tights and funky ankle-high black boots. "Colour. I need colour." She rummaged until she found a gauzy green scarf. She even put on lipstick, a pretty coral pink. As usual, she cheered up when she looked at her reflection. Dark red hair, blue-green eyes, freckles. "Enjoy yourself!" she urged, thinking of the bones. "Life is short."

Before she got in her car she called for Bob and checked the shed. No Bob.

When she got to the inn, one of the Parsley teens was there to direct her to a parking place. As she gave her coat to another teen in the lobby, she joked, "Don't your parents ever give you kids time off?" The girl smiled sourly. Gerry slunk into the dining room, then straightened, glad she'd dressed up.

Live music — a singer and a guitarist — performed softly from one corner. A roaring fire blazed. And many, many Parsleys and other notables of Lovering filled the room with happy chatter.

Gerry took a glass of white wine from a youngster behind a table and looked around for her hosts. Betty Parsley was probably supervising in the kitchen. A roar of laughter told her she'd located Phil Parsley, standing with a group of men. Gerry walked over to the group. "And then I said, 'Will no one rid me of this nagging wife?'" The men burst into laughter.

Gerry flinched but nonetheless said, "Merry Christmas, Phil. It's nice to be here."

"Gerry!" A large man, Phil gave her a bear hug. Obviously, he was already full of good cheer. "Glad you could make it. Cats not keeping you too busy? Not coughed up too many furballs?"

He roared with laughter at this incredible piece of wit and his cronies joined in.

Gerry's eyes widened but she kept her smile fixed in place. "No, no. They're no trouble. Oh, is that — ?" She pretended to see someone she knew over by the buffet table and retreated.

She knew it. The town saw her as a laughingstock. A solitary female living with twenty-three cats. She fumed as she piled food on her plate. She'd show them. She'd —

"Hey, Gerry, leave some for the rest of us," a quiet voice urged at her elbow.

She turned, ready to lash out, but saw only Doug Shapland's nice face and unassuming smile. She looked at her plate. It was laden with mini-quiches, fried shrimp, roast turkey, stuffing, mashed potatoes. "Oh, my gosh, Doug. You take half." She scraped a portion onto his empty plate. "I guess I was blinded by fury."

"Sounds serious. Let's get a table."

The restaurant tables had been bunched up on one side of the room so people could circulate, chat or dance. They found a good spot near a window and ate their supper. Well, Doug ate. Gerry just stared at her food.

"It's the cat thing. People make remarks. I get angry."

He paused eating to say, "Your quiches are getting cold."

She bit into one and relaxed. "Spinach, nutmeg, Swiss cheese. Yum. As good as Cathy's."

"She may have made them," he replied. "I think Betty buys from her. That's better. As for the cat thing, embrace it. Make it work for you."

"How would I do that?" She took another quiche from Doug's plate — mushroom and thyme in a cream sauce.

"I dunno. You're an artist. Paint portraits of the cats. Support a spay and neuter clinic with the profits. Protest pet stores selling cats when so many are in shelters."

Gerry said slowly, "You mean really become a crazy cat lady, but do good with it."

"Something like that." He shrugged. "But in the mean time, let 'em talk. After all, what can they say that will actually hurt you? I should know." Doug, a recovering alcoholic, raised his ginger ale. "Cheers!"

"Cheers, Doug!" They clinked glasses. "You're right. They're just teasing. But I'm not used to it. I never stood out for any reason before. How are the boys?"

"Oh, you know — distant as only young adults can be."

"That reminds me, I have a gift for David. And one for you. Want to see me home and I'll give them to you?"

"I don't have a car yet, but I can drive yours," he suggested. "You've just had a drink."

"Good idea. That's the last thing I need: to lose my licence out here in the country. Oh!" She covered her mouth with her hand. "Did you?" When he nodded, she apologized. "I didn't know."

"It's all right," he said, getting up. "I got it back. I just can't afford to operate a second car and the boys are using Margaret's tonight. You'll have to drive me home later."

"Deal." She looked around for her hostess to thank her but only saw Phil. She shrugged. No way she was approaching him again!

As Doug helped her on with her coat in the lobby, Gerry thought how comfortable it was that he was a man of only medium height and build. It was nice not to have to look up so far.

After his initial gawk at her damaged car, he drove them home, where he took in the blue tarp over the shed roof. "Want me to have a look at repairing that?"

"Yes. But not tonight. I'll tell you inside."

A few of the cats greeted Doug. They knew him from his cutting the grass and gardening for years for Aunt Maggie, and lately, for Gerry. She put on the kettle as Doug built up the fire. "Would you like one?" she asked, seeing him stroking the kittens.

"David might like it." She brought him a cup of tea and his gift. "Thanks, Gerry. I didn't get you anything."

"No need. This is to say thank you for all the odd jobs you do. Open it."

It was a book cataloguing the work of Chihuly, the world's greatest glass artist, with coloured photographs. "Oh, wow," breathed Doug. "Look at that." They pored over the book together.

"I thought you could try doing in neon what he does in glass," Gerry suggested.

"Well, obviously," Doug teased. "I'll be world famous in no time."

"Like me with my future cat portraits," Gerry teased back.

They clinked mugs. "To Art!" they exclaimed in unison.

Gerry handed him another flat package. "And that one's for David. A graphic novel. I know he draws."

Doug leaned over and kissed her cleek. "Thank you very much, especially for remembering David."

Gerry smote her forehead with one hand. "Oh, no, I've forgotten to do Cathy's house *again*. That's almost four days. I was in it on Christmas. All this skeleton business distracted me."

"What?!" Doug almost dropped David's package and his book on the kittens. "What skeleton business?"

"I'll show you. Well, not the skeleton, but where I, I mean Bob, found it." Grabbing her coat and the flashlight from the kitchen, Gerry led Doug outside.

"Oh, Bob. Well, if Bob found it, that's okay," joked Doug.

They entered the potting shed and walked through into the larger woodshed. "I'm sure the police won't mind if we just *look*," said Gerry.

The police had moved some of the junk so they could fully open the interior door. The piled-up farm implements, lamps and other small objects loomed from the tops of desks and tables. Likewise, wood had been thrown from the neat stacks Gerry had made in the fall, to form a pile away from the hole in the floor.

"What a mess!" said Doug, looking down.

Gerry swept the light around the room. "Yes. But the wood will be gone by spring, and then we can have a good turnout of all this stuff."

"You could have a sale," said Doug, dropping to his knees beside the hole. "Can I have the light?" He shone it into the hole. "I wonder how long he was down there. Wouldn't it smell?"

"The police said they were old bones. Maybe they were put here as bones, so there'd be no smell. Or maybe —" Gerry looked at the hole in horror. "Maybe the person who killed him was the only person who came into the shed. In the old days, the women wouldn't come in here. The men would, or the servants, to get things."

"You're, we're, assuming the bones belong to a male, not a female, and that the person was murdered."

"Oh, it's a male all right. I *feel* it is," she added with less assurance. "The way Prudence described her experiences, I felt sure it was a male."

"Prudence's experiences? Tell me inside the house. It's cold in here."

As they stood in the kitchen, Gerry told him of the tap on Prudence's shoulder, the tug on the rope. "So we're going to see Mrs. Smith and see if anyone over there can help us."

"Over there."

"You know. Mrs. Smith and Prudence believe they're talking to Prudence's mother, for one. Sometimes Gramma Ellie is around too."

"Gramma Ellie."

"Look. If I don't support Prudence in this, she may not want to return to The Maples. She's spooked enough about Aunt Maggie's death here. This shed guy may make it worse."

"Shed guy."

"Are you repeating me to be annoying on purpose, or is it just happening?"

"Just happening," he said with a grin. "Come on. I'll help you check Cathy's. Then you won't have to do it tomorrow."

"In the dark?" Gerry said doubtfully.

"No, silly, we'll turn on Cathy's lights. Come on. Fifteen minutes and it'll be done. Then you can drive me home." When Gerry still looked doubtful, he added, "You're not afraid, are you?"

"N-no. Not afraid exactly. And it would be nice to have someone with me. I can't drag Prudence over there again. It's not really in her job description. Let's go." Stopping only to pick up the flashlight again, they set off towards Fieldcrest.

They passed Andrew's house. It was dark and, again, his car was absent. "Andrew is away at night a lot lately," commented Gerry.

"He's sleeping at his mother's sometimes, I believe. She doesn't like being alone."

"Poor Andrew. He's the only —" Gerry stopped, aghast.

"You were going to say, he's the only sane or likeable person left in that family, now Geoff is gone. You're right. I feel sorry for Andrew, too. I just drop the boys off at Mary's. She doesn't want to see *me*."

"Her loss," Gerry said softly and took his arm.

They passed the stone crypt of the Coneybears, nestled in a thicket between Andrew and Cathy's properties. "I always forget about this thing. Why is it here again?"

They paused and stared at the squat, flat-roofed structure. "I imagine it was because people died before there was a church or churchyard," Doug explained. "One of your forebears is in there, I believe."

"Really?" Gerry played the light on the two sides of the crypt she could approach. "Coneybear on one side and Muxworthy on the other. Funny. Just last names. She flashed the light towards Cathy's driveway. "Let's get this over with."

A light snow began to fall as they walked up Fieldcrest's long driveway. In the sombre light, the dark house looked asleep. Gerry thought of the many people who'd slept beneath that roof over the 150 or so years the house had existed. She saw them: in their long gowns and sober suits; they sat or stood in the public rooms downstairs; loved or suffered or died in the private ones upstairs.

She shook herself, as if coming out of a trance, and climbed the front stairs.

7

Gerry took off her gloves to unlock the broad front door. After she fumbled for a few seconds, Doug, saying, "Shall I?" took the keys from her. Their bare hands brushed and Gerry felt — what? That old sweet magic? A thrill in the pit of her stomach? Like swooning?

She felt something all right and heard something too, a "meow," as Bob appeared on the porch stairs and brushed past her legs and into the house. They followed him in.

"He's fascinated by this place! That's the second time he's followed me here. Bob, what is it?"

"Big old house like this must be full of mice," Doug suggested. "No cats. Just a lazy old dog."

"Hey," Gerry replied indignantly, "Prince Charles is my friend. And there are plenty of mice at my house for Bob to chase."

"Ah, but lots of competition." Through the balusters, Doug stroked Bob, who sat six steps up the staircase, grooming snow off his sleek black coat. Then the cat turned and bounded up the remaining steps.

"Shall we?" asked Doug, bowing so Gerry could precede him. She flicked the light switch. Nothing. Somewhat annoyingly, Doug then flicked it once or twice.

Gerry went halfway up the stairs, reached into the fixture and tightened the already tight bulb. Nothing. "That's funny. It worked when Prudence tightened it."

Doug joined her, loosened then retightened the bulb. No luck. "Not our problem," he shrugged. "Bulb, wire, even the fixture could be at fault." They followed the cat who was running from one side of the long upstairs hallway to the other, pausing at bedroom doorways, and checked the bedrooms together.

Standing at the window of what she thought of as "her" room, Gerry remarked, "I never noticed when I was staying here, but you can just see a corner of The Maples from here, my bedroom, actually. I wonder if people ever looked from there to here, long ago, you know? Lovers, perhaps," she added dreamily.

"You're in a funny mood," was all he said. For some reason, she felt disappointed by this response. "Probably can't see The Maples when the trees are in leaf. Let's check the main floor now."

The big reception rooms downstairs looked even emptier at night than they had when Gerry had inspected them by day. "Be sure to check all the windows," she called from the dining room. "I don't know if Bob is getting in on his own or following me. He's so clever, he —"

"Gerry." Doug's voice, calling from the living room, sounded serious. "You better come in here."

"Oh, what's he done? If he's shredded any of Cathy's upholstery, it hardly matters, it's so —" She looked where Doug was pointing.

The fireplace contained sizeable chunks of charred wood. A few bits of twig and bark marred the otherwise clean floor and carpet. Gerry gaped. "Someone's had a fire?"

"It's still warm," he said quietly. "Someone's been here. May still be here."

Gerry tried a laugh. It failed. "Probably just kids looking for a place to party."

"Yeah, probably." He was trying to sound reassuring, but to Gerry he sounded more wary than anything. He continued, "Maybe we should —"

"Leave?" Gerry's voice cracked on the word. She took a breath. "Well, we know there's no one upstairs. And no one on the main floor." She looked at Doug, who completed her train of thought.

"Which leaves the basement. I'll go. You wait in the kitchen so if there is a problem, you can go for help."

"And leave you to get beaten up? Don't think of it! I'm coming too. After all —" She grabbed a weapon. "What are pokers for?"

He grinned, but only slightly, as they moved quietly to the basement door. She switched to a whisper. "You really think they're down there?"

He flung open the door and answered in a loud voice. "Yes, I do. You call the police. I'm going down."

They waited. Gerry rather wildly said, "All right, dear," and stomped heavily in stocking feet to the phone. "I'm pretending we're married," she hissed in answer to Doug's bemused stare.

"Yeah, that'll scare them," the once-divorced man replied in a quiet voice. He went down a couple of steps.

"Here! Here!" She brandished the poker at him. "Take it!"

He retraced his steps and took it from her. "If I don't come back —" he began in a sad voice.

She clucked her tongue in annoyance and pushed him towards the basement door. He snorted. "Oh, now you *want* me to go." And down he went.

His voice floated up the stairs. "I guess you were right. About kids."

She edged over to peer down where he stood at the bottom of the stairs. "What's all that stuff?"

"Broken wine bottles. The rack's tipped over. No, don't come down, but can you find a garbage bag and maybe a dustpan and brush? I'll sweep it up."

She rummaged in Cathy's kitchen, muttering, "House-sitting? Never again. Broom cupboard? Under the sink? Where *I'd* keep them." She went into the hall, found another cupboard under the stairs where Cathy's vacuum cleaner and other housecleaning tools were stored. She added a pair of rubber gloves and Doug's boots to her armload and went downstairs.

"There's no one here now," he said as she joined him. "Oh, thanks." He sat on the stairs and laced up his boots. Gerry sat and watched him right the tipped-over rack and clean the mess.

"Really, I should be doing that," she commented.

"You might wreck your nice dress."

She preened a bit. He concentrated on his brushing. They spoke at the same time.

"Doug —"

"Gerry —"

"You go first," she said.

"All right. What are you doing tomorrow?"

"What everyone else will be doing: phoning my insurance company. Why?"

"Well, your insurance company won't be open in the evening. Would you like to go curling?"

"Curling? I've never tried. Oh! The brushing reminded you." She paused, then asked suspiciously, "Are you very good?"

"It's not competitive. I mean, it is, but we'd be on the same team. If you like."

"Hmm. Sure! I'll try it."

He'd finished his task and looked around the rest of the basement briefly. "It's a bit damp."

Gerry, now in a hurry to leave, said hastily, "Oh, it's always damp. Especially around the edges. Come on. I've had enough."

They put the wine-soaked brush and pan in a sink full of soapy water and threw the broken glass-filled bag in the garbage can.

As they walked back to Gerry's, they nervously glanced around. Gerry took Doug's arm. Then she drove him home. As he leaned over to kiss her cheek, she presented her mouth instead.

"Oh." He seemed a bit startled, then became confident. "That must be what you were going to say in the basement," he said, and got out of the car as she lightly smacked his shoulder. Gerry smirked in the car's rear-view mirror as she drove home. It was only when she got into bed and snuggled down that she remembered Bob.

She sat upright. "Well," she told the Honour Guard, "there's no way I'm going back to Cathy's house tonight. He'll just have to sleep there." It was some time before she could settle, picturing Bob roaming the big cold house, its walls echoing with his futile meows. And when she woke in the morning, it was to the sound of someone letting themselves in to her house.

She had a moment of panic before she heard, "Gerry? You up?" and relaxed at the familiar voice. Prudence was the only person Gerry allowed a spare key.

"I'm up." She sat up, yawning. "Come in."

Prudence stuck her head in the room. "I know you gave me the day off, but I'm going crazy stuck at the neighbours'. It's a small house and they're both deaf. Plus they've been married forty years so they sound angry all the time. Charlie — that's the husband — was coming into town so he gave me a lift. Can I just spend the day here?"

Once again, Gerry wondered about Prudence's husband, about whom she never spoke. She had such a negative view of marriage. "You sure can. I'm sorry you've been suffering over there. And if you want to work, I could use some help. I think I forgot to do the cat boxes last night."

"I could tell, or, should I say, smell," said Prudence, wrinkling her nose.

"Oh no. And after I went to all that trouble giving them a full clean last week. Do you want to sleep over here instead of your neighbours'?"

"I'll think about it." Prudence scanned the room. "Where's Bob?"

"Cripes! He's at Cathy's. He followed me and Doug over there last night. I'll get him first, then have breakfast."

"All right. I'll feed the beasts and get some more wood in."

"Did I already use what was on the porch?"

"Nearly." Prudence left, followed by the Honour Guard, who by now recognized the phrase "feed the beasts" or at least the word "feed."

Gerry dressed and then, remembering last night's kiss, was having another smirk in her bedroom mirror when she heard Prudence call her name.

Expecting some psychic manifestation or more bones, when Gerry met Prudence in the kitchen she was surprised to see her holding Bob, struggling to join his friends already eating. "Look what I found in the shed."

"He must be freezing!" said Gerry.

Prudence let him go. "Not him. He popped up out of that hole in the floor."

"How did he get in there? I'm beginning to think the only ghost around here is that cat!"

Prudence handed Gerry a coffee. "What's been going on in the shed? You been having a tidy?"

Gerry stared. "Oh my gosh. You don't know about the bones."

Prudence slammed her cup down on the kitchen counter. Coffee slopped everywhere. "What?"

"The police moved the furniture and wood. They wouldn't let me in while they worked. Bob brought me a bone. And then I found the whole skeleton — I assume the whole skeleton — when I went for wood yesterday. I can't believe it was only yesterday."

"There was a body under the floor in the shed? Right where I felt a tap on my shoulder? And when I felt the pull on the tree rope, I was standing outside right near that end of the shed. Gerry. Someone's been lying there for years."

Gerry felt the skin at the back of her neck move. "I'm afraid so. But the police said the bones have been there so long that it's not going to be considered a suspicious death. Nobody living could have —"

"Could have put the body there," Prudence finished. "That almost makes it worse. That someone got away with — murder, I suppose — and lived their life out, perhaps lived in this house, *knowing* that right over there —" She shivered.

Gerry asked anxiously, "Is this going to put you off coming here, Prudence?" She had a bright idea. "Maybe, now the bones are gone, the spirit — or whatever it is, was — has gone too."

Prudence didn't look convinced. "I have to make some phone calls."

The day fell into its usual rhythm. Gerry washed the cats' breakfast dishes, then worked in the living room for a change. She wanted a break from *Mug the Bug*, and left him in the dining room. At the living room table she began doodling cats, thinking about cat portraits she could try to sell.

She meant them to be close-ups, whimsical, telling a little about each cat's personality, but found she was also doodling cats jumping, stretching in mid-air, twisting, landing. "Cats jumping," she muttered. "Cats jumping over objects the way horses do. A cat jumping competition." She drew a scene of two cats jumping simultaneously while an absurd collection of people and other cats watched from the sidelines. Like a track meet, she scrawled at the bottom of the page.

Prudence vacuumed, washed cat towels, dusted. The women met for lunch in the living room. Gerry pushed aside the sheets she'd covered with sketches and bit into her favourite ham and cheese.

Prudence, munching *her* favourite — a peanut butter and pickle sandwich with a small bag of potato chips — looked the sketches over. "What's this?"

"Oh. An idea for a book. Cats jumping or something. I'm not sure. To be continued. Or not."

"Looks like a children's book. Pictures on top. Words beneath."

Gerry pulled a couple of pages over. "And then you switch the position to keep the eye engaged. I remember. We worked on illustration at art school." She pushed the papers away again. "I'm bored with *Mug*. I'd like to do something completely different. I wonder how kids' books pay? You make your calls?"

Prudence ticked off numbers on her fingers. "Insurance first, of course, for the house. You should phone yours. Then a contractor, who *says* he'll be over tomorrow morning. Hah! I called several but he was the only one picking up. People are still on holiday. It couldn't have happened at a worse time. Then Mrs. Smith. She can see us tomorrow afternoon at 1:30. You still coming?"

Gerry blinked. She'd agreed to accompany Prudence when it was just a case of a tap on the shoulder. Now there were bones. "Are you kidding? Of course I'm coming. Maybe she'll have some answers."

In the patient voice of one who'd had to explain this many, many times, Prudence gently remonstrated. "It's not her, Gerry. It's the others. The dead. Mrs. Smith is just more sensitive to them than most of us."

Gerry nodded vaguely. She was out of her depth here. "And do we tell her about the bones, the tap, the rope?"

Prudence shook her head. "Maybe after. She'll have probably already heard about the bones. Gossip moves fast around here. No. We just wait and see what she can pick up from the other side." She rose. "I better get to work upstairs. You want me to change the sheets?"

"Yes, please, Prudence. I slept in Aunt Maggie's bed again last night. I'd like to move back to my room. If you're not staying. Are you?"

"No. I better be on the spot if the contractor actually shows up. Pick me up around one tomorrow."

Gerry nodded and made her insurance calls before returning to work. More sketches followed: of cats jumping, cats sitting chatting with people, cats in a castle, in a field. She didn't know where this was going, but it sure was fun.

As Prudence drove them to her street that afternoon, Gerry mentioned that she was meeting Doug at the curling rink after supper.

"That's nice," Prudence absently replied.

Gerry continued, "And we kissed. I thought we might at Cathy's house last night, but the moment passed when we found the wine rack tipped over in the basement and—"

"You were over there at night?"

"With Bob. He followed us, as he must have when we found him in the basement cupboard last week."

"And you're sure he didn't follow you home?" Prudence sounded thoughtful as she pulled up to a stop sign.

"No, but, I didn't see him. He must have. And then followed you into the shed this morning." Gerry didn't see where this was going.

Prudence was temporarily silenced as she attempted to engage first. "We didn't actually see him follow us over there the other day either," she persisted, as the Mini jerked forward.

"No. You're right. But how else—?"

Prudence pulled into her own driveway and the women surveyed the damage. Gerry was again appalled at how her friend's neat little cottage had been crushed all down one side. The women looked at each other. "Am I to understand," Gerry began, "that you think there is some underground *connection* between my shed and Cathy's basement?"

Prudence shrugged and arched her eyebrows. "How else does Bob keep popping up in both places when we haven't put him there?"

"An underground passage," Gerry mused. "I don't know. It sounds far-fetched. Bob's a cat, after all. A mysterious creature, able to slink silently and all that."

"A black cat invisible against snow? Are you telling me we missed that, and you and Doug missed it again last night?"

"N-no. I just assumed Bob followed Doug and me home last night, wandered off and slept outside. He's done it before. But you're saying we forgot him in Cathy's house and he took a tunnel under the road —" Gerry's voice sounded incredulous in her own ears. "And that he came out in the woodshed in time to meet you this morning."

"That's about it," said Prudence. "And when we found him in the basement cupboard, he'd gotten locked in the woodshed, got bored with that, and went off to Cathy's house to hunt for mice."

"I'm going to check that hole in my shed as soon as I get home!"

"Not without me," cautioned Prudence. "You're going to eat supper, get changed and drive to the curling rink, right?" She let herself out of the car. "Goodnight, Gerry."

Gerry grumbled goodnight as she shifted over into the driver's seat. She's right, she admitted to herself. I'd probably fall in and meet the zombie apocalypse. She reversed the car and headed up to the highway. She was in the mood for fast food. After all, it was the holidays!

Back at the house with her delicious repast steaming in front of her, Gerry sang, "Five golden onion rings," and tried to remember the other lines of her absurd personal Christmas song.

8

Gerry showered carefully, shampooing her hair, not wanting to smell of her greasy supper. As she changed into stretchy pants and searched for a pair of clean running shoes, she thought about all the curling she'd watched on TV or, rather, not watched. How many Saturday afternoons had she spent peeking in her father's little TV room to hear him say, "I'm still watching," which was her cue to stomp off, feeling TV deprived?

He'd explained. "You watch your kid shows in the morning. I watch sports in the afternoon. You're welcome to watch with me. After all, I like watching Bugs Bunny with you. Maybe you'd like curling. Or football. Or hockey." She'd stared at him, incredulous that he could think she'd ever like such dull viewing. Curling: slow. Football: brief periods of violence but basically, slow. Hockey? She couldn't follow the puck, her father's TV reception was so fuzzy.

And her mother in the background to all this, shopping, preparing their meals unobtrusively, happy to be at home with her family.

And now I'm going to *play* curling, Gerry mused, scraping her car windows. Fun! I hope.

As she walked into the little community centre that housed the rink, Gerry contrasted once again her old life in Toronto with her new life in Lovering.

Toronto had streetcars and buses and a good subway. In Lovering she had a car. Toronto was full of cafés and ethnic restaurants, movie theatres and museums. Lovering had, to be fair, lots of eating establishments, but obviously not the other accoutrements of a big city.

Lovering had fresh air and plenty of trees. Toronto — not so much. It was the city of her birth, where she'd grown up living with her parents. She'd always love it. But she was glad to be out of it.

She went shyly into the curling rink lounge. Might have saved the bother of shampooing her hair. The air was redolent with the scent of hot dogs and french fries — snacks for the curlers.

She'd been here before for craft fairs. The local art club exhibited here. She looked nervously through the big glass window that separated the lounge from the ice. She'd never been down there.

She saw Doug and rapped on the glass. He pointed to one side of the rink. She changed her footwear and left her coat and boots behind as she went down some steps, found the door and cautiously stepped onto the rink's slick surface.

"Glad you could make it," Doug said, handing her a broom. "A little sweeping first, I think, to see how you move. Just do what I tell you. This is Rick."

Rick waved a hand as Gerry and Doug took up positions facing each other. Gerry copied Doug's stance, broom at the ready, feeling ridiculously excited. There were a few lanes, each with its own small group playing or practising, but all Gerry's focus was on her own.

Rick crouched and slid the rock forward, twisted and released it. Gerry stared down at it briefly but kept most of her attention on Doug. Rick started shouting, "Hard! Hard!" Doug scrubbed the ice in the rock's path. Gerry did likewise and they bumped brooms.

"Me closest to the rock," Doug muttered. Gerry got a little ahead of his broom with her own and kept brushing. "Off! Off!" he said suddenly, and she leapt back.

"Hard!" shouted someone else at the rapidly approaching end of the rink.

"No, off!" shouted Doug. She decided to obey him. The rock slid neatly past another and came to rest behind the first. When Doug joined their fourth player behind the stones to confer, she trailed him and stood uncertainly.

Here was the tall red-haired man who'd been speaking with Betty Parsley at church the previous morning. Rick slid all the way from the far end of the rink and said, "What were you thinking, Steve? Doug called it. I called it."

Steve stared coolly at Rick. "I just thought it could use a bit cleaner ice, that's all. Don't make a case of it. And who's this?" He turned his attention to Gerry, who felt uncomfortable with the testosterone level in the immediate area.

Doug introduced her as his cousin. That gave her a moment's pause. His cousin. Not his — ? Fine. She flashed Rick and Steve brilliant smiles. "I'm really excited to be learning to curl," she began, when Rick interrupted her.

"Doug! She's a beginner? We've got the match this weekend!"

"I thought she could sweep a bit tonight," he replied mildly, "as Jimmy is away and Ralph is sick. And if she likes it, she can sign up to learn."

Gerry's heart sank. Learn? Sign up? As in a curling class? And apparently, she was causing some tension within Doug's team. This "date" wasn't turning out at all as she'd hoped.

"Doug, Rick, can I get you over here?" A guy with a clipboard was beckoning. Doug hesitated while Rick hurried off.

"Don't worry about me," Gerry assured him.

"We'll grab a coffee, won't we, Gerry," said Steve with a smile. She nodded and Doug, relieved, slid over to the organizer. Steve and Gerry left the rink, walking up the stairs back to the lounge. "You take a seat. What do you like in your coffee?" She told him.

Gerry sat in one of a row of seats facing the window. Doug looked over in her direction. She lifted a hand. Steve brought her a coffee and sat down next to her. "Cheers!" he said.

Gerry sipped and almost choked. There was something stronger than cream and sugar in there. "I don't really like it," she said, putting the cup on the floor, thinking, it must be half whisky.

Steve looked blank. "Oh. Sorry. I thought you might be chilled standing around on the ice."

"No, I'm fine."

"I'll get you another." Gerry watched as he returned her coffee to the barkeep, offering it to him with a laugh. He brought her a fresh cup.

There was an uneasy silence, which Steve broke. "When my dad and his buddies used to play, they had a can of rye and ginger ale in one hand and a cigarette in the other."

Gerry laughed. "What did they do when they actually had to play?"

"See that little ledge running down the side wall? Now it's for water bottles, but back then it was for drinks and ashtrays."

She laughed again. "I don't see other women playing with men."

"Not tonight. But it's a thing. Called mixed doubles."

"Oh. Like in tennis," she said. They subsided into silence again.

This time Gerry spoke first. "So what are they discussing?" She jerked her head to where Steve's teammates stood with the clipboard guy.

"Our rink is hosting a tournament this weekend. Rick and Doug have got themselves on the planning committee." He flashed a grin. "Me, I just turn up and play."

"Very sensible," she commented. "I stay away from committees myself."

"And what do you do, Gerry?"

Gerry was surprised. Usually men didn't ask women her age about their jobs. "I'm a commercial artist. Comics, greeting cards. Paintings of your house, spouse, child, pet."

"Well, I don't have any of those, so I'll pass. Unless you'd like to paint me. For myself, of course."

Gerry looked at his face more closely. Long and thin, with hollow cheeks and high prominent cheekbones. Ruddy, but pale underneath it. And that red hair, much redder than her own, a real russet. "I see you as a Viking or an Elizabethan privateer. A white ruff would set off your colouring and maybe a cloth-of-gold cloak. Background another red than your hair, with lots of brown undertones."

He looked surprised. "Hey! You really are a pro!"

She inclined her head. "Thank you. That's just the patter. The proof is in the execution."

"Well, I'm impressed, anyway." He rose. "Look. I see Doug coming. I don't think we're going to practise anymore tonight. Good to meet you, Gerry. Maybe see you around sometime."

She was going to say, "Yes, like I saw you at church yesterday," but just then Doug arrived and, after discussing their next practice time, Steve left.

Doug took his vacant seat and sighed. "I can't believe how many details there are in planning an event."

"That's why people hire professionals." She spoke rather more tartly than she'd intended.

Doug looked somewhat taken aback. "Oh. Yes. That would be nice. But we're a small club with few benefactors. We have to pay for everything out of members' dues. Are you mad at me?"

Gerry felt contrite. "No. Yes. A little. I thought —"

Doug spoke slowly. "You thought this was a date. Geez, Gerry, don't you think I know what a date's supposed to look like? And that this isn't it?"

She felt miserable, and stupid.

Doug continued, "I just thought, maybe start to get to know each other better, away from your house, where I work for you, you know?"

Now she added embarrassed to her list of negative emotions. She stood. "I'm going to go now, Doug. Your friend needs you again anyway." True enough, the organizer was advancing on them, clipboard to the fore, Rick trailing behind. Doug swore under his breath.

Gerry stooped and gave him a quick kiss on the cheek. After all, she still liked him. When she got into her car, she blew her nose and wiped away a few tears. She looked up where the roof bulged down into the interior. She sang, "And my car crushed under a tree."

Tuesday morning, the familiar routine reasserted itself. Feed cats, make coffee, clean litter boxes — "Six litter boxes," chanted Gerry — drink coffee, make fire, work.

It felt good to get back to drawing. She roughed out a few cat portraits: the elusive calico Lightning; Bob's inquisitive face with its white whiskers and dickey; Mother's benevolent marmalade-coloured expression; and little Jay's round-eyed innocence. She was just choosing her colours when the phone rang. The kitchen phone had a long cord. She stretched it so she could still look at her work on the table in the living room. "Hello," she said, absently.

"I'm calling to make sure you don't forget we have an appointment at 1:30."

"I haven't forgotten, Prudence. I'll pick you up but you have to drive us there."

Silence at the other end of the line.

"Oh, come on," coaxed Gerry. "You missed a lot of practice time because of the storm and sleeping over at my place. You need to drive in winter. The roads are clear today." She added, "I'll buy you a lollipop."

"Very funny," Prudence replied coldly. "I'll be ready at one," and hung up.

"Eat or draw? Eat or draw?" Gerry eyed the clock on the mantel. She compromised by taking a banana, which lay, uneaten, and another coffee, which cooled as she began colouring in Jay's black and white. At five past one, Gerry caught sight of the clock, squeaked, gulped coffee, grabbed banana and wallet, and dashed to her car.

It was ten past by the time she pulled into Prudence's driveway, and a quarter past by the time a red-faced Prudence had the car backed out and onto the road.

Gerry reassured her. "Don't worry. It's a lovely sunny day and we're fifteen minutes away from Mrs. Smith's. It's that condo at the end of the river road, right?"

Prudence nodded, her hands gripping the steering wheel. Once she got going, she was fine.

Gerry looked out the window at the lake. "Almost frozen." She thought about the previous evening. Somehow, none of that seemed important. She resolved to put Doug, his teammates, and curling out of her mind. Stick to work, she told herself.

Prudence parked and they walked into the modest foyer. They buzzed Mrs. Smith and took an elevator to the fifth floor, the topmost. Mrs. Smith's door was decorated with a little artificial wreath. Prudence knocked.

"Hello, Prudence. How are you, dear?" Mrs. Smith gave Prudence a little hug. "Miss Coneybear," she politely greeted Gerry, shaking her hand. "Please come in."

"Call me Gerry. Oh!" Gerry stopped in amazement. She'd been expecting a dark, drapery-lined room with a round wooden table covered with a cloth. Instead everything was painted white and the narrow, door-lined hallway opened into a rectangular living, dining and cooking area, which sprawled along a glass-lined fourth wall, outside of which was a long balcony with glass railings, so the view was unimpeded. And what a view!

Where Gerry's waterfront home looked at a section of the river up close, Mrs. Smith's abode took in miles of it, stretching from the northwest down to and beyond the bridge to Montreal.

Prudence was already seated at the glass-topped dining table and Gerry remembered they were here on business. She sat down next to Prudence. Mrs. Smith sat so she was facing them.

There was no clasping of hands in a circle. Mrs. Smith's eyes didn't roll back in her head. She simply closed them and sat quietly. Prudence did the same, so Gerry followed suit.

A clock ticked somewhere. A plane droned overhead. The room was comfortably warm and Gerry contrasted Mrs. Smith's worry-free existence with her own wood-hauling, tree-dodging, cat-litter-infused one. The fridge clicked on. Mrs. Smith spoke.

"A family. No, two families. Deeply unhappy individuals in both." There was a pause.

"Is that Mother speaking?" asked Prudence in a low voice.

Mrs. Smith wrinkled her brow. "This is someone new. Someone I've not spoken with before. A man? There's a lot of emotion here. Love. And hate."

Gerry immediately thought of the bones under the woodshed. Maybe they belonged to the man who was communicating through Mrs. Smith. Gerry opened her eyes a crack, checked Mrs. Smith's and Prudence's were still closed, and shut her own again.

"He knows — knew — some people belonging to someone here. Is it the Catford family?" Gerry supposed Mrs. Smith began with Catford because it was Prudence's maiden name. There was a pause. "Is it from the Parsleys?" Mrs. Smith continued.

Bound to be, thought Gerry, then remembered Prudence's mother had been one. And Prudence was Mrs. Smith's client. Another pause.

"No? Is it from —" and here Mrs. Smith hesitated. "Is it a Crick?" Gerry almost gasped and felt Prudence draw in a tiny audible breath. Prudence had been, might still be, married to one Alexander Crick, but Gerry hadn't yet learned the man's history.

"So not a Crick." Prudence and Gerry both relaxed. "Prudence, do you have any names to suggest? Gerry?"

Prudence said softly, "Shapland, Coneybear, Muxworthy. Who else, Gerry?"

"Petherbridge?"

"Is the person — the people — named Petherbridge?" Silence. "Is the person a Shapland?" Silence. "Do you know anyone called Coneybear?"

Gerry held her breath and cracked open one eye. She was in time to see Mrs. Smith clap her hands over her ears. Gerry opened her eyes wide, reached over and pressed Prudence's arm.

"Yes, yes! I understand. Coneybear. Yes? Another name?" Mrs. Smith's voice sounded loud and strained. She uncovered her ears and asked Prudence, "Which names have I not yet tried?"

Prudence whispered, "Muxworthy."

"Is the other person's name Muxworthy?" Mrs. Smith had to cover her ears again. "I have to stop," she gasped, got up and walked over to the long glass wall, stared out at the view.

"Coneybear and Muxworthy!" Gerry said excitedly.

"Shush," cautioned Prudence, getting up. "Mrs. Smith, I'm leaving the money on the table. Mrs. Smith, are you all right?"

The medium turned and looked at them with a weak smile on her face. Her eyes were moist. "I'll be fine after a cup of tea. I hope you heard something helpful. Your mother wasn't forthcoming today, Prudence, or maybe this other was so much stronger, she got out of his way."

"Well, thank you, anyway. Maybe next time. You take care of yourself, now." She jerked her head to indicate to a reluctant Gerry it was time to leave.

They rode down in the elevator in silence, and it wasn't until they got into Gerry's car that she burst out with, "My family, Prudence! This has something to do with my family!"

9

The ever-sensible Prudence replied, "Well, that's no surprise. It's your family's woodshed." She started the engine. "Where am I going?"

"I need to eat," Gerry said. "Let's go to that patisserie that's so good. My treat."

After a roast beef panini with caramelized onions, mustard and Swiss cheese, fries and a salad, and two cups of excellent coffee, Gerry felt better. Prudence had had lunch, so settled for an almond croissant with her coffee. "Well," she said, ruminatively.

"Yes?" Gerry replied, wondering if she had room for dessert.

"Just — well," said Prudence. "Go on. You know you want to."

Gerry beckoned to their waitress. "Do you have any of those big chewy cookies with chocolate and nuts in them? I'd like one, please."

"And so order is returned to the universe," Prudence commented, drily.

"What? So I like a cookie." She leaned forward. "To be honest, Prudence, I'm getting a bit sick of fruitcake."

Prudence waved a hand, dismissing all fruitcakes. "What we have to discuss are Coneybears and Muxworthys."

Gerry tried to make a joke. "It sounds like a company. Coneybear and Muxworthy. May I help you? No?" Her cookie arrived and she began eating.

Prudence continued. "I'm assuming we're talking about individuals, one of each name. That's how it seemed to me."

"Well, Mrs. Smith kept saying 'person' in the singular, but I don't think we can assume. Until we know the exact date of the bones, how can we know in which generation to start looking? It's pretty vague. Can they even date bones with any degree of accuracy?"

"I'm afraid my life in Lovering and work as a housekeeper hasn't qualified me to answer that," Prudence replied sarcastically.

"Very funny. I'm trying to remember from crime shows and mystery novels, but I can't. So we'll just have to go back 100 years — at least we know that much — and see where Muxworthy intersects with Coneybear. Gramma Ellie was born around the start of the First World War. Grampa Matthew a bit before. So the generation of my great-grandparents is where we start. Let's get going. I need my family tree."

The sun had set and they joined a light version of the regular commuter traffic on the road back to Lovering. Across the lake, the lights of other habitations shone. The wind blew against the still-open water, making little stiff waves.

Gerry felt exhausted and over-stimulated at the same time, yet she was surprised when Prudence turned at Station Road. "You're going home?"

"I'm tired, Gerry. At Charlie and Rita's I can lay down before supper, then have a nice quiet evening. I suggest you do the same. I'll see you tomorrow morning."

When she got home, Gerry had all the business of cat stomachs to fill and cat boxes to empty. She was too distracted to make a fire and settled for cranking the thermostat. The oil furnace crashed on in the distance and soon little blasts of warm air began coming from the vents. It was easy to locate said vents: some of the cats were fond of lying in front of them.

Gerry got the Coneybear family tree and sat staring at it, elbows on table, hands either side of her jaw. The generations marched across the page, the descendants and ancestors slid up and down. "Snakes and ladders," muttered a sleepy Gerry. Tired out by the séance, she went for a nap.

A couple of hours later, she woke up, refreshed. Eight o'clock. She went downstairs in robe and slippers, made tea, and rummaged through her collection of Christmas treats.

Not fruitcake; she really was sick of that. Ooh, there were some of Cathy's Viennese crescents left. She took her tea and the tin to the living room table and had another look at her family tree.

So, based on dates of birth, she could eliminate the last four generations. She drew a pencil line across the page. Nobody below there could be the "persons" involved," she told Bob, who lolled on the table, waiting for cookie crumbs to fall.

She realized she could even eliminate the great-grandparents' generation — most of them born in the 1890s. "Unless they were child psychopaths," Gerry explained to Bob, flicking him a bit of nut from a cookie. He spat it out and looked at her, disgusted, as if to say, "What? I look like a squirrel?"

She erased the line and raised it up one generation. So, the great-great-grandparents. People born in the 1860s, '70s and '80s. There were others on the tree whose times fit, but they were Petherbridges, Parsleys and Catfords.

My grandparents would have known these people, their grandparents. She stopped and looked out the window at a clear, cold night. If she leaned down and looked up, she could see through tree branches a half moon, set like a bowl low in the darkness.

Similarly some others, 100, 200 years ago, could have sat by this window, doing accounts or writing letters or nursing a restless baby — or, perhaps, a broken heart. And the moon would have shone or not, depending on the date and the weather.

She sighed and returned to the tree. How amazing that all these people had once lived, some of them in this house, all the way back to —

She froze, looking at the names at the top left-hand corner of the tree, back another generation from the one she'd been considering. The original couple: John Coneybear and Sybil Muxworthy. John: 1810 to 1893. Sybil: 1837 to 1865. Coneybear and Muxworthy. Two people, whose names had caused an uproar, at least in Mrs. Smith's head, as she communicated with a restless spirit.

"Look at this, cats!" None of them did. Gerry got up and stood in front of the cold fireplace, holding the tree. "Margaret Coneybear: 1855 to 1945 — the only surviving child of John and Sybil, besides my great-grandfather Albert. Somebody who's alive now might remember her. Dad and Uncle Geoff would have. I remember Dad speaking about Great Aunt Margie and how funny she was. Married a Petherbridge who died young, leaving her with her son Jonas. I bet she lived here. How can I find out? I need someone really old. Drat the Coneybears, dying in their fifties. (Sorry, Dad. Sorry, Aunt Maggie.)"

Gerry bent over and tickled the kittens, who were waking at the sound of her voice, while Mother slept on, curled half on her back with her paws over her head. She dropped her voice to a whisper. "I take your point, Mother. It is getting late." She leaned on the mantel and gasped. "Oh, no! I've still got the shed guy's finger bone. At least I think it's a finger bone. I wonder if the medical people have noticed."

She thought, should I return it? Does it matter? And more soberly, was he a relative? Surely not. A relative would have been noticed if missing, accounted for. A servant? A stranger? A passerby who happened to die at the house or in the street?

As her brain ran riot with possibilities, she hardly noticed as she replaced the bone and picked up the cookie tin. She ate absent-mindedly until her searching hand discovered the tin's emptiness. "Aw, now I'm sad," she moaned, and went foraging for real food in the kitchen.

By now, it was after midnight. She munched a piece of cold meat pie with chutney, then another. Eating made her sleepy.

When she got upstairs, Bob and Lightning were already stretched (Bob) or curled (Lightning) on her bed. She peeked into Aunt Maggie's room. The Honour Guard was in place. All was well. Surprisingly, she fell quickly asleep.

A freezing cold draft coming through her bedroom door (always left ajar so the cats could come and go while she slept) woke her. The little light on the bedroom's portable heater still glowed, so the power was on. The furnace? The drop in temperature as she exited the bedroom confirmed her guess. Well, there was no way she was going to try to fix the problem herself in the dark early morning hours. The furnace was located in a kind of lean-to built onto one side of the back porch and could only be accessed by going outside.

She went downstairs where the grandfather clock in the foyer told her it was six-thirty. "Fair enough," she said. "I've had enough sleep." She went back upstairs to get dressed. She unplugged both the heater from her room and the one from Aunt Maggie's. "Sorry, cats." The members of the Honour Guard stretched and one by one hopped off their dead owner's bed. Gerry plugged one heater into the upstairs bathroom. Then, trailing cats, she made her way downstairs and placed the other one under the living room table.

"Brrr," she said and exhaled. "Can't see my breath, so hopefully no pipes have frozen." She quickly made a fire: newspapers twisted then knotted as her father had shown her, twigs gathered from the property, and kindling split off logs. She put on the kettle and fed the ravenous mob.

As she brought in wood from the back porch, she remembered she and Prudence would be checking the hole under the floor in the shed. And I should give Cathy's a quick look. There would be no time for the family tree. She put it away in the table drawer.

Time to get Prudence. She turned the keys in the car's ignition. Nothing. Again. Again nothing. She noticed the lights were switched on. She groaned and phoned Prudence's neighbour.

The wife, Rita, answered. "Yes?" Gerry explained the problem. Without covering the speaker, Rita yelled, "Charlie!" Gerry jumped.

"What?" was Charlie's answering bellow from elsewhere in the house.

"Ya gotta drive Pru," Rita yelled again.

"She's in the shower."

"Not get her, drive her. To work. And bring yer cables. Sounds like the young miss needs a jump start."

"What?"

"They'll be there soon," snapped Rita and hung up.

Poor Prudence! thought Gerry. Quite a contrast to her normal quiet home life. While waiting, she made a piece of toast. She was shovelling walkways when Charlie and Prudence arrived.

Charlie affixed the jumper cables and Gerry's car started right up. "Got to keep her running for twenty minutes," he shouted. "Recharges the battery."

"Groceries?" suggested Prudence. "I have a list."

"Thank you very much," Gerry said to Charlie before he drove off.

At the store, Gerry was one of its first customers of the day. She looked at the items on Prudence's list. Must be in the baking aisle. She added a box of cat litter to her own mundane collection of milk, eggs, ham, cheese and bread. She bought a frozen quiche and another meat pie, then went to the vegetable department. She looked around rather cluelessly, then got a bag of carrots and a broccoli. "Different colours are good," she muttered. "I read that somewhere, I think."

"Good thing you came early. We'll be swamped later," growled the middle-aged cashier. When Gerry looked blank, the woman added, "You know: New Year's Eve?"

Back home, Prudence was vacuuming. Gerry unpacked and put away the items, arranging those on Prudence's list on the counter. Currants and dried apricots seemed reminiscent of the now boring fruitcake and Gerry sighed. The allspice was a mystery. She opened the package and sniffed. Mild, like nutmeg. Disappointing. The almond extract in its tiny bottle smelled delightful. She brightened as she looked at the shortening. That might mean pastry. The four little bottles of food colouring were the real mystery, as was the package of unflavoured gelatin. She'd never cooked or baked with either of those before.

The drone of the vacuum cleaner stopped and Gerry went through to find Prudence in the dining room, removing cats from chairs and replacing hairy towels with clean ones.

Of all the rooms in Aunt Maggie's house, the formal dining room was the one Gerry least warmed to. The huge heavy mahogany table, which could seat fourteen, was so wide one couldn't reach the middle of it without standing up. Well, Gerry couldn't. She had to admit it made a good winter work area with her various art projects scattered about its surface. The chairs, with lightly upholstered seats and straight backs, were comfortable, and the chandelier elegant, but there was something dark about the room, despite the windows in the lake and roadside walls.

The massive marble fireplace was surmounted by a convex mirror that bulged and distorted the room's reflection. Gerry remembered, as a child, dragging a chair over to the mirror, and standing at its level, making the most dreadful faces into it. It creeped her out a bit, and she wondered why someone had hung it there, rather than a simple flat mirror. She supposed she could replace it. Heavy sideboards and dark ancestral portraits completed the furnishings. Gerry shivered.

Prudence noticed. "It should warm up in here soon. I changed the furnace fuse. Let me show you."

They put on coats and boots and walked outside along the back of the house. Prudence had shovelled a skinny path around the porch foundation to its far side. There, she produced a key and unlocked the door.

They stepped into the miserable alcove inhabited by the furnace. Gerry had been assured that it was not unusual to situate a new (relatively new, anyway) oil furnace outside a basementless old house, but she still found it bizarre.

Prudence showed her the little fuse box just for the furnace. "I used up the last fuses so I'll put them on the next grocery list. Get them at the hardware."

They trooped back into the house and returned to the dining room where Gerry sat on a clean towelled chair and asked, "What's the food dye for, Prudence?"

Prudence continued replacing fresh towels for used ones. "Thank you, Min-Min. Sorry, Mouse. We just need the red dye today." The cats, used to the routine and used to Prudence, mostly went limp when she lifted them up and resettled placidly on their chairs, maybe grooming a bit first. The three grey tigers — Winston, Franklin and Joe — chose the occasion to stalk the newest member of their gang, Ronald, the little white with the thin black moustache, all four becoming a ball of joyous energy that mock-fought its way out of the room.

Prudence fumbled in the pocket of her apron. "Here's the recipe. It's one of my mother's. Squares. You can make the base this morning if you want."

Gerry took the tattered and stained little piece of paper. Mrs. Catford, Prudence's mother, must have clipped it out of a magazine fifty or more years ago. Marshmallow Squares, Gerry read. But Prudence hadn't put marshmallows on the list.

Gerry began to prepare what she quickly recognized was a cookie base. She pressed it into a square pan and put it to bake. The soothing smell of buttery, sugary shortbread soon filled the kitchen and adjacent living room.

She made a pot of tea and told Prudence to take a break. The house was warmer as the two women sat in front of the fire.

"They've grown since I was here." Prudence tickled the tummy of one of the kittens.

"Do you want one?" Gerry absently asked.

"I get enough cats coming here three times a week," was the reply.

Gerry refrained from asking if Prudence wasn't ever lonely and instead remarked, "That big dining room is wasted space. I don't need such a huge table taking up the whole room."

"You wouldn't get rid of it?" Prudence sounded shocked.

"It's hideous. So dark and heavy, and the sideboards and chairs: they're not my style. I'm uncomfortable working in there."

"I doubt if any of the house is your 'style'," Prudence replied tartly, "but your aunt left it to you to maintain the family heritage."

"I suppose once the Borduas sells, I could insulate the place and use the bamboo room full time."

"That's a very good idea," said a relieved-sounding Prudence. "When's the auction?"

"They said sometime in the spring. Oh well, I can tough it out for one winter, I guess. Though I miss the bamboo room."

"It was Maggie's favourite as well," Prudence said softly. "She was so happy in spring, when she could open all the windows and take possession of it again. Well," she said briskly, "those cat towels won't wash themselves. Do you think you can carry on with the baking?"

Gerry stood up. "Of course." This was progress. Prudence leaving her to bake alone *and* using a treasured family recipe.

The shortbread base was done. Gerry put water in a pot and added the gelatin. She measured out the next few ingredients and stirred the mixture on the stove, then added the icing sugar and left it to cool.

She made her ham and cheese sandwich and ate it, then poked the mixture with a finger. It was cool. Feeling somewhat nervous, she got out the electric beater. This was where the magic was supposed to happen. She beat until the mixture was foamy, then added the almond extract and drops of red food colouring and beat again. When the mixture was stiff, she poured it onto the shortbread.

The artist in her loved the soft pink colour. Prudence arrived, sandwich in hand. "Oh, Prudence, isn't it pretty? If you wanted to make a display, you could tint another batch pale green, and another pale blue, and arrange them together. It would look professional!"

"Why don't you do that next time you teach your art class or have a tea party? You can fold other ingredients in like chopped candied cherries or coconut, or put sliced almonds on top."

"No, I like how it looks, just all pink and shiny."

"Well, that shine disappears. It gets a thin crust, but it's still pretty." A small smile appeared on Prudence's face. "You can keep the recipe. I know it by heart."

Gerry blinked. Some line has been crossed when Prudence gave her this scrap of browning paper. "Thank you," she said quietly. "I will treasure it," and put it away in the drawer where Aunt Maggie's recipes lay in a folder as yet to be explored.

10

"Well," said Gerry, "we can't put it off any longer."

"I suppose not," agreed Prudence slowly. "Better to go in the daylight than after dark."

"Right."

After lunch they'd brought wood from the shed to the back porch, nervously looking at the hole with every trip. The porch was packed with wood and they stood together in the shed, gazing down. Bob, who Gerry had purposely brought outside, was perversely hunting among the bits of furniture and tools, about as far from the hole as possible.

Gerry called him; then, that failing, crawled behind a worm-hole-filled bureau and caught him. "Come on, Bob. I'll come with you." She handed him to Prudence and lowered herself into the hole.

Where the bones had lain, the police had dug the earth to a depth of a few inches. Gerry said, "Oh, this is what he likes — fresh soil. I'll watch where I go. Hand him down."

Prudence handed her Bob and the large flashlight from Gerry's car. Gerry crouched and shone the light. "Well, it's a crawlspace, that's for sure. I'm heading in the direction of the road."

Prudence walked carefully towards the front of the shed as Gerry kept up a running commentary from below. "There's old rotten lumber somebody forgot about. Quite a few stones. Ow. I kneeled on one. No, Bob, no! Not in my face! Oh, gross."

"What?"

"He pooped, then kicked it at me."

Prudence laughed.

"Okay." Gerry thumped the floor above her head. "I'm here. That's as far as I can go."

Prudence stepped into the front portion of the shed and called, "I'm in the little potting room. Is the foundation blocking you from going any further?"

"Yes. No! Prudence, Bob's gone through! There's a little door, about two feet high, rotted away enough for him to fit!" There was silence except for the sound of Gerry grunting. "I can't get it to open. No." The sound of splintering wood. "Gosh, it's in bits. I'm going on."

"Gerry, maybe I —"

Gerry's voice, muffled, interrupted her. "It's no good. Earth has fallen. It's blocked. But Bob, or another animal, I suppose, has burrowed through the dirt. It goes down. But it's tiny. I'm coming back."

Prudence walked quickly back to the hole in the floor and waited impatiently for Gerry to reappear. It was a pretty grimy face that showed a moment later.

"My goodness, Prudence, there used to be a secret way out of the shed under the road! It could come out anywhere. Maybe in Cathy's house!"

"But we know it does, Gerry. Bob keeps popping up over there."

"Oh," a disappointed Gerry agreed. "But isn't it exciting that someone, some human, made it, and not just a groundhog followed by a cat?"

"Yes, that is interesting," Prudence grudgingly admitted. "I wonder if it's something to do with the bones. Or just a coincidence. Anyway, we better bring the flashlight in case we find the tunnel's other entrance." They walked the short distance along the road towards Cathy's driveway. "How was the curling?"

"Uh, not great. Doug's teammates were there. Well, two of them were away but the other two played with us. Briefly. I didn't even get to roll the rock down the ice."

"Curl the stone down the sheet," Prudence corrected.

"You curl?"

"Don't sound so surprised. I may have curled. In the past. Who's on Doug's team?"

"I met Rick, who seems very possessive of Doug or the team or something. And Steve, who seems okay. Jimmy and Ralph were away. That's why Doug thought it would be okay to bring me. Apparently, you can't have a practice with two-fifths of the team missing."

Prudence murmured, "Rick Catford and Steve Parsley."

"Oh, that explains why I saw Steve talking to Betty Parsley at church. Relatives. She seemed a bit upset with him."

Prudence sniffed. "Relatives? Betty's only a Parsley by marriage. *She* comes from *Puckton*."

"You don't like her, Prudence?"

Prudence paused by the stone crypt in its lonely position by the road at the edge of a field. "There's something — oh, I don't know. She's worked at the inn and raised all those kids to be hard workers too. Now the twins are another story."

"Twins?"

"Steve and Ralph Parsley. Second cousins to Betty's husband Phil. Or is it third cousins? Steve's all right, I guess. But Ralph. In and out of trouble since he could walk."

Gerry felt uneasy. "What kind of trouble?"

"Oh, burning down the farmer's hay barn, for one. When he was little, he was caught drowning kittens in a bucket. Now he's older, he graduated to house breaking and car theft."

"You mean he's been to prison?" squealed Gerry.

"Some." They resumed walking.

"But, he's on Doug's team!"

"You can bet he's the spare. Doug wouldn't rely on Ralph Parsley for much. Probably he's doing Steve a favour."

"Poor Steve," Gerry murmured, her heart softening.

"Liked him, did you? You got the key?"

They stomped their snowy boots on the veranda and went inside. "I'm not coming here again in the dark," commented Gerry, "but this isn't so bad." The house in the afternoon was just a big old empty house. Creaking floors and the distant crash of the furnace coming on were not alarming.

Prudence went to flick the light switch to light the stairs.

"We don't need that today," Gerry said. "Besides, it wasn't working when Doug and I —"

Prudence flicked. The wall sconce bulb glowed.

Gerry's jaw dropped. "Every time it's one or the other. Working. Not working. Working. Not working. Now working."

Prudence shrugged and flicked the switch off. "Upstairs first?" Upstairs, all was as it should have been. Gerry ran the taps in the bathroom. "Not frozen yet," she called cheerily.

"Wait. It's not January yet."

"Tomorrow it is," Gerry replied, "and it's getting colder. I promised to look in on Mr. Parminter tonight. Toast the New Year in. Want to come?"

They walked downstairs. "I think I will. Another evening in with Charlie and Rita will have me going bonkers. Thank you. I'll phone them. And don't worry about changing bedrooms. As long as the cats are with me, I don't mind sleeping in Maggie's bed."

As they checked the many windows of the main floor, Gerry asked, "Has Maggie ever, you know, communicated?"

"It's funny. She never has."

They entered the kitchen. "Oh, look at that." Gerry crossed to the sink, pulled the plug and ran fresh water on the dustpan and brush. "I wonder if the basement will still smell winey."

"What do you mean?"

"I didn't tell you? Well, when we got here late Sunday night, ashes were still warm in the living room fireplace and, in the basement, the metal wine rack had been knocked over. We had to clean up the glass. Maybe I should wash the floor down there today."

Prudence wasn't thinking of floors. "And you didn't call the police?"

"Just kids, Prudence. It's not like the police are going to swarm the place looking for DNA and fingerprints."

"But don't you want to know how they got in, Gerry? Cathy will."

Gerry spoke slowly. "I never thought of that." She rested the pan and brush in the dish rack, then caught Prudence's look of disapproval. "What? They're clean. Let's check the basement. There's only one window and that's near the armoire where Bob appeared. Bob. We forgot about him." She opened the basement door, half-expecting him to shoot into the kitchen.

They stood at the top of the stairs. A smell of stale wine wafted upwards. "Ick," said Prudence. "I'll get a pail and mop."

"In the hall cupboard under the stairs," Gerry called. She descended a couple of stairs and heard Prudence running water in the kitchen. Wine had also splattered the bottom steps. They were painted, so perhaps hadn't stained. Not that it mattered. She surveyed the decrepit basement with a shudder. Prudence joined her.

Gerry took the wet mop. "I guess Cathy has so much to do keeping the part of the house people see nice, she's had to let the basement slide." She wiped the stairs from above, then gingerly stepped down onto the wet surface.

"You're getting your socks wet," cautioned Prudence.

"They're old ones." Gerry swabbed the floor until the odour dissipated.

"How about the rack shelves?" Prudence suggested.

"Mucky."

"I'll get a rag." Prudence noiselessly padded back up to the kitchen, returning with a faded tea towel.

Gerry used it to dry the stairs. She bowed before Prudence with a flourish and, in an exaggerated British accent, said, "Modom."

Prudence stepped down onto the clean stairs. Gerry moistened the cloth and wiped the sticky rack while Prudence cautiously looked around. "I don't see Bob," she said.

"Check inside that armoire under the window."

Prudence walked slowly to the armoire and opened its bottom doors. Then she got down on her knees. "I checked it last time, Gerry. It's solid wood at the back. He can't have come through here. He was just hiding in it the other time."

Gerry joined her on her knees. "Oh. That's disappointing. Maybe he's just fooling around in the tunnel today. Must be lots of hibernating mice and voles underground in winter. Do mice hibernate?"

This question was fated never to be answered, as at that moment they heard a muffled noise. "Over there." Gerry pointed to a corner adjacent to the window where they knelt. They rose and walked to a door, rounded at the top, ajar just the width of a cat.

"I bet I know what this is," Prudence said.

"What?"

"A cold room. For potatoes and such." She opened the door. A smell of earth met them. They both looked down. Bob sat, staring at the cement floor, where a beetle crouched, immobile. As they watched, the cat batted it gently with one paw. The beetle hopped once, then froze.

Gerry scooped her cat up. "The bug doesn't appreciate your sense of humour, Bob."

Bob struggled to escape. Prudence found an empty jar and inverted it over the beetle. Bob, released, resumed the interrogation, but now through glass.

The room was quite long, but narrow. It contained, as Prudence had guessed, sacks of potatoes, carrots, turnips, onions and beets, as well as shelves loaded with Cathy's preserves. "She's almost out of marmalade," Gerry observed.

"You make it in January," her companion replied.

Gerry stopped in her tracks, astonished. "Why?"

"Because that's when the bitter oranges you need are imported."

"Oh." Gerry put all thought of Cathy's excellent marmalade out of her mind. "So, Bob, where's your bolt hole? Eek!" She'd brushed against something hanging from the ceiling.

Prudence, busy flashing the light around the floor of the cold room, looked up. "Garlic," she said, adding, "Look at this."

The stone foundation had at one time been secured with mortar, but the latter had crumbled and loosened with the years. Some animal, or animals, had poked its way through a gap into Cathy's cold room. The gap was low down and toward the back of the room and might not be seen by a middle-aged person relying on the light cast by the single low-watt bulb hanging from the ceiling. Prudence held her hand in front of the hole. "No draft."

"So it doesn't lead outside." Gerry took the flashlight and let the light play over the end wall of the room. "See how the roof gets lower towards this wall? Would the original room have had a dirt wall or stone like this one?"

"Originally? Probably no wall. They would have had a trapdoor in the floor and a ladder. We're just below the kitchen. But this is a fancy house for rich people. They might have walled their cold storage."

"Look. This mortar that's falling away. What if, behind these stones, there used to be a passageway under the lawn, linking Fieldcrest with The Maples?"

Prudence sniffed. "Unlikely. Why ever would they have bothered with one? They weren't smuggling or hiding priests or royalty on the run. They left those activities behind in the old country. No slaves were escaping around here, either. The people were trading, farming."

"Maybe they were eccentric and thought it was fun; or paranoid, needed to feel they could escape their houses."

Prudence looked doubtful. "You'd have to study the history of the area since the two houses were built and see if there was any reason to be afraid. There are bullet holes in a church's walls the other side of the lake, but that was —"

"Bullet holes," Gerry interrupted, thoughtfully, then, "Where's Bob?"

"Well, he didn't go in the hole. We've been staring at it the whole time."

They left the cold room, first releasing the beetle, closed its door, and moved around to the other corners of the basement, calling for the cat.

"You don't suppose there's another way for him to get out, do you?" Gerry sounded anxious.

"No, I don't," snapped Prudence, "but this place is in such a state of disrepair, I wouldn't be surprised to see half a dozen holes in the walls, bursting with groundhogs, skunks and rabbits."

"I don't want to meet any more skunks," said Gerry. "Once was quite — wait. Is that him?" She shone her light in the far corner of the room, was in time to see a black shadow slip behind a big old bureau. "Bob, I —" She rounded the corner and looked behind the bureau. "Oh, my God! Prudence! Quick!"

Later that afternoon, a still tearful Gerry and a more than usually thin-lipped Prudence ate pink marshmallow squares and drank strong sweet tea sitting in rocking chairs near the fire. Bob dozed on the hearth rug. The kittens played with a catnip mouse someone had dropped into their box. Mother was taking a break crunching kibble in the kitchen.

Gerry mopped her eyes. "It's not even that I *knew* her, just to nod to, you know?"

Prudence nodded. "She was younger than me and had children. We never clicked."

"I mean, until last weekend, I never even exchanged more than 'Hello, how are you?' with her." She sobbed.

"It's shock," Prudence reassured her, patting her on the back. "You feel it more when you're young, but you get over it sooner."

"You mean like Aunt Maggie's death? Oh, but Prudence, that was different. You knew her well and you — you found the body. Oh!"

Prudence nodded. "Exactly. You found it this time. Or Bob did."

"Bob was more interested in the water drips coming from the pipe to the sump pit." Gerry shuddered reliving the scene so recently played out. Bob sitting next to the sump pit, feinting at drops of water, the small inflow pipe set in a slimy wall, the woman face downward at the edge of the pit, one hand trailing on the water in it.

Touching the body (reluctantly); Prudence gently turning it over to confirm life was extinct; seeing the battered but still recognizable face of Betty Parsley. Both of them stumbling away to the kitchen, where Prudence made the call. Gerry going back to the basement to get Bob. Closing the basement door and sitting in Cathy's cold living room to wait for the police.

Then all of that. The questions. The information given. The police officer in charge's assessing looks, taking in Gerry's shock, Prudence's stern resignation, the absence of any signs of struggle on their hands or clothes, though they were both a bit grimy at the pants' knees. Bob sat on Gerry's lap patiently, though every time the double doors of the living room opened or closed, or someone went in or out the front door, his ears and tail twitched with curiosity.

Finally, the body was taken away. The police officer asked for Gerry's key to Cathy's house. They were free to go. There would be more questions tomorrow.

Numbly, the women put on their coats and boots. Gerry tucked Bob, protesting, inside her coat with his quizzical face peeking out, and they slowly walked back to The Maples.

Prudence phoned her neighbours to tell them she was sleeping at Gerry's and would return the next day.

"You didn't mention Betty?" Gerry asked drearily.

"Of course not." Prudence sounded indignant. "What if Phil or one of the children hasn't yet been notified? I won't tell anyone until it's general knowledge. Then — you'll see — we'll be pestered with 'well-wishers' wanting to know all about it."

"Some of them really will be well-wishers," Gerry said humbly. "Doug, Andrew. I wish Bea was here. And Cece. Oh my! Do you think the police will tell Cathy?"

"Bound to. Perhaps she'll cut her trip short." Prudence rose. "Want more tea? No? I'll do the dishes. Good squares, by the way. Just like Mother used to make."

The man materialized in front of the living room fireplace. Black and white kittens were fast asleep in a box, curled into a large marmalade cat's side. She opened her eyes.

The man looked at the objects on the mantel. One provoked no more than a look of resignation, but another brought a tender smile to his diaphanous face. He looked around the room helplessly, as if wondering why he was there.

She had brought him, as she always would. He drifted from the living room into the dining room, in neither of which he'd ever been welcomed; looked at the paintings on the walls.

He barely noticed the multitude of cats, sleeping or not, each on its own chair; a big black one with four white paws, sprawled in the middle of the massive table, blinked at him. The man looked for her portrait.

He found it at last in a smaller room next to the larger. There she was, her sweet expression, those loving eyes. Sybil.

He stared at it for a long time. Well, this was some compensation for being disturbed in his long rest under the woodshed. He wafted into the hallway with its large staircase and stiffened, if smoke could be said to stiffen.

If he'd had any moisture in his wispy mouth, he would have spat it at the large portrait that faced him. Medium brown hair, medium brown eyes, the slight jowls that told of middle-class comfortable living. An old man when he'd married her, yet he'd lived the longest. Of them all.

He tore himself away from the portrait. Past. It was all in the past. And they were at rest.

But he was not. How could he sleep when she was so near? But he couldn't get to her. Not in there. Not unless he was invited. He sighed and a grey cloud condensed in front of him.

He let himself rise to the second floor, not noticing the black and white cat following. His gaze played from one family portrait to another. The old man's descendants, no doubt.

He stopped and returned to one of the paintings. The image of a young girl awoke something in his memory. Surely that was how his mother used to look, long ago, when he was a small boy.

A thin face, dark hair and dark eyes, a shy smile. His gentle mother, before life coarsened, toughened her. But his mother's portrait would hardly be likely to be gracing the walls of the Coneybear home. Who could it be? The girl also had a look of Sybil. Her daughter?

He lost interest and returned downstairs to the room with the dying fire. He began to stretch out his hands to its warmth, then grimaced. It was no use to him now. As if to mock him, the black and white cat stretched and yawned, then curled up on the braided rug, as close to the fireplace as it could get.

The man gave a sigh of infinite weariness and let himself go. The kittens in the box mewed in their sleep. The marmalade cat closed her eyes as he faded from her sight.

PART 3

OLD FRIENDS

11

Gerry, feeling a bit sick to her stomach — and not just because of the seven pink marshmallow squares she'd eaten — went upstairs to lie down. No cats followed her, she thought, but as she went to close her door, Lightning slithered in.

Gerry knew better than to pick her up. She got wearily into bed and the little calico jumped up and settled by her feet.

Where her predecessor, Marigold, had been a long-hair, Lightning's fur was short. Where Marigold had been a white cat with clearly defined large patches of beigey-orange and black, mostly on her back and sides, Lightning was mostly black, with muted orange zigzags throughout her coat, and a striking orange blaze across her nose.

And where Marigold had had a clear sense of her superiority — after all, she was a calico — and position as First Cat, Lightning was conflicted. She both craved Gerry's affection and rejected it. Gerry had learned that as long as she let the cat come to her, there was peace between them.

She felt rather than heard the faint purring coming from the end of the bed. The room darkened as the winter sun set, and then she slept.

She slowly came to consciousness. She was deliciously warm. Lightning, having crept up the bed and curled into her side as she slept, immediately jumped off the bed. Apparently, she was willing only to trust a sleeping Gerry, not an awake one.

Gerry yawned and sat up. Now for a nice, relaxing evening at home. Then she remembered. A death. A violent one, by the looks of it.

She put her robe on over the clothes she'd slept in and flumped downstairs. Prudence must also have gone for a nap. "I need a coffee," Gerry told Bob, who was stretching on the hearth rug, raking it with his claws.

The phone rang. She picked it up and got the cream from the fridge. "Oh, Mr. Parminter. I'm so sorry. Yes. I fell asleep. No. No. I'll come over. May Prudence come as well? Yes. I got some wine. All right. All right. Bye." She hung up. "Oh, rats. Well, not before my coffee." Prudence appeared, bleary-eyed. "Did the phone wake you?" When she nodded, Gerry poured her a cup of coffee. "Here. Want to come over to Mr. Parminter's? Bring in the New Year?"

"Why not?" Prudence weakly replied. "We'll keep each other company. Should we bring some food?"

"No. He says he's got cheese and crackers and nuts. I bought a bottle of Prosecco. Cheap and fizzy. Just let me splash my face with cold water."

They picked their way carefully along the edge of the road. A few cars, no doubt full of revellers, passed them.

Mr. Parminter let them in, his face wreathed in smiles. "How very nice of you to come spend your New Year's Eve, your Silvester, with me. Drop your coats there. Come through. Come through. We're in here."

Here was a large living room with a sofa and chairs drawn up to a glowing electric fire. Gerry had to admire its efficiency, and, of course, there was no way Mr. Parminter could be expected to haul wood inside or, in fact, even kneel to lay a fire.

In his nineties, and still able to make short drives in his ancient Toyota Camry ("They have to send to California, you know, when she needs spare parts."), he was in good health, but frail.

Now he settled himself in one of the chairs, gesturing to the low table in front of the sofa. "Help yourselves, please. I will have a morsel of Oka, Gerry, if you will prepare it for me."

She cut into the little round and handed him a wedge impaled on the tip of the cheese knife. He broke off a crumb and dropped it in front of Graymalkin, basking on the stone hearth.

Gerry asked, "Shall we have the fizz now?"

"Oh, let's wait a bit, until we're closer to midnight," Mr. Parminter requested. "Now, what have you ladies been up to?"

Prudence and Gerry looked at each other. Prudence opened, then closed her mouth. Gerry took a deep breath and said, "We found something." When she saw Prudence's eyes bulge a warning, she hastily added, "In the woodshed." Prudence relaxed.

"What kind of something?" Mr. Parminter queried.

Gerry decided to start small. "A bone. Bob found a bone. Which he brought inside and which freaked me out when I stepped on it."

Mr. Parminter interrupted her. "Oh, I know what you mean. Sometimes — well, not now it's winter — sometimes Graymalkin drags in a dreadful bit of something he's killed, and with my eyes, I sometimes don't see it before I tread on it. I always wear slippers now." He stroked the cat, who had jumped up and was kneading his lap.

"Well, I was in bare feet and it hurt as well as freaking me out. So, I assumed it was a chicken bone until I went for wood. You know how my shed floor got caved in from the storm?" Mr. Parminter nodded. "Well, Bob jumped in there. He's like a dog, likes to follow me when I'm outside."

Mr. Parminter interrupted her again. "Where are my manners? Prudence, there's some port over there, and glasses. I think it would go well with the cheese."

Prudence brought and poured them all a glass of port. White, it tasted to Gerry like plums. "Perhaps a bit of Brie?" Mr.

Parminter requested. Gerry put it on a thin wafer and handed it over. Graymalkin, purring, lapped at his little portion.

"So. Bob tried to drag out another bone from under the shed, but when I looked at it, I realized, or guessed, it belonged to no animal. The skeleton was laid out on its front or back. I don't know. Animals may have shifted bits of it."

She shivered and sipped her port. Mr. Parminter leaned over and touched her hand. "You know, Gerry, we are all bones. They are nothing to be frightened of."

"I know. I wasn't frightened so much as sad. Here was this poor person, forgotten by those he loved. Or maybe they worried about him, never knew where he wound up?"

"I just meant to say, don't let it oppress you. After all, we have a lovely brand new year opening up in a few hours. We have our good health, our friends, our families." At this, Gerry, thinking of the Parsley family and how they must be feeling, felt her chin and mouth wobble and had to rush from the room. She heard Prudence reassure a dismayed Mr. Parminter. "She misses her parents. And the bones upset her. You weren't to know."

Gerry, in the bathroom, mopped up her tears. She *did* miss her parents. *And* Aunt Maggie. And Uncle Geoff. She blew her nose into a wad of toilet paper, flushed and wandered into the hall.

Graymalkin (She really was getting better at not calling him Stupid!) had followed her, she supposed out of cattish curiosity, and sat on the hall runner. She timidly offered him the back of her hand to sniff and heard Mr. Parminter reading aloud from the volume of Cowper she'd given him. She stepped closer and stood in the living room doorway.

Prudence sipped port and stared at the fire while Mr. Parminter, magnifying glass in hand, read. The poem, entitled 'A Fable,' ended with a stanza called 'Moral.'

'Tis Providence alone secures
In every change, both mine and yours.
Safety consists not in escape
From dangers of a frightful shape,
An earthquake may be bid to spare
The man that's strangled by a hair.
Fate steals along with silent tread,
Found oft'nest in what least we dread,
Frowns in the storm with angry brow,
But in the sunshine strikes the blow.

He said, "That's a bit grim, isn't it? What about this? 'The
Pineapple and the Bee.'" Gerry, still loitering in the doorway,
smiled at the image. "I'll just read the ending. It's about a bee who
wastes her time trying to get into a tightly sealed hothouse. They
grew pineapples under glass in England in those days. It's a poem
Maggie marked."

Our dear delights are often such,
Exposed to view but not to touch;
The sight our foolish heart inflames,
We long for pine-apples in frames,
With hopeless wish one looks and lingers,
One breaks the glass and cuts his fingers;
But they whom truth and wisdom lead,
Can gather honey from a weed.

"Let's see if we can find another one." He flipped carefully
through the old pages. Gerry came into the room, exchanging a
weak smile with Prudence.

"What about this? Maggie marked the whole poem. 'The Jackdaw.' The jackdaw sits up on the church steeple and watches the world."

> He sees that this great roundabout
> The world, with all its motley rout,
> Church, army, physic, law,
> Its customs and its bus'nesses
> Are no concern at all of his,
> And says, what says he? — Caw.

They laughed. "Oh, I remember, these are Cowper's translations of another poet, Bourne, who wrote in Latin. My God, people used to be cultured."

"Like pineapples," quipped Prudence.

He looked at her over his reading glasses. "I take your point, but still. Ah. Let's see what he says of 'The Winter Evening.'"

Graymalkin returned and, seeing his master occupied, jumped onto the sofa next to Gerry and, after putting out a tentative paw, climbed into her lap. Gerry said, "You're certainly a civilizing influence, Mr. Parminter."

"Yes, well, poetry is — ah, you mean on the cat."

"Him too." Gerry sweetly smiled.

He peered at the bottom of a page. "Oh, here he's written in a letter to his friend Hill in 1783. 'I see the winter approaching without much concern, though a passionate lover of fine weather and the pleasant scenes of summer. But the long evenings have their comforts too; and there is hardly to be found upon earth, I suppose, so snug a creature as an Englishman, by his fireside, in the winter. I mean, however, an Englishman that lives in the country.'" He took off his glasses and added, "In a well-insulated and heated house. I won't read the poem. It's quite long."

"Read us some of your poetry, Mr. Parminter. Would you?"

"It will sound poor stuff after this classical work."

"It will sound of its time as Cowper's sounds of his," Prudence said absently.

Mr. Parminter gave her a look. "A very penetrating thing to say, Prudence. All right, Gerry. You'll find one of mine over there. Yellow cover. Find it?" She brought it to him. "No, I'm tired. My eyes are tired. You read what you fancy."

The poem's title was the same as its first line.

> The fields begin to sheathe themselves in some
> Soft metal underfoot as they ripen
> Into hardness. The air quiets. Except
> For Christmas' three-week hum, traffic thins.
> Some life has left the earth, been driven down
> And in. The metal spreads its silent hymn
> That sings of hardship, night; of frozen beings,
> Their signals lost; records the broken keen
> Of almost-dogs. They spread out as they run
> For meat. Under the trees their lines bisect
> The rabbits' shorter curves. Life joins life:
> Gray fur, brown fur, metallic scent of blood.

Prudence murmured, "Beautiful."

Mr. Parminter commented. "Yes, well, I used to walk in the woods where I lived and would see the tracks but never the animals."

Gerry turned a page. The poem was called "This Cold Winter."

> Why do I think such desperate thoughts in winter,
> Such separate thoughts. I lie in the coffin
> My bed, unattached to any thing, any one.
> No one, no thing can undo my dread.

No cup or touch can attenuate this cold whimper,
This cold winter.

"Brrr," said Gerry.

"Donne. I'd been reading Donne," he explained.

Gerry read the book's title. "*Elegies in Elysian Fields.* Could you explain that to me?"

"Certainly. Elysium was the place the dead passed through before entering the other world, also known as the Islands of the Blessed or the Fortunate Isles."

Prudence asked, "Where my mother is?"

"'Where life is easiest for men. No snow is there, nor heavy storm, nor ever rain, but ever does Ocean send up blasts of the shrill-blowing West Wind that they may give cooling to men.' Homer, from his *Odyssey*."

Gerry had a quizzical look on her face. "But it doesn't sound like, I mean, in the poems, that you were in Elysian Fields, Mr. Parminter."

"Elegies, Gerry," Prudence answered.

"Oh. Right. Here's one. It's called '#6 Mermaid Road.'"

When every taboo great or small is broke,
And, landed on the sun, we sweat to plant
Our last gardens; when moon-pull that pressed sweet
Flesh to flesh, passed over each fretted face,
Aroused, soothed, each one of owned, kept demons,
Has lost its home — blasted, mined, and smelted
Free of any precious ore — and we count
The change left after our dubious purchase;

We will fill with feather, red bark, shell, bone,
The one handmade bowl, lip across from lip,

And perch it in some temporary space,
Construct imaginary rafts of light
To bring us to an archipelago
Of the heart — of still water over stone.

"Huh." Mr. Parminter reflected when she'd finished. "That one, believe it or not, was a love poem."

"I can see that," commented Prudence, "especially at the end. It's intimate after all that planetary stuff."

"I'm going to get the Prosecco," said Gerry. "Us visual types don't really get poetry, eh, Graymalkin?" She went into the kitchen and returned with the chilled bottle and three fresh glasses. After the cork had popped, and they were ready to toast, Mr. Parminter made a speech.

"I would like to say that this year was a very mixed year. We lost Maggie — and Geoff — but we gained Gerry, and I gained Graymalkin here." The cat lazily blinked, sitting erect in front of the flickering gas flames. "Something else," the old man added. "I would officially request that both of you address me as Blaise." His voice trembled. "There's no one else left so to do."

Gerry said, "To Maggie," and they sipped.

"To Geoff Petherbridge," Prudence said. They sipped again.

"To Gerry's arrival." Mr. Parminter raised his glass at her.

"To Graymalkin. To the love of a cat," Gerry suggested, thinking of Marigold.

"And to Blaise," both women chimed.

Prudence twinkled as she added, "Easily the most handsome man in the room."

Blaise laughed. "And I used to be, you know. I used to be."

"Blaise." Gerry had remembered something. "What did you mean when you called New Year's Eve Silvester? Isn't Silvester a name?"

"Yes. It's most interesting. Pope St. Sylvester lived in the fourth century. He slew a dragon with a prayer and what is described as a thread on its mouth. December thirty-first is his burial day and his feast day. In some parts of Europe this day is known as Silvester." He leaned forward anxiously. "I hope I haven't upset you talking about burial." When Gerry looked blank, he continued. "You know: those bones you were telling me you found in your shed."

And the other, more ghastly find of the recent hours rose up before Gerry and Prudence. "You know, Blaise," Gerry said, rising to her feet, "it has been a terrifically long day. I'm awfully tired. But I'm going to phone you tomorrow and fill you in with more details of the bones. We'll talk about it then." And with sincere wishes for a happy New Year, they took their leave.

They walked arm in arm. "I just couldn't tell him tonight."

"I should hope not. It might shock him."

"He may have known her. He may have *taught* her."

"No. Remember I told you she didn't grow up here?"

"So you did. Poor woman. Poor woman."

Silently, they let themselves in to the house and wearily went to their beds.

12

Next morning Gerry drove Prudence to collect some of her clothes from her neighbours' house. It just seemed easier if Gerry drove. Both women were exhausted. "The worst part," Prudence said, glumly looking at her house, swathed in tarps, "is that everyone is on holiday until at least this Monday, and even then, some workmen are away on vacation. God knows when I'll be able to get back in."

"You're welcome at The Maples for as long as you need. Maybe you should take that trip to St. Lucia while your house is being repaired."

Prudence nodded. "That's an idea. Though I wonder if the police will let me leave the country now we've found this new body."

Gerry was aghast. "I never thought of that. Can we really be suspects?"

"I touched her."

"Well, I cleaned up the broken wine bottles and washed the floor. They might — no, Doug cleaned up the glass. Oh, now he's involved, too! What a terrible start to the year!"

"When we get back, call Mr. — call Blaise and break it to him gently. Word can't have gotten out yet. Everyone is sleeping in this morning."

Gerry smiled for the first time that morning. "Charlie and Rita weren't asleep. I could hear them from outside."

Prudence sighed and said nothing.

They planned to spend a quiet day.

The police phoned and asked some more questions: the same ones they'd asked the day before but in different words. Prudence explained that The Maples was only her temporary residence and why. Gerry explained again how she and Doug Shapland had checked the house late at night after the Parsleys' party, but hadn't looked at the part of the basement where the sump pit was located.

Prudence got back on the phone to ask if she could go on vacation and was told, no, they'd rather she didn't.

Then Doug called, expressing his surprise at receiving a phone call from the police that morning and being told to come to the station for a talk that afternoon. Then Gerry phoned Blaise and told him why she'd been so upset the previous evening.

Then they had lunch.

Gerry bit into her tuna sandwich. "Blaise says today is the Feast of Fools and that Christmas gets crazy from now on. People used to switch their roles. If you want to be the boss, I'll be the sassy housekeeper for a while."

"No, that's okay. I have some Christmas sass saved up that I need to get out."

"Prudence, I don't really know what to do. None of this makes any sense. Why was Betty Parsley in Cathy's basement? How did she get in? Who was with her? And who —" here Gerry's voice grew hushed — "who *killed* her?"

"I don't feel so sassy anymore," Prudence said soberly.

"Me neither. 'Eight somethings something' suddenly seems way too frivolous." She finished her sandwich and pushed the plate away. "I know. Let's just think about our bones in the shed — who *that* was. Want to read some letters?"

Prudence shrugged. "Might as well." She followed Gerry upstairs to her little office and watched as she shifted some boxes about.

"These I've been through. So cute. Gramma and Grampa Coneybear's love letters from before they were married. They had nicknames for each other. These are bills. Okay, this box contains deeds. I've been through it but don't know where the properties are, exactly." She handed the box to Prudence. "One for you and one for me. Let's go back down by the fire."

Prudence sat at the table and unpacked her box. Gerry moved the banana box and sat on the rug with hers. They worked in silence for a moment, sorting.

"Whatcha got, Prudence?" Gerry asked absently.

"Deeds, like you said. Bills of sale for land. Someone was busy buying property in the mid-nineteenth century."

Gerry got up and extracted the family tree from the papers on the table. "So that would have been —" She scanned the generations. "These Catfords don't go back far enough. Here are some Parsleys at the right time. A Muxworthy — Charles — no, he was born in 1840. He'd be a bit young to be wheeling and dealing. So, who? Ah." Her finger came to rest on one name that stood alone. No parents, no siblings. "Him again. John Coneybear," she murmured.

"One of the founders of Lovering," Prudence informed her.

Gerry's finger slid across the page. "Married to Sybil Muxworthy, Prudence. Remember the reaction from Mrs. Smith to those two names?"

"Through Mrs. Smith," Prudence patiently reiterated. "It's not her reaction. It's the spirit's."

"Yes, yes." Gerry was scanning documents. "So you sort these according to time frame and especially pay attention to the ones with Coneybear or Muxworthy on them." She returned to the rug. "I've got letters to read."

For a while there were just the sounds of the crackling fire, purring cats and paper being unfolded. Gerry, being the hostess, plugged in the kettle and made them each a coffee. She noticed

Prudence was making notes on a separate piece of paper. She finished her letters and moodily stared into the fire, stroking the kittens as she sipped her drink.

Prudence went to the kitchen, returning with Lovering's little phone book. She unfolded the map in the back and smoothed it on the table. "Come look at this." Gerry sat next to her.

"Some of the lot names I don't recognize but some I do. See, this one. Birch Wood. That's here." She pointed on the map and shaded in the land with her pencil. "And here is the Sugar Bush. You know where that is."

Gerry made a face but said nothing. The Sugar Bush: where, last fall, she'd been scared, then skunked, just before she'd found Uncle Geoff's dead body. Prudence shaded it in on the map.

By the time she'd finished, there were a few gaps, but many miles of the shore, former farmland and woods that surrounded The Maples were marked. "He bought some and some he got when he married Sybil."

Gerry looked fascinated. "John Coneybear?"

"Yup. This is all part of old Lovering, the land the first traders squatted on when they began to settle. By John's time, The Maples was built and he was turning it into quite an estate."

"For his children," Gerry said slowly, looking at the family tree and remembering the plaque inside St. Anne's Church, with its sad list of children, most of them dead in childhood or infancy. "These two made it. Margaret Coneybear, 1855 to 1945, and Albert Coneybear, 1865 to 1921. Born ten years apart and poor Sybil died the same year Albert was born.

"I think there's a drawing of her, Sybil, I mean. Remember that sweet-faced woman? She's still hanging in the gallery." Gerry led the way to the little room off the dining room and went to one of the drawings. She took it off the wall and read what her Aunt Maggie had scribbled on the paper pasted on the back. "'Sybil Muxworthy Coneybear, artist unknown, circa 1860?'

Pretty. Light brown hair, hazel eyes. Where was this one hanging, Prudence, before we brought it in here?"

"Upstairs, I think, in the hall." Prudence led the way. They stopped and looked at the space where Sybil's portrait had been. A landscape was to the left while a simple sketch of a little girl hung to the right. Gerry removed the latter and flipped it over. Aunt Maggie had written "Margaret (Margie) Coneybear Petherbridge, 1855–1945."

"It's hard to tell from a pencil sketch, but she seems to have been dark haired and dark eyed. A thin face and long. Not like her mother's heart-shaped one."

Prudence grunted. "Must have taken after her father. Do you want to see him?" She carried Sybil while Gerry brought Margie. They descended into the large main foyer and surveyed John Coneybear, the founder of the family. Gerry placed Margie's portrait on the table under John's and gestured to Prudence to do the same with Sybil's.

"No portrait of Albert, is there?"

Prudence thought. "Maybe in one of the photo albums. There should be some of him and lots of Margie, she lived so long."

"That can be another project, looking through the photographs. Gosh, I haven't done that since I was around ten." Gerry surveyed the family group before her. "Both parents with light brown hair and eyes; mother's jaw heart-shaped, father's squarish. He looks like he enjoyed his food. And a little dark girl with long straight cheekbones. Who did she look like, I wonder?"

Prudence spoke doubtfully. "Cecil Muxworthy is dark with a long face. She could look like some other Muxworthy relation."

"That's probably it," agreed Gerry.

They went back into the living room and sat by the fire. "What was in your letter box?" Prudence asked.

Gerry replied, "Mostly the letters of Elizabeth Parsley, Albert's wife. From him and her children."

"Oh, I remember her from when I was a little girl. She was one of Mother's great-aunts and used to have us to tea once a year. Around Christmas, come to think of it. She was very strict and stiff. Not at all like her sister-in-law, Margie, I've heard. She died before I was born. They were both widowed young. Then Margie's only child died and she moved back into her childhood home. With Elizabeth."

"I wonder if that was difficult for them," Gerry said.

"Elizabeth would have considered it her duty and Margie her right, so I guess it worked out okay. You have any thoughts about supper?"

"Well, if it weren't New Year's Day, I'd say, let's go to the Parsley for sup — oh, Prudence! I forgot all about Betty Parsley!"

"Good," her friend replied. "I'm going to rummage in your freezer and then we should feed the cats."

They dined on Bea Muxworthy's homemade stew and garlic bread, also from the freezer. The phone rang as they were doing the dishes. Gerry took the call. "Doug! How did it go? Uh-huh. Uh-huh. Well, I'm sorry about this, Doug, but I did explain to the — what? Oh. Yes. I see. Goodbye." Prudence tactfully said nothing as she continued to wash the cutlery.

"That was Doug," Gerry said slowly. "He's a bit upset. The police kept him in for hours."

"That's not your fault," Prudence replied briskly.

"No. But he seems to think we should keep our distance from each other until the matter is resolved."

"They may never find out who did it."

Gerry frowned. "When the business with Uncle Geoff and Margaret happened, he wanted us to keep our distance until the spring. Then he asks me curling and that was a bust. Now it's off again." She sighed and added dejectedly, "I honestly don't know how he feels."

As Prudence didn't either, she wisely said nothing.

"I'm going for a long hot bath, then to bed to read. Good night, Prudence."

"Goodnight," Prudence said distractedly. "Do you mind if I read the letters in this box?"

"Help yourself," Gerry yawned.

"It's Friday," announced Prudence.

"So?" Gerry buttered her toast, then slathered on marmalade.

"So, I work on Fridays. This place is awful hairy."

Gerry looked around casually. There were dust bunnies in the corners of the room and a layer of dust particles on that part of the table undisturbed by their breakfast. "All right," she said doubtfully. "But you could postpone until Monday, if you want. Have a real rest."

"I'm uncomfortable living in a messy house," said Prudence rather primly.

"Then go to it. I too shall work. Maybe I'll go shopping this aft. Make a list of what you want to eat over the weekend." Prudence was already dragging the ancient vacuum cleaner out of its cupboard and grunted by way of reply.

Gerry cleared the table, then spread out the cat portraits she'd begun what seemed like weeks ago. As she sketched, the portraits took on a more cartoonish flavour and she began to exaggerate the cats' gestures and movements.

Bob, who'd been lying on the dining room table the night before, gave her an idea, and she began to draw human characters as well. There was a tall thin old woman, a little girl, a butler. She seated them, except the butler, at a huge table adorned with all kinds of fancifully decorated cakes and desserts. And, for some reason, the cat modelled after Bob began jumping over the cakes.

"'The Cake-Jumping Cats of —' What would be a good name, Mother?" Mother stopped grooming the kitten of the moment, blinked, then resumed her task. "Of Lickspittle? No. Too yucky.

Of Hairball-on-the-Marsh? Hairball-on-the-Lake? I know. It's not a house. It's a *castle*. Lots of turret things and suits of armour in the hall."

Gerry was amazed when Prudence plunked a sandwich down in front of her with the announcement, "It's one o'clock. I've made a grocery list." She examined the sketches while Gerry munched hungrily. "What's all this? A children's book?" She smiled her thin-lipped smile as she flipped through the sheets of paper and looked at the illustrations. "They're funny."

"'The Cake-Jumping Cats of —' I haven't got a funny name for the place yet. For some reason, the people of this castle or village get their cats to jump cakes. I don't know if there's enough to make a book."

"Children's books just need a short plot, a moral, if possible, and, in the case of this one, jokes. No? I don't think it's beyond you. After all, you can do the writing and the drawing."

"I better go shop or I'll get sucked into it again. List?"

"Next to your wallet and keys. I'll do this room while you're out."

"Don't touch —" Gerry indicated the sketches on the table.

"Yes, yes. I know how to dust around your art by now."

As she drove to Lovering, Gerry felt the exhilaration she'd come to associate with starting a new project. She always forgot the hard graft that would be necessary to bring a project to its conclusion.

She got a small grocery cart, then groaned when she checked Prudence's list. Three boxes of cat litter. She put the cart back, taking one of the larger ones.

Because it was the holidays, she amused herself by going up and down all the aisles, choosing little treats she and Prudence could enjoy together. Prudence had put peanut butter, crunchy, large, and bread-and-butter pickles together on the list. Gerry grinned, knowing her friend would usually eat nothing else for lunch, at least on a weekday. "Ooh, chocolate-coated digestives," Gerry noted, and took one package each of dark and milk chocolate. They weren't on the list, but what the heck.

She paused by the tinned fish. Kippers? Kippers with scrambled eggs and buttered toast. She was just reaching for a couple of cans at the top of the pile when a voice at her elbow spoke.

"Hi, Red."

She was so startled she turned abruptly and found herself looking up into Steve Parsley's face. The cuff of her coat caught the stack of canned fish and many, many tins cascaded onto her shoulder and from there to the floor.

Steve stooped to help her with the tins. "Red's herrings," he said.

"What?"

"Red's herrings," he repeated. "Not so funny the second time but I don't know your name, so —"

"Yes, you do. It's Gerry. We met at the curling —" Gerry's voice trailed off as she realized she was in the presence of Steve's twin. "Are you Ralph Parsley?"

"Yep." He finished restacking the tins. "Sorry I distracted you. And sorry I'm not Steve." He smiled. "He seems to have made quite an impression."

"You mean, so much so that he gets tins of kippers hurled at him?" Gerry said, a trifle sarcastically. She put two tins in her cart and mumbling, "Sorry about that," walked on.

"Hey, I've had worse." He was having no difficulty keeping up with her. She stopped in the pet supplies aisle and heaved a ten-kilo box of litter into her cart. "Let's start again," he pleaded, as he assisted her with the other two boxes. "I'm Ralph Parsley, bro of Steve, member of Doug Shapland's curling team. And if I'd known you were coming to our practice, I'd have gotten over that flu bug much quicker."

It wasn't working: his charm, or whatever he called it. He looked and sounded like his brother, but there was something "off," something Gerry couldn't warm to.

"I'm sorry about your relative," she said.

He paused with the final cat litter box resting on the edge of her cart. He looked confused. "Relative?"

Assuming he hadn't yet heard, Gerry was horrified. She wasn't going to tell him about Betty Parsley's death in the pet supplies aisle of their local supermarket. She dropped the box into the cart and hurried on, saying, "Forget I said anything."

He followed her, though. "Oh. You must mean Betty. I thought you meant, you know, a *real* relative. She's just married to Cousin Phil, you know. Not blood. So, what about a coffee?"

Appalled, Gerry blurted out, "Now?"

"Yeah, now. Or whenever you like. Tomorrow? Tell ya what. I'll take you for brunch tomorrow. They do a great buffet at that place up by the highway."

Gerry was unloading her groceries as fast as she could. She paid the cashier. As Ralph went to steer her cart to the car, she removed his hands, and, drawing herself up to the length of her five-foot nothingness, said, in full hearing of the cashier, bag boy and next customer, "Mr. Parsley, I am sorry for your family's loss but I have no wish to accompany you to brunch, lunch or dinner." She gestured at the bag boy to accompany her, and added, "Or coffee!" Her last glance back was of a scowling Ralph Parsley, standing, staring after her.

She felt tears coming into her eyes as she fumbled for a dollar for the boy. "Thank you, miss," he mumbled, as he dragged her cart away.

She sat in her car and fumed. "So irritating! So pushy! No filters!" In her rear-view mirror she saw Ralph burst through the doors of the store with a case of beer under his arm, narrowly missing an old lady creeping in, and slid down in her seat, snapping the mechanism that locked the car doors. At least he didn't appear to know hers was the red Mini with the dent in its roof. He got into an old black pickup truck and burned rubber pulling out of the lot.

As she drove carefully home, she quickly forgot about him, looking forward to unpacking the groceries in Prudence's peaceful presence, to enjoying a cup of coffee, and then getting back to work.

13

"Dibble!" shouted Gerry. "It's Dibble, Prudence!"

"All right, all right. What's Dibble?" Prudence was taking the armloads of wood Gerry was bringing from the woodshed to the back porch and stacking them neatly on the tarp.

"I saw one on Aunt Maggie's little potting bench and remembered the word. You know: that tool used for making holes in the earth for seeds. A dibble!"

"Surely a tool invented by Eve in the Garden," muttered Prudence.

"What? No, I don't mean *a* dibble. I mean Dibble! The village where my cake-jumping cats are going to live!"

"Ah," Prudence said wisely, "*That* Dibble." She was happy Gerry had this new project to distract her from Betty Parsley's mysterious death, and even from the discovery of the body under the woodshed floor. Prudence didn't know which made her more nervous: the old bones or the new. "Dibble, indeed," she said, as Gerry, shadowed by Bob, disappeared around the corner of the house to get more wood.

Prudence stretched and looked out over the frozen lake. She supposed life would get back to normal after the weekend. For most people, that is. She wondered when she'd be back inside her own cottage. She was getting accustomed to staying at The Maples. Not that it was the first time. One winter, Maggie Coneybear had had a flu turn into pneumonia and had needed nursing. Prudence had stayed for a week, rather than leave Maggie to the mercies of her sister Mary or niece Margaret. Not that they'd offered to stay, anyway.

And, on another occasion, Maggie had sprained her ankle and needed crutches, so Prudence stayed for a few days. She'd been happy to do it. Maggie had been her best friend. Hard to believe she was gone. Prudence's reverie was broken into by the reappearance of Gerry's happy face.

"And Marigold is going to be the Queen of Dibble Castle and I'm going to put Aunt Maggie in it too. Well, just someone who looks like her. And dogs and some of the other cats. Bob, of course, will be the hero. And a little girl who's very bored at first but then tries to train the cats to jump, which we all know won't work. Prudence, did Aunt Maggie have a cookbook with photos of really fancy cakes in it? You know. Old-fashioned giant things with decorations?"

"I'll have a look. That's enough wood now, Gerry."

"Okay. I'll just lock the shed."

Prudence made coffee and got a stack of old cookbooks from a cupboard. She was flipping through the pages when Gerry joined her. "Ooh, I've got to have that one." She pointed at a Gâteau Saint-Honoré, its top piled with creampuffs.

"We don't have to make these, do we?" begged Prudence.

"I'd like to, but no. Expensive ingredients and just us to eat them. Look at that! Floral Basket Cake," she read. "How on earth do they get it to stand up?"

"There are things called dowels, not unlike dibbles, special cake-reinforcing sticks."

But Gerry had moved on. "Chocolate Swans. I'm in awe. Battenberg Cake. Very royal."

"I can make that," said Prudence. "It's just finicky."

"Lucky Horseshoe Cake. Rose Garland Cake. Lovely names. Lazy Daisy Cake. Apricot Ribbon Cake. Prudence, I'm getting hungry."

"Have a marshmallow square," said Prudence, handing her the tin.

Gerry spent the rest of the day roughing out the first half of the book. She hooted with laughter as she named her characters: Atholfass, a calico cat, Queen of Dibble in the province of Fasswassenbasset; Max Scarfnhatznmitz, a border collie, courtier to the queen; Tess, Lady Ponscomb, a retriever, lady-in-waiting; and the humans: Latooth Élonga, a middle-aged authoress; Languida Fatiguée, a twelve-year-old girl; and Sneathe, a supercilious butler.

She was sketching the book's opening scene — a tea party — when Prudence called "Supper!" Gerry walked into the kitchen.

"Smells yummy. What did you make?"

"I roasted the chicken with peppers, onions and mushrooms, opened a can of tomato sauce and boiled some spaghetti."

"Did you ever consider moving in here permanently, Prudence?" Gerry loaded up her plate and they ate amidst the pages of her prototype book.

"Huh," Prudence grunted. She lifted pages and studied the characters. "I like your dogs. Did you ever have a dog?"

"No. But lots of my friends did when I was a kid. I want the book to appeal to cat and dog lovers alike."

"And who's this?" Prudence pointed to a long skinny middle-aged woman with glasses, her hair in a bun. She wore a long baggy dress and loads of necklaces and bracelets.

"That's Latooth Élonga. She's the queen's best friend and lives in the castle. She writes mystery novels."

"Of course she does. Languida Fatiguée." Prudence snorted with laughter.

Gerry explained. "Every little girl reaches an age when she gets depressed. It could be because something happens like a family move, or it could be when she gets her period."

Prudence interrupted. "You're not going to write about that, are you?"

"No, no. It's not that kind of book. I just mean she doesn't speak, sits alone a lot of the time; in a word, mopes. She'll cheer up though, when the cats get jumping."

"Works for me," Prudence said drily. "If you don't mind, I'm going to have a long hot soak before bed."

"Of course, Prudence." Gerry jumped up. "Here, I'll do the dishes. And don't forget, over the weekend, you are not working. Do what you'd do at home. Relax."

"I'd be cleaning my house on the weekend," Prudence responded. Then she smiled. "I'll find a book or something. Maybe I'll make a Battenberg cake."

Gerry worked on *The Cake-Jumping Cats of Dibble* for hours that evening, remembered the dishes at ten o'clock. She cleaned out the cat boxes, planned the next day's work and went to bed where she conked out immediately.

Both women were groggy next morning. "It's the pasta," Prudence yawned. "It's heavy."

Gerry made Prudence sit down while she boiled the kettle. "A British breakfast this morning, Prudence. Kippers, eggs, toast and tea. Yes?"

"All right. I like kippers."

"So do I. But they remind me I met Ralph Parsley yesterday, an experience I do not care to repeat. Ugh."

"Mm. Funny how one twin is quite charming and the other — not. Was he driving that dreadful old truck of his?"

"Yup. Screeched out of the parking lot like he meant trouble for someone. Can you tell him apart from Steve?"

"Sometimes I think I can but then find out I was wrong, so I'd have to say no. I expect their close relations can, though."

"So it might have been either of them talking to, or rather, being talked at by Betty Parsley last week."

"Where?"

"I saw them at church, after church. Betty seemed angry. The tall redheaded man was just listening. Then I met Steve the next day and assumed it had been him."

Prudence finished her thought. "But it could have been Ralph. Anyway, they both work at the Parsley Inn. Steve is Phil's manager for the pub side. Betty managed the restaurant. And Ralph does part-time manual labour. Unloads beer barrels and boxes, takes empties out to the truck after the weekend."

Gerry placed a plate of food in front of Prudence and began to pick at her own. "So, I saw Betty at church that Sunday morning. Presumably, her family saw her that afternoon. But I didn't see her at the party that evening. I wonder if she was already down in Cathy's basement when Doug and I found the broken wine bottles."

"Well, I don't think Bob knocked that big rack over himself. He might jump on it but he doesn't weigh enough to tip it." Prudence took in Gerry's downcast face. "Eat your nice breakfast, Gerry," she said sharply. "You didn't kill Betty Parsley and you're not responsible for her death."

"But if I'd checked the basement better! She might have still been alive!"

"It's no good," Prudence said gently. "We'll never know."

Gerry finished her cold breakfast and Prudence cleared the plates. "Don't do the dishes," Gerry called out.

"I wasn't going to. I need some new clothes. A friend is picking me up around eleven and we'll have lunch out."

"Oh, that's nice." Gerry was already fingering her cake and cat drawings and spoke absently. "If you want to bring her in for tea after, feel free."

"Thank you, Gerry. And what makes you think she's a she?"

But Gerry was already too engrossed in the dialogue of her Dibble tea party to give much thought to a possible Lovering one and hardly noticed when Prudence left.

The Cake-Jumping Cats of Dibble

Chapter One
The Idea

Many cakes ago, in the village of Dibble, in the province of Fasswassenbasset, the queen and her friends were enjoying a game of cards as they drank their tea.

"Pass the Battenberg, would you, Max," purred Queen Atholfass.

The haughty monarch, resplendent in her white ruff and magnificent calico coat (long-hair, don't you know), delicately pried apart the little cubes of alternating chocolate and white cake with one elegant nail.

"Delicious." Through lazy slits, she eyed the courtier, Max, Count Scarfnhatznmitz, an energetic border collie, who'd slid it to her with his nose. "How clever of you."

"Not at all, Your Majesty. My pleasure." Max bowed deeply and suddenly, which brought his nose down with a smack onto the table, knocking over his teacup and soaking the cards. "Sorry, sorry." He mopped the tablecloth with a napkin.

With a sigh, a little girl got up from her place at the table and slowly fetched a damp rag. She handed it to Max before wisping out of the room.

"What's wrong with Languida?" queried Max, as his tongue, pink and thick as a thickish slice of ham, drooled dangerously close to the Queen's plate.

"Nothing at all," snapped the Queen, jerking her plate away.

Gerry stretched and stood up. She was pretty pleased with the first illustration. Latooth, Languida, Max, Tess and the Queen sat at a round table with a partially demolished Battenberg cake and cups, cards and a huge ornate teapot. Humans and dogs sat on regular chairs while Atholfass adorned a kind of high chair with a big round cushion on top. She wore her crown and her wonderful calico coat. The dogs had cloth capes. The humans wore long old-fashioned dresses. Sneathe, the butler, sneered from a doorway, bearing the next cake.

"No lesson. No moral. A wonderful world of endless cake and play," said Gerry to any of the cats who were in the room. "Like you guys have." She tossed a catnip mouse into the kitten box and was delighted to see them react to it. She teased Mother. "Are they too young for catnip, Mother? What is the legal age to give catnip to kittens?" Mother blinked and looked inscrutable.

Gerry built up the fire and turned back to her book. The trick was to put as much information into the big illustrations as possible and then insert mini-sketches where subsequent actions demanded. She'd drawn one little picture of the moment when Max's nose knocked over his teacup, so the next should zero in on him mopping, his tongue dripping on the Queen's plate and her jerking it away. She set to work.

She was stretching her fingers when she heard a car door slam, then another. Three-thirty! And she'd missed lunch. She hurriedly shuffled the sketches and notes into a pile and put them on the bench at the other end of the room. She was wiping the table as Prudence and her friend entered through the kitchen.

"Hello, ladies! Good shopping? Let me put the kettle on." For Prudence's friend was a she—Lucy Hanlan. They'd known each other for years, apparently.

"I bought a tin of Danish butter cookies," Lucy said. "And Prudence thought you still had fruitcake."

"Still," Gerry agreed, flashing a dangerous smile at Prudence.

"I told you you'd be glad we made so many," Prudence replied evenly.

Gerry made a pot of Earl Grey tea and sliced some cake while the ladies unpacked Prudence's purchases and snipped off all the tags and little plastic pieces. "Honestly," said Lucy, "you'd think these socks were made of gold the way they staple them together." Gerry decided she liked the woman and relaxed.

"Get a lot done?" Prudence asked. Gerry nodded. "Gerry's writing a book. For children, she says. But I think it's for herself."

"Isn't that why every author writes or creator creates?" Gerry asked.

"Lucy sews."

"What do you sew?"

"Anything. Dresses, skirts, shirts, pants. I help with the amateur plays and musicals in the town, with the costumes."

"And you wouldn't do it if you didn't enjoy it, would you? Cake?"

"Absolutely not. Yes, please."

"What did you buy, Prudence?"

Prudence exhibited a pair of grey pants, two white shirts, five pairs of undies and five pairs of socks. And a black cardigan. Lucy and Gerry looked at each other and grinned.

"Prudence's uniform," Lucy said.

"I just don't care about clothes," Prudence sputtered. "I don't see what all the fuss is."

"You wore a perfectly nice green dress to my art show last fall."

"Yes, well," Prudence grudged, "that was to please you and to fit in with the others. But I don't want to stand out."

"Why is that, Prudence?" Lucy asked quietly.

As quietly, her friend replied, "Learned my lesson."

There was an awkward pause. Gerry rose. "Fresh tea. Do you live in Lovering, Lucy?"

"In the heart of."

"Lucy comes from one of the oldest families in Lovering."

"Hanlan," mused Gerry. "That's Irish, isn't it? My mother was Irish."

"Holt?" queried Prudence.

"Her mother was a Fitzpatrick."

"Sounds like an upper-class name," said Lucy. "Oh, no offence, I'm just interested in names. Now, I'm descended from the indentured servants who were brought in the 1850s to work and help the settlers."

"That's a kind of slavery, isn't it?"

"Oh, no. Though there were bad masters who starved their workers or refused to free them when the period of indenture was up."

Gerry spoke slowly. "So there would have been servants brought over from Great Britain by the early settlers hereabouts?"

Lucy nodded. "Absolutely. As many were Catholics, there are quite good records at the Catholic Church. Of their marriages, their children's births, deaths."

"Huh. A whole other part of the history of Lovering I never knew existed. Thank you for telling me, Lucy."

Lucy smiled. "My pleasure. The past is always with us. Prudence told me about the bones in the shed. You're thinking they might have belonged to a servant, as the family wouldn't have been able to hide one of their own members missing. And why would they?" She rose from the table. "Well, it's been lovely to meet you finally, Gerry, and to have tea in this marvellous old house." She kissed Prudence, and, impulsively, Gerry as well.

"What a nice person," Gerry said, scrubbing the breakfast and tea dishes while Prudence stood by with a tea towel.

"One of my oldest friends. I bought a quiche and some salad for supper."

Gerry groaned. "How did you know? I missed lunch and then ate too much fruitcake. And cookies. Quiche and salad will be perfect."

"Well, it's the holidays. It's expected we make the wrong dietary choices." Prudence looked guilty. "We went for fast food burgers for lunch."

"I'm a bad influence," laughed Gerry.

Prudence went into the living room to wipe the table, then called Gerry. "Come see this. What were you saying about the catnip mice being duds?" Gerry stuck her head around the corner of the room.

Almost all the cats — all twenty-three of them — were in the living room. About half of them were playing with catnip mice: flipping them in the air and biting them; on their backs wrestling with the mice on their bellies. Even the kittens were solemnly sitting up, batting a mouse from one to the other.

"Ten catnip mice," sang Gerry, and couldn't stop laughing. Slowly, the cats became aware of her and stopped their various games. They recovered their dignity, sat up and groomed, then most of them stalked from the room.

"Now you've given offence," said Prudence. "I'm going to put my new clothes away. Oh, yes. Is it all right if I do a laundry?"

"Prudence, you are a *guest*. Of course it's all right." Gerry retrieved her pile of papers and spread them out on the table. "I'm just going to do the next little bit."

"Huh!" said Prudence, and went about her tasks, as Gerry returned to her imaginary tea party.

Her dearest friend, Latooth Élonga, an older lady, an authoress, and vaguely related to Languida, joined in the conversation. "Well, dear, it won't be long before she's gone." Latooth's many necklaces and bracelets swung and glittered as she reached for the teapot.

"What?" said Queen Atholfass, momentarily distracted by the shiny glass and metal. She emerged from her trance and again became her aloof self. "Leave me? Why would she do that?"

"It's what they do, dear," replied Latooth, her glasses glinting. "The young things. They leave."

Tess, Lady Ponscomb, a black long-haired retriever, chief lady-in-waiting at court and cousin of Max, had been sitting quietly nibbling cake. "Your Majesty, I think —"

"When I want you to speak, Ponscomb, I'll ask you. Always barking about something or other." The Queen lashed her tail angrily.

Max leaned in. "Your Maj, if I may?"

"You may, Max," purred the Queen, fluttering her tiny eyelashes.

"Well, Your Maj, the young like action. They like to move." To illustrate this point, Max jumped up and ran about the room, knocking a flower arrangement from its stand and sending a hat rack flying.

"Em, sorry about that."

"No problem, Max," cooed the Queen. "Ponscomb, tidy that up."

Max helped Tess with the mess. "Sorry, Tess. I couldn't help it."

"I know, Max," replied the downtrodden Tess.

At this moment, the butler, Sneathe, oiled his way into the room, ignored the two grovelling dogs, and with much bowing and flourishing, placed a chocolate sponge cake with satin icing where the Battenberg cake had been.

Gerry chortled. "I feel another illustration coming on," she warned the cats still keeping her company. "Just a quarter page. Sneathe stepping over the two dogs. Does that sound good?"

Prudence, passing through the room on an errand, stopped, realized none of this was meant for her, and continued on her way. She heated the quiche and prepared the salad.

Gerry worked on into the night, pausing only to eat the meal brought by a silent Prudence. Later she went to top up the tub of kibble in the kitchen and clean the cat boxes. "Drat the woman," she muttered. The cat boxes were clean and the kibble container brimming. "Can't get her to relax." She went to bed and read for a while but couldn't turn her brain off. Visions of cakes and cats and bones in the ground disturbed her long after she fell asleep.

14

A bell tolled. The bones lay down, arms folded neatly across ribs. Bob crouched at the skull, Marigold at the feet — or was it the other way around? Gerry opened her eyes, saying, "But, Marigold, you're dead!" and saw Bob's quizzical white whiskers. He sneezed, spraying her. "Ew, Bob!" The bell rang again, then stopped.

"Oh, heck!" Gerry threw back the bedclothes, startling Lightning, who was just waking. The cat slunk toward the door. "Sorry, Lightning," Gerry called after her.

She'd meant to attend church to see if anyone who'd been there last week was there again, and to talk to them about with whom Betty Parsley had spoken. "Well, of course they're there again," she muttered as she slipped on dress slacks and a sweater over a turtleneck. "That's why they're called the faithful. Unlike me." A sudden thought struck her. What if Betty had been unfaithful to Phil, and what Gerry had witnessed between her and one of the Parsley twins was a lovers' quarrel? Sex or money, she thought, then doubted that all murders could be so easily explained.

She brushed her hair and teeth and splashed water on her face, then raced downstairs to care for the cats. Breakfast would have to wait.

The minister was preaching when she arrived in the porch of little St. Anne's and crept to a pew at the back. Overnight, the temperature had dropped again and the church was cold.

No red-haired men in the congregation. Gerry relaxed. One less thing to worry about.

The minister was speaking about Christmas, how it was still going on, this being the eleventh day, and how its message should be with them all year, not just when they were flushed from wine, good food and fellowship. Gerry agreed, then let her thoughts slip away to Dibble, where it was always summer, at least in her mind. Hearing Betty Parsley's name at the end of the sermon brought her back to the present.

Though sobered by the minister's prayer for Betty and her family, Gerry enjoyed singing the offertory and concluding hymns, then loitered with the others, exchanging greetings as they arranged their winter garments.

One elderly man, bent over and fat, looked roguishly at Gerry. "Well, young lady, I hope you've got your long johns on today. I'm wearing mine."

Gerry, who ordinarily would have cringed at being called "young lady," just laughed and handed him the cane he'd hooked over the end of the pew. "I'll have to buy some soon."

He looked at the cane. "That's not mine," he cackled. "Wife!" he called to a tiny thin lady, very frail, who was still sitting. "Your cane."

She slid along the length of the pew and hauled herself upright. She had no coat or hat or gloves to put on, as she'd never divested herself of them. A gash of lipstick and two dots of rouge decorated her little face. A fox wrapped itself around her shoulders, biting its tail in chagrin. She grasped the cane with one hand and her husband with the other and majestically left the church.

"The Clarkes," a woman whispered when they'd left. "Used to be big farmers. Past the ferry. Sold their land now. No sons." Her voice rose to a normal level and she pointed her chin at Gerry. "I know who you are." Gerry wasn't sure if the woman considered this a good thing or not. The woman lowered her tone again. "Isn't it terrible about Betty Parsley?" Gerry nodded. "Do you know how — I mean, how she —"

Gerry was disappointed. This woman was fishing as she herself had hoped to do. Gerry felt a bit ashamed, then decided to play. "I — we — found her."

The woman's mouth dropped open. Jackpot! "No!" she breathed.

"Yes. I was checking the house for the owner while she's away and found Betty. In the basement." The woman seemed stupefied by this amount of information so easily retrieved. Gerry pushed. "Did you know her? Did she have any enemies? Old grudges? People she fired?"

The woman drew her chin back. "Well, I, hardly, yes, I suppose."

Gerry faked a move. "Oh well, if you don't want to tell me —" and turned away.

The woman fell for it. "I work there. Sometimes. When things get busy. In the kitchen or waiting tables. Or even as chambermaid if the regular one is sick." She drew back, satisfied, and added, "I'm not sure I want to work there anymore."

"Why not?"

The woman leaned in. "Well, it's usually the husband, isn't it? And he's still there."

"Do the Parsleys live at the inn?"

"Yes. They've got an upstairs bit and a downstairs bit, round the side. It's the kids I feel sorry for."

Gerry could see no sign of sympathy in the woman's face but agreed anyway. "And Phil? How does he seem?"

"Oh, he *looks* shocked; all thin and pale in the face, though he's a big beefy man. But he would, wouldn't he, if he did it? Afraid of being arrested!" As if that proved his guilt, the woman nodded, looking triumphant.

"And you don't know of any enemies, at the inn or elsewhere?"

The woman snorted. "Elsewhere? The Parsley Inn was Betty Parsley's life. Just a waitress somewhere else she was when Phil found her and brought her home, and suddenly she's running the place. Not that she wasn't a good manager. Made it pay. And kept those kids of hers out of trouble." She shook her head. "I don't know what'll happen now. To my job. Inn's closed."

"It'll reopen," Gerry reassured her.

"I hope so."

"Were you at church last week?"

"Yes. Why?"

"Did you see Betty talking to anyone in particular?"

"Can't say as I did. You think her killer was at church?" The woman sounded horrified and looked furtively around at the last few stragglers, chatting with the minister.

"Oh, I was just wondering who the last one to see her was before —"

"I talked to her at the party."

Gerry got excited. "The party Sunday night? What time?"

The woman nodded. "About eight. I was in the kitchen and she told me to get Ralph to bring up more boxes of liquor and beer."

"And did you?"

"Yeah. He was smoking a joint out back in his pickup, as usual, but he did what she wanted."

"And did you see either of them after that?"

"Her — no. Him? He wouldn't normally come through the kitchen with the alcohol. There's another staircase. So, no."

Gerry decided to make her escape. "Well, thank you, er —"

"Annette. Annette Bledsoe." They shook hands and parted.

Gerry adjusted her scarf so it covered her mouth and walked home, her eyes watering from the wind that blew off the lake. What had she learned?

Not much, she was forced to admit. She wondered if the police had released Betty's body for burial. It being the holiday period meant everything was much slower. That reminded her — her car needed to be at the body shop this week. She hoped it could be repaired in hours, not days.

When she entered the kitchen, there was the sweet smell of cake baking and Prudence was just finishing cleaning the kitchen. Gerry sniffed hopefully. "What is it?"

"You'll find out later. I haven't made it for years. I think I'll send you out for a walk this afternoon. You've been hunched at that table drawing for days."

"Prudence, I'm not ten! And it's windy today. Too cold. No, I'm going for a junk lunch and then I'm going to hang around the Catholic church."

Prudence looked scandalized. "Hang around St. Pete's?"

"I'm hoping to catch the priest after service, after his lunch. To ask about parish records. I think, if our bones weren't those of a stranger, and we have no way of finding that out, they must have been a servant, a person without family. Do you want any lunch? I could bring it back here to eat."

"No, thank you," Prudence said firmly.

"Okay. See you." Fifteen minutes later, Gerry was happily hunched over her burger and onion rings in a fast food restaurant booth.

"Hey, Red, good to see you," someone said lightly and slid into the seat across from her.

She choked. "Don't call me Red," she managed, before drinking half of her root beer.

He looked surprised and a bit taken aback. "I'm sorry. I didn't know you were sensitive about your hair."

She looked closely at the twin. "Steve?" she said cautiously.

He laughed. "Oh, you've met Ralph and thought I was him. Let me guess: he annoyed you." He sighed. "I'm tired of apologizing for my brother, but anyway. Sorry if he did."

"No, you're right. Why should you?"

His order was ready. He brought it back to Gerry's booth and gestured at the empty seat. "Is it all right if I — ?"

She nodded, having taken an enormous bite of her hamburger. They ate in silence for a few moments.

"Doing any curling lately?" he asked.

"No." She wondered if this was his way of asking if she was seeing anything of Doug. "No. I think if I do any curling in the future, it will be with women."

"Ah." He finished his burger and attacked his fries. "Look, I heard you found the body at Fieldcrest and I just wanted to say —" He seemed to be searching for words. "I just want to say, I wish it hadn't been you who found her."

Gerry was astonished. "Why on earth are *you* sorry?"

"What? Oh. Well, you just moved here. You're kind of young. It wouldn't have mattered to that old lady who owns the place, if she found it."

"Cathy? Cathy's not old. How old are you?"

"Me? I'm thirtyish."

"I thought you were at school with Doug." Gerry sounded bewildered.

He looked sheepish. "Okay. You caught me. But he was finishing high school when I was starting."

"So you're thirty-six," Gerry said crisply.

"Yeah. In a couple of months. Sorry. I just was hoping — I mean — I didn't want to seem —"

"Steve," Gerry said, rising, "one of my best friends is in his nineties. Now *that's* old."

He smiled and also got to his feet. "Yeah. That's old. Look, can I call you sometime?"

She hesitated. Then thought, why not? She nodded. He saw her to her car. She was checking her face for traces of condiments in her car mirror, when she saw him exit the parking lot in Ralph's beat-up old pickup. She reassured herself. That wasn't Ralph.

Steve's just borrowed his truck. Maybe they share it. But it made her think.

She drove down the long bumpy road towards Lovering. It was one-thirty. Surely the priest would have had his lunch by now. She walked up the wide steps of the big old brick house next to St. Peter's and raised and lowered the knocker twice. There was a pause. A dog barked briefly. The door opened. A short fat man stood holding a Jack Russell terrier. "Yes?" The terrier was struggling.

"Oh, hello. You don't know me, Father Lackey. I'm an acquaintance of Lucy Hanlan. Gerry Coneybear."

"You better come in, Gerry Coneybear, before this woman-eating monster gets the better of me." Gerry stepped in, the priest closed the door and put down the terrier. It rushed to sniff Gerry's legs, then backed away, appalled.

"Are you a puppy killer?" asked the priest mildly.

"No. But I have twenty-three cats," Gerry explained.

"Ah ha! That'll be it, no doubt. And is that the problem you've come to me about? Are you a cat hoarder?"

Gerry laughed. "No, no. Nothing like that. I won't keep you long, Father. I'm curious about your parish records. How far back they go."

He looked interested. "Has your family been here long? Are you Catholics?"

"Yes. And no, we're not. Anglican. But Lucy said there was an influx of Irish servants in the middle of the nineteenth century. It's possible they were Catholic, isn't it?"

"Let's go into the study." He led her through the wide central hallway to a large, high-ceilinged room at the back of the house. The terrier followed, still in shock.

"What's his name?"

"Smitty. Now, your servant or servants may have been Protestants, in which case I won't be able to help you. Sit down, sit down."

She sat in one of the armchairs in front of his desk. If these walls could talk, she told herself.

Father Lackey drew a piece of paper in front of him and prepared a pen. "Now. Let's be methodical. What exactly do you want?"

So she told him about her cat finding the one bone and then the whole skeleton, the fact that the bones were old, and her reasoning about how they must belong to a servant or a stranger. She concluded, "And then it was just luck meeting Lucy yesterday and her remarking about indentured servants. Although our bones may be those of a regular servant." She didn't tell him about the bones haunting Prudence. Nor did she confide in their consultation with the psychic Mrs. Smith.

All this time, Smitty lay next to his owner's massive desk, where he could keep an eye on both the priest and Gerry. When she'd finished talking, he sat up and gave a single bark. Then he lay back down with his nose on his paws.

The priest put down his pen, sat back in his chair and also appraised her. "Why do you want to know who this person was?"

Gerry blinked. "He, or she, was found on my property. I feel responsible. He'll have to be buried eventually, and I'd like that to be in the appropriate place. Is that enough?"

"Yes. That's good. Now, if you'd like to give me the pertinent dates, I'll see what I can do."

Gerry hesitated. "The police haven't given me a date for the skeleton, but based on when the woodshed was constructed, which we know, I'd say from about 1850 on? So 1840 to 1890? They said the bones were at least 100 years old."

The priest nodded. "St. Pete's was here. Oh, not the present building, but the parish was in existence. It's quite interesting. The priest would have had several congregations and have travelled from one to the other on Sunday." He smiled. "Now, we're spoiled. One church and instead of a horse I have a car for visiting."

"Does Smitty visit with you?"

"Sometimes. But he usually waits in the car." He rose and held out his hand. "Well, my dear, I will spend a few pleasurable hours looking up possible candidates for your man under the floor. Or woman." He gave her a quick shrewd look. "You think it's a man, don't you?"

She took a deep breath. "Yes, I do. It's a feeling I and my housekeeper have. It's a man."

"All right. I'll look up both genders, though. You never know what you'll find."

Driving home, Gerry pondered the little priest's final words. Indeed, what would he find in his centuries-old records? "Probably nothing," she told her reflection in the rear-view mirror.

When she entered the kitchen, the cake smell had dissipated and something lay under a tea towel on the counter. "Prudence?" Gerry called idly, lifting a corner of the towel.

"In here and leave that cake alone. It's setting." Gerry walked through into the living room. Prudence had all Aunt Maggie's old recipe books out on the table. She handed Gerry a list. "These are the cakes that would look spectacular with cats jumping over them. I've made one today because I have a fondness for it, but don't expect me to make one every week."

"Cool! Which one did you make?"

"The Battenberg."

Gerry's jaw dropped. "Have you been peeking at my work?"

"You left it on the table," Prudence defended herself. "I used to make it with Mother and later with Maggie. How did it go at the church?"

"Very good. For a start. He'll look into it. Er, when will the cake be ready?"

"I'll make the tea."

The Battenberg in the cookbook showed a checkerboard of two chocolate and two vanilla squares of cake sandwiched together, so Gerry was surprised when Prudence exhibited her cake. No fewer than twelve pink and white squares alternated delightfully. "Fancy," breathed Gerry. "I'll have to change my text. Pink is much prettier than chocolate. And is that marzipan icing?"

Prudence put a slice on Gerry's plate. "Yes. Apricot jam holds the sections together."

"It tastes great. Thank you so much. Maybe I'll try to make one of the cakes on this list." Gerry noticed a couple of old photo albums on the table. She drew them near her. "Find anything?"

Prudence had inserted slips of paper to mark interesting pages. She opened the topmost book. "This is from around the time of Albert Coneybear's marriage to Elizabeth Parsley." The photo showed the pair: the man standing, looking at the camera; the woman seated, looking at a point off to one side.

Gerry reached for the family tree. "So, the 1890s then. There's that grim mouth again." She pointed at Elizabeth's face. "The same as in her portrait. It's hard to tell people's colouring from looking at sepia-tinted reproductions." Then, after checking a few dates, she added, "So you couldn't have known Margie, but did know Elizabeth."

Prudence nodded. "I told you. My great-aunt. She was reserved. Like me." Gerry left that comment alone as Prudence turned to the next place in the book. "Here's Margie."

The contrast couldn't have been greater. It was another courtship photo. Again the man stood while the woman sat, but Jonas Petherbridge had a hand on Margaret Coneybear's shoulder and she'd reached up to cover it with one of her own. Both stared happily at the camera.

Where Elizabeth was small and pale, with blond or light brown hair, Margie's darker skin, hair and eyes crackled with energy you could still feel over 100 years later. And she'd been a big woman — filled the chair. Gerry tapped the photo with a finger. "I like her," she mused softly. "Are there any later ones of her?"

Prudence laid that album aside and opened another one. She pointed. "There. A family party at The Maples in —" She carefully removed the snapshot from its position and read the back. "1932. So, this is Margie, her son Jonas, and his wife Sarah Muxworthy. Maybe Margie was already living here with Elizabeth. That's her. Her husband Albert was long dead."

Gerry perused the family tree. "As were two of her children. That's sad."

Prudence replied crisply. "People expected to bury some of their children back then. There's your Great-uncle John and his wife, Mary Parsley — no kids. I vaguely remember him and, of course, she lived until I was in my twenties. She was my mother's twin."

Gerry stared. "So the Parsleys run to twins, do they?"

Prudence nodded. "Not excessively. Once a generation. No more. Mother was very upset when Mary predeceased her."

Gerry waited respectfully for a few seconds, but, no more information forthcoming, changed the subject. "Again, it's hard to tell people's colouring from black and white photos, plus, they've all gone grey in this one."

"Yes, but look at Margie's son Jonas — dark hair and eyes like she had."

Gerry thought. "Uncle Geoff was dark, wasn't he? Who's this?" She indicated another couple in a different picture.

"That's your grandparents — Matthew Coneybear and Ellie Catford — before they were married."

Gerry peered at the tiny faces, especially Matthew's. "He's not dark. Fair, I should say."

"Yup. He was. A handsome man, too."

Gerry smiled. "Did you have a crush on him?"

"He was my Uncle Matt. He used to pick me up and spin me around by the arms. My father never did that."

Again, Gerry waited in vain for explications. A knock at the door surprised both women. "I wonder if Andrew's cake radar has gone off," Gerry joked over her shoulder, then peeked through the kitchen window. "No car." She went to the door. "Cathy!"

15

Cathy looked exhausted. "Come in! It's so good to see you! Merry Christmas!" Gerry hugged her friend, then helped her slowly disrobe. "How's Charles?"

Prudence brought another plate and cup and served Cathy. "Charles is sleeping at home," Cathy replied. "We've been on the road since four this morning. Is this Battenberg cake?" She took a mouthful. "Where did you buy it?"

"Prudence made it."

"Professional quality," murmured Cathy the caterer, who herself was renowned for her baking. "I should be sleeping but I had to come over and talk to you about Betty Parsley. Gerry, how ghastly. Maybe just another small piece, Prudence. The airport and airplane food was atrocious."

"We were both there," Gerry said, "and Prudence was the one who held it together. I got all teary."

"Well, what a shock. I'm so sorry. I had no idea she was using the place for —" She halted. "Anything."

"Did you give her a key?" The possibility had just occurred to Gerry.

"Well, I do catering for special events at The Parsley, and sometimes, if I'm not at home, I let Betty pick up the food. It's convenient for us both. We're not, we weren't friends."

"She doesn't seem to have had any," Gerry said thoughtfully.

"That's sad," Prudence commented.

Gerry continued. "And did anyone else ever use the key to pick up food? Phil? The Parsley twins?"

"Well," Cathy said doubtfully, "they may have. If Betty was too busy, she might have delegated. I don't like the idea that Ralph Parsley might have a key to my house. Oh, how am I ever going to get to sleep tonight?!"

"I could come over and check the house for you," offered Gerry.

"We could," Prudence stated.

"Oh, would you? Thank you! I'd feel so much better."

"Come on. You're tired. You can tell us about your trip and your sister another time." Gerry covered the cake as she spoke.

Cathy looked confused. "My sister? Oh, right. Yeah. Another time."

The women trudged by the side of the road. "How's Mr. Parminter?" Cathy asked.

"Good," Gerry answered. "We were there for New Year's Eve. It was the day we —"

Cathy spoke wearily. "Everything leads back to Betty, doesn't it?"

Prudence comforted her. "It just seems that way. You've had two shocks: hearing about it and now coming home to confront it."

They crossed the road and turned into Cathy's house's driveway. She'd left many lights switched on, and the house looked more like the welcoming abode it usually was.

"Before I forget, Cathy," Gerry began, "there's a switch or a fixture next to the stairs going up to the bedrooms. It's on, then it's off. Maybe it needs an electrician."

"Oh, that old thing. I've had it checked. They couldn't figure out why it's like that. Sometimes I light guests to bed with a candle. They like that."

"Very atmospheric," murmured Prudence.

They stood, a nervous little group, in front of the front door. "Come on, Cathy," Gerry urged, "Prince Charles is waiting."

Cathy, who had been hesitating with her key, found her nerve. "Yes. Of course. I must be brave for Charles."

Inside, the normal warmth of an occupied house made a difference to at least Gerry and Prudence's moods. This was Cathy's home. She should be made to feel comfortable.

"Basement first, I think," Prudence suggested.

Cathy shrunk back. Prudence tucked her arm in Cathy's. "My dear, it will be far worse imagining than seeing. Come along."

They walked down the long corridor to the back of the house. Gerry, coming last and peering into the reception rooms, saw Charles on his side on a rug, snoring. "I see Charles is glad to be home."

The other two were focused on making it to the kitchen. Prudence distracted Cathy with talk of food. "Why not take something out of your freezer, dear, and defrost it so if you take a nap now, when you wake up, you can eat your supper."

Cathy rummaged for a moment and extracted a tub of homemade soup. She placed it in the sink, then looked furtively at the basement door.

"Now, Gerry will go first, then you, then me," Prudence suggested. Gerry made a face only Prudence could see and opened the door. With as much assurance as she could muster, she tried to descend the stairs in a normal fashion. Once at the bottom, she turned and watched the others.

Cathy crept down, her eyes wide in a white face. She looked with horror at the floor upon which Gerry was standing. Gerry looked down too.

A dull red stain oozed from a dark centre to faded edges. "Oh, no, no, no," she expostulated. "Your wine rack was tipped over and some of the bottles broke. Doug mopped it up and I cleaned it later, but we didn't really scrub it. It's just wine, Cathy."

Cathy reached the basement floor and stood next to Gerry. "There was a struggle?"

Gerry shrugged. "Who knows?"

They moved from one section to the other. "This is where we found Bob, in the armoire." When Cathy looked bewildered, Gerry clucked her tongue in exasperation at herself. "Of course! You don't know. Bob has a way into your basement. We think from my woodshed."

Cathy asked in an incredulous voice, "And he comes out through my armoire?"

"No," said Prudence, glaring at the incompetent Gerry, "your cold room. Look." And they showed her the hole in the wall.

Finally, there was nothing left to look at except the corner where the sump pit gurgled and dripped. Cathy held Prudence's hand as they approached. They turned the corner made by the pieces of old furniture and looked. Cathy dropped Prudence's hand. "There's nothing to see. It's just my horrible old sump pump in its hole. I'm very tired."

Slowly, she mounted the stairs and checked Charles in his slumber. Finally, she climbed the stairs to her room. Gerry squinted at the wall sconce, which today was working. Prudence went ahead to fill Cathy's hot water bottle, then slipped it under the covers.

They left her sitting on her bed, yawning, and tiptoed downstairs. But some creak or shift in the old house must have alarmed Charles, for he bugled as he woke and scrambled to his feet.

"Charles! Shush! I know." Gerry rushed to the kitchen, Charles skittering after. She left him, nose deep in his bowl, crunching his supper. After scrawling "Fed Charles" on a notepad, she joined Prudence at the door. "Will she be all right?"

Prudence nodded. "I don't think she's very imaginative. She'll be fine."

"And you, oh sensitive one? Did you pick up any vibrations from Betty Parsley?"

Prudence busied herself about her boots. "Nothing. About her."

Gerry paused in adjusting her scarf. "What does that mean?"

"It means I feel something. But not in this house."

"In mine?" They stepped out the front door into the biting wind and began walking back to Gerry's, their heads down.

"No. Not really. Actually, it's strongest right here." Prudence paused as they reached the bottom of Cathy's driveway and passed the above-ground burial vault of Gerry's family.

"Coming from the crypt?" Gerry sounded incredulous and Prudence responded peevishly:

"You don't have to sound so skeptical! I don't want to feel it. I just do!"

Gerry felt baffled. "I think I need to know more about my family's and The Maples' histories. Do you feel like reading old letters this evening?"

"I don't mind. I'm not very hungry."

"I am!" Gerry said with the enthusiasm of youth. "Tinned split pea soup and grilled cheese sandwiches. Easy, quick, good."

After she'd attended to the cats and they'd eaten their simple supper, the women each brought a box of letters and family papers down from Gerry's office. Prudence sat at the table, while Gerry worked on the rug in front of the fire.

At first, Mother and the kittens watched gravely from the banana box, but the kittens were larger and strong enough to hoist themselves over the box's sides, and when Gerry caught one of them peeing on an ancient bill for horse feed instead of in their nearby cat box, she had to join Prudence at the table.

Gerry sorted. "Tax records from the 1920s, 1930s. Oh, look, the *Lovering Herald* must have started back then. Here's Ellie and Matthew's engagement notice. How quaint. 1932. Oh, this is sad. Matthew's brother, Alfred, killed in the First World War. A picture of the plaque when it was installed at the church after the war. Another engagement. James Parsley and Sylvia Catford. 1939. Are those Phil Parsley's parents?"

"Yes."

"But Phil's not that old." Gerry lifted up her family tree, which was never far away.

"No. I think they married after the war and had their family then."

"That makes sense. See? Bill, the newspaper's editor, born 1950, and Phil, from the inn, in 1953."

Prudence pushed her own stack away. "What has all this relatively recent history to do with my haunting?"

"What we need is a list of everyone in the crypt."

"Gerry, it's written on the tablets on the outside." When Gerry looked blank, Prudence continued, "Around the back of the crypt."

Gerry's face cleared. "Oh. Right." She felt foolish. "I forgot about that. I just read the family names carved in the rock facing the street. Well, tomorrow I'll go over and copy all that down. What's in your box?"

"Letters. Love letters. Letters from sons away at school or on business. Letters from family who've moved away or are on vacations. All from the twentieth century."

"That's not our period. But it's good you eliminated that box from our inquiries."

Prudence shook her head and laughed. "Our inquiries. Next you'll be trying to find Betty Parsley's murderer."

"Absolutely not. Whoever did that is a dangerous person. I am staying far away from that inquiry."

They discussed their plans for the next day, which was to be a busy one, and went to their rooms.

As Gerry settled in with another Miss Read paperback, she had a real sense of the Christmas holidays being over at last.

The next morning was a scramble. As they were eating, Prudence's neighbour Charlie phoned to let her know a contractor was at her house. They hurriedly cleaned the cat boxes, figured out the day's schedule, and drove over. Gerry left a well-bundled-up Prudence supervising the dismantling of her broken roof and made the half-hour drive to her car dealer.

After waiting for an hour, she was told her car wouldn't be ready that day and offered the use of a courtesy car. The Mini they gave her was lemon yellow and had the number 12 painted in black on each door.

She had some time to kill before picking up Cece and Bea at the airport, so she went for a coffee and a doughnut. She was staring absently out the window at the bleak landscape of new and used car lots, stirring sugar into her cappuccino, when a familiar black pickup truck pulled into the space in front of the restaurant. A Parsley twin got out of the passenger side, leaned in to shout a few words, then slammed the door. The other twin drove off in a fury, it seemed, swerving violently to avoid a car entering the area.

Gerry sat, frozen, not wanting to meet either twin when they were obviously so angry, but the one who'd come in only wanted the toilet and a takeout coffee, and soon left by the same door by which he'd entered, not noticing Gerry, hunched in her seat.

He — whoever he was — got into a small light green car parked at the doughnut shop and, more calmly than whoever was driving the pickup truck, left in the same direction.

Ralph and Steve: Ralph, presumably, driving his pickup; Steve in his own vehicle. None of my business, thought Gerry. But it had made her uneasy, all the same.

She checked the time. Cecil and Beatrice Muxworthy's flight was due in at 12:30. If they were on time, she wouldn't have to park. She drove to the airport in the yellow Mini. Well, at least I'm visible, she thought.

It was a busy time of day and loitering on the arrivals level with a car, however compact, was impossible. Gerry couldn't see Cece or Bea. "My nerves can handle one more pass," she murmured, dodging SUVs, buses and taxies, and circled the airport again.

This time she was lucky; spotted Cece's tall gangly frame, bent over, pushing Bea in a wheelchair. Gerry beeped briefly, pulled over to the curb and hopped out. Bea, as usual, was laughing. "Gerry, you simp! There's designated wheelchair pickup parking. It's right over there and it's free!"

"No one told me," she replied cheerfully, throwing their bags in the back.

"And what have you done to the Mini?" her friend queried, sliding slowly into the front seat. Cece disappeared to return the wheelchair and a parking attendant bore down on them. Quickly, Bea whipped a square handicapped parking permit from her purse and held it up to him. He waved them to a spot further along the curb. "Making MS work for me," Bea chortled. Moments later, a sprinting Cece flung himself into the backseat, folded up his legs sideways, and clicked on a seatbelt.

"Nice paint job, Gerry, but why 12?" Cece's eyes twinkled at her as she glanced in the rear-view mirror.

"Have you guys been paying any attention at all to the rest of the world outside of Jamaica?" She could see both were tanned and had that relaxed-around-the-eyes-good-vacation-look.

"Nope," said Bea. "Been eating and laying around and breathing soft sea air."

"Iree, man. Been chillin'," Cece chimed in.

"Iree?" Gerry asked.

"Rastafarian," Cece explained with a wink. "Means, um, in a relaxed frame of mind."

"Huh. I see. Well, we had an extreme weather event on Christmas Eve, and," Gerry added in a more sober tone, "a death."

"Who?" they chimed in unison.

"Betty Parsley." She filled them in with as much as she knew.

"Almost the last person I would have expected to die that way," murmured Bea.

"Why?" a curious Gerry asked. "Had you known her long?"

"Since she married Phil. A quiet person who just focused on her family and, by extension, the family business."

Cece harrumphed self-importantly. "Yes, my dear one," his wife enquired sweetly. "You have information?"

He cleared his throat again. "It was always my impression that Betty was the business, while Phil just played host."

"Well, he'll have to step up now," his wife suggested grimly. "Their kids are still teenagers. They can't run the place."

"N-no," Gerry agreed. "But isn't Steve Parsley a kind of manager at the inn?" She felt Bea's eyes on her and then a flush mounted her cheek.

"Gerry's blushing!" Bea announced. "Have you been seeing the dashing Steve? A dash of Parsley. Get it? Yuk, yuk."

"Shush, dear, you're being yourself again," chided Cece. "Do tell us, Gerry," he continued in a polite voice, "what you know about Steve Parsley?"

Gerry blurted out, "Almost nothing! I've met him twice! Saw him this morning, by coincidence. He was shouting at his brother and didn't notice me."

Cece sounded serious as he said, "Ralph Parsley is something else, Gerry. I'd steer clear."

Gerry said, "Oh, I don't like *him*!" And blushed again.

Bea pounced. "Aha! So she does like the Steve twin." She grabbed the dashboard. "Wait! Wait!"

"What! What?" A flustered Gerry reacted, braking.

"You just missed the smoked-meat place. We're taking you there for lunch. Turn around!"

Grinning and grumbling at the same time, Gerry manoeuvered the car off the highway and into an industrial park where she could turn around and head back onto the highway in the opposite direction. Minutes later, they were sinking their teeth into succulent smoked-meat sandwiches with sides of fries and cole slaw.

Cece returned to the subject of the car. "I know it's a different car, Gerry. The dash is different as well as the colour. What happened?"

Gerry told them about the storm on Christmas Eve, the damage to her trees, the car roof and the woodshed. And then she had to explain about the bones.

Bea almost choked on a fry and had to guzzle most of her cherry Coke. When she'd recovered, she blurted, "So *two* bodies? *Two* deaths?"

"Well, the bones are old, maybe 150 years. So, a long-ago death. And we've discovered a long-ago way from my woodshed under the road into Cathy's basement."

"Really?" Gerry could hear the skepticism in Cece's voice.

"Weren't there local fears of Fenian activity in the area in the 1850s or 1860s?" said Bea, a member of almost every group, club or association Lovering had to offer, including, Gerry supposed, the historical society. "And before that, around 1837 or '38, it was the Patriotes scaring the English settlers."

"I remember," said Gerry slowly, "being taken as a child to see bullet holes in the walls of a church. Prudence mentioned them, too. But that was the other side of the lake, no?"

Bea nodded. "There was activity here, too. At the Parsley Inn, actually."

"So you're thinking some kind of escape route from one property to the other?" Cece still couldn't keep that note of doubt from his voice.

"Or an early warning system," Bea stated triumphantly. "Send a servant scurrying through the tunnel to alert the people at the other house of trouble."

"And trouble would likely come from the river as the most easily navigated route," Cece concluded. "Do either of you ladies have room for strawberry cheesecake?"

Gerry nodded, while Bea groaned, "Oh, to be young again. But I'll have a bite of yours, dearest, if you're having some." Cece rolled his eyes and ordered two servings and coffee and, when the desserts arrived, positioned one midway between himself and his wife. Meanwhile, Bea, after rummaging in her capacious beach bag, thrust a small package at Gerry.

Gerry unwrapped a six-inch-tall wooden carving of a sitting cat, tail erect, and with a face that looked remarkably like Bob's. She ran her hand over its back. "Thank you."

Cece responded, "Thank you for picking us up."

"So what do the police say?" said Bea, picking up her fork.

"Not much. Nothing, actually, since the initial discovery. Or did you mean about Betty?"

Bea's mouth was full but she nodded. "Bofe," she managed. Gerry heard Cece sigh.

"Well, they interviewed me and Prudence, of course, and Doug because —" for the second time that day Gerry felt her cheeks grow warm.

Bea swallowed a big gulp of coffee. "Oh ho! Doug as well? My, my." She turned to her husband. "We have to go away more often, hon. Apparently, our absence does wonders for Gerry's love life!"

"Shush. No. Yes. Oh. Doug was the only person I really knew at the Parsleys' party, so we hung out and he offered to accompany me to check Cathy's house. Oh. Cathy just got back yesterday. You know, now that you guys are back, too, I feel like having a Christmas party."

"But Christmas is over, Gerry," Cece pointed out.

"Not really. In fact today is the twelfth day. Yes, a party this Saturday. All done?"

During the drive home to Lovering, and beginning with "Twelve Austin Minis," Gerry entertained her friends by trying to remember and sing her version of "The Twelve Days of Christmas."

*B*ob's whiskers and paws twitched as he dreamt. The crawling thing was coming to get him. He had nowhere to hide, was rooted to the spot. It put out a bloody hand to touch him and — he woke up, his tail fluffed to twice its normal size.

He groomed it back down to its usual slender sleekness and looked around the dark room.

The girl slept, snoring gently, her red hair outspread on the pillow. He put out a paw, touched its brightness. Strange how she had no sensation in it. His own hairs were mini-receptors, sensitive to any change in temperature or breeze.

He felt a slight motion now and knew the same insubstantial presence from before had entered the room. He turned his head to view it.

At the foot of the bed, the other cat briefly awoke, noted the emanation and blinked once at Bob, clearly indicating this wasn't her ghost and that he was on his own. As she went back to sleep, Bob calmly regarded the man.

He could feel his exhaustion from across the room. The man paused in front of the disused fireplace where the room's electric heater ticked and glowed. He examined the objects on the mantel, then turned away, seemingly dissatisfied. As he looked in the cheval glass in a corner of the room, Bob saw him pass a hand back and forth in front of his face.

Bob jumped off the bed and stood next to the mirror. He looked up and saw in it a tall, thin man with sensitive lips, large dark eyes and black hair.

The loose assemblage in front of the mirror put out a hazy claw as if to touch his former self. His hand passed through the glass and the image there dispersed.

Now the thing moved to another corner, where the girl had thrown her cast-off clothes over a rocking chair. Under the clothes, Bob knew she kept a large rag doll he was forbidden to play with. Its soft head, flopped to one side, was just visible.

The ghost looked at the doll and drew near it. Bob followed. The ghost began to tremble. It pointed at the doll, then at Bob, then back at the doll, making rending motions with its hands. It was obvious what it wanted.

Bob methodically pulled the girl's underwear, jeans, sweater and pullover to the floor. He jumped up onto the rocker, which began to shift forwards, backwards, forwards, backwards. He put one paw on the doll, which was longer than he was, and looked at the vibrating spirit. It nodded once, twice, then, as if its excitement made it impossible to remain, it melted away, leaving behind the odour of something burning.

Bob wrinkled his nose at the smell and joyfully set about his task.

PART 4

AND TRUE

16

After she dropped the Muxworthys off at their modest home in Lovering's town centre, Gerry picked up a few supplies. "Always cat litter," she muttered, pushing a shopping cart, its wheels protesting, with six boxes balanced precariously. "I should have asked for some for Christmas." She dropped them at home, looked longingly at *The Cake-Jumping Cats of Dibble*, attended to her own hungry mob, and went to get Prudence.

The light was fading as Gerry pulled into Charlie and Rita's driveway. Across the street, contractors were rearranging the tarps over Prudence's bedroom. Prudence must have been watching from her neighbours' window, because she quickly joined Gerry in the car.

"How'd it go?" Gerry asked, putting the car in reverse.

Prudence rested her head on the headrest, closed her eyes and sighed.

"I bought a meat pie and some broccoli," Gerry continued. "I thought I'd do some baked potatoes. And we still have your marvellous cake."

Prudence sighed again.

"What is it, Prudence? You're making me nervous."

"I spoke with the insurance. Apparently, it could take months for the claim to be settled."

"So?"

"So I have to pay the contractor now. There goes Maggie's legacy to me. There goes the money for a new car of my own."

"But, Prudence, you wouldn't be able to buy a car until you get your licence and that won't be until next winter." There was another sigh. Sensing her friend was gloomy, too, because of a day spent listening to Charlie and Rita shout, watching part of her house being dismantled, Gerry thought of something. "You know what? Now would be a perfect time for you to take that week down south. I insist you go. Check with the police if it's all right, then book the flight for next week. If you want, I'll visit your house and make sure the work is ongoing."

Prudence roused herself. "Oh, Charlie can do that. He's a retired carpenter himself, among other things. He's itching to be involved. Could I really just leave everything and go?"

"Absolutely. I don't have any students for at least another month, and I'll just have to drag the vacuum cleaner around and do cat towel laundries myself."

"I'll do it," Prudence vowed.

As they passed Cathy's house, they saw a tall figure — not Cathy — following a rotund, red-coated Prince Charles about his business. The person stooped, picked up a snowball and flung it near Charles, who paused, gave the ball an incurious sniff, and continued cocking his leg on all available protrusions.

"But that's —" Gerry thought she heard Prudence say.

"Who?"

"I was going to say the Stribling boy, but he'd be a man now. And anyway, that was a woman."

"Must be a guest," Gerry offered. "Doesn't Charles look like a walking tomato in that coat?" Prudence laughed.

They'd arrived back at The Maples, where Gerry surveyed her own reconstruction dilemma. "You know, I think I'll just wait until spring to get the shed repaired. We'll have burned all the wood by then and the workers will have more room to manoeuvre. Doug suggested I have a sale to shift all the old furniture and junk."

Prudence stood in the driveway taking in the garish courtesy car. "How long for your car to be fixed?"

"Couple of days. Hungry?"

"I could eat."

Gerry prepared supper while Prudence uncharacteristically relaxed. "You wouldn't think standing around watching other people work could be so exhausting," she complained, a purring Bob on her lap.

"Why not?" said Gerry, coming from the kitchen with two glasses of red wine. "I get tired watching you work around here."

"Nonsense. You work too. All this." Prudence gestured at the mess of drawings and text Gerry had pushed down to one end of the table.

"Yeah, I suppose. I can't imagine teaching in that gloomy dining room. Maybe in here where I have the fire. It'll be so nice to get back into the studio in the spring. Which month will it be warm enough?"

"May, probably. Early May."

Gerry groaned. "Four more months."

Prudence thought for a moment. "I don't know why we didn't think of this before. Let's set you up in the room off the big dining room. You're not planning another show, are you?"

Gerry considered. "Not until spring. Would it be warm enough?"

"Warmer than the studio. I could help you move your stuff in there if you like."

"I wonder if the art class would fit."

"Probably. Anyway, you can try it and if you don't like it, move back to either the dining room or in here."

The oven timer went off and they ate their supper. Prudence helped with the dishes, then trudged off to her room. Gerry reread some of the cake-jumping book and worked on it for a while. The tea party in Dibble was ongoing.

"Latooth, would you serve?" asked the Queen. "Now, Max, what were you saying about the young — and moving?"

"I forget," said Max, eyeing the recently arrived confection. "But did you hear about Crumpet? They're claiming to be the champions of the world."

"In what, dear?" asked Latooth, who, after first serving the Queen, put a slice of chocolate sponge in front of Max's nose.

"In cake jumping." Max had barely uttered the three fateful words before his ham tongue neatly drew the entire slice of cake into his mouth.

Queen Atholfass almost fell off her chair. Well, she did fall off her chair, or rather, jumped to avoid the droplets of drool flying from Max's mouth towards her face.

Gerry paused to make a small sketch of the angry, fur-fluffed Queen in mid-air, crown askew, dog spit everywhere, cake half in, half out of Max's wide-open mouth.

"What?" she roared. "Those, those, alley cats are claiming to be the world champion cake jumpers?!"

Languida drooped in and slumped in her chair. Latooth eyed her uneasily for a moment and then asked the question. "What on earth is cake jumping?"

Though Gerry had a pretty good idea of what cake jumping involved, she decided to call it a night. She stretched and yawned, did her last cat-related chores and climbed the stairs to bed.

Bob and Lightning were already there and she regarded them affectionately, carefully stroking Lightning between the ears (practically the only spot the damaged cat allowed caresses) and giving Bob a good tummy scratch. He lolled on his back, squinting up at her.

She changed into pajamas and crawled into bed. Half an hour later, she crawled out again, grumbling. "I hate when I'm tired but not sleepy." She shrugged on her Winnie-the-Pooh robe and SpongeBob slippers and shuffled down the hallway to her office.

She picked up one of the boxes of family papers and carried it back to bed. She turned on all the lights in her room, placed the box on a chair next to the bed and climbed back in.

Lightning remained a tightly coiled calico ball at the foot of the bed, but Bob, like some ancient lawyer, gravely indicated which papers he thought were important by placing one paw delicately on them.

Gerry amused herself and him by putting two papers side by side on the coverlet and letting Bob's paw decide which one she read first.

"These are interesting, Bob. These must be the oldest papers I've read so far. From the 1800s. A letter from England from a Jonah Coneybear, dated 1820. 'This is my son, John Coneybear, legal issue of myself, Jonah Coneybear, and my wife Anne Grey of Luton-on-Marsh, Devon.' Huh. A letter of introduction. Rats, I need my family tree."

She got out of bed again and tromped downstairs to retrieve it. Once back, she checked John Coneybear's birthdate. "1810. 1810! He was only ten years old when he emigrated! Poor little soul."

She added the two new names to the tree, then scrabbled in the box. She began to lay things out, oldest on top. Bob, his advice no longer required, jumped off the bed and, rooting around in a corner under the rocking chair, found a catnip mouse and amused himself flipping it around.

There was nothing between 1820 and 1830. He'd have been working as a sailor, she seemed to remember, so would have had little need for paper. "Now what is this? 1831. A letter offering him a job. He's twenty-one and he becomes an employee in a trading company, The North West Wood and Timber Co." Gerry's voice grew excited. "In Lovering! I remember! That's how Uncle Geoff and Andrew's furniture company began. Wood!"

She picked up the next paper. "1838. From his father, telling him his mother has died." She paused, remembering her own mother's premature death, how difficult it had been for her father to comfort her. And here was John, receiving such news months after the fact and having to cope, alone.

She looked at the old envelope the letter had come in. It was addressed to the care of Thomas Muxworthy, Main Road, Lovering. Again Gerry referred to the family tree. Thomas was Sybil Muxworthy's father! So John had been a lodger in the very house where his future wife had just been born in 1837.

"Fantastic!" Gerry said, quite loudly. Loud enough to make Bob pause in mid-bite of the catnip mouse. And loud enough that Lightning jerked, uncoiled, stretched, made sure all was well, gave Gerry a peevish look and went back to sleep.

Gerry, at this point wide awake, went downstairs and made a cup of tea. While she waited for the kettle to boil, she wandered around the main floor of her house, thinking about the man who'd built it, imagining him picking the lot of land, supervising its construction, bringing home his bride, raising his family. She brought her tea upstairs and returned to the papers.

First, she wanted to know when John and Sybil had married. Her tree told her 1854, when John was forty-four and Sybil only seventeen! How had such an age difference worked out for them? What had occurred during those seventeen years while Sybil grew up and John established himself as a man of business?

She listed the subsequent papers. Receipts for wood purchased from various landowners along the Ottawa River. John's own lists of men hired by him to transport the wood.

Dates of log booms and calculations of how much wood was lost as it floated down the river.

And more personal papers. A receipt for a suit of clothes he bought in Montreal, and another for a purchase he made at a Montreal jeweller, dated December 15th, 1853.

Gerry smoothed the little paper out. "Cley or," it said. She stared at the words, puzzled. Clay or what? And why buy clay — she assumed a misspelling — at a jeweller's?"

She restacked the papers in the box, turned out the lights and fell asleep to dream she was standing balanced precariously on a log out in the middle of the lake. She woke, knowing something was wrong.

It was still dark. She heard a groan, followed by the sound of retching. "Prudence?" she called, peering into the bedroom next door. Not there. She ran to the bathroom and found Prudence lying on her side on the bathmat, shivering.

"Flu," she croaked.

Gerry patted her shoulder, covered her with a towel and ran downstairs, rushing past several startled cats. She grabbed a large plastic bowl and ran back upstairs. She found a hot water bottle and a heating pad and put them both in Prudence's bed. Then she returned to the bathroom, washed Prudence's face — her teeth were chattering with fever — and supported her back to bed. She placed the bowl next to her pillow. Prudence promptly filled it. "Oh, poor you," Gerry wailed softly and ran to rinse it out. When she returned, Prudence seemed more comfortable, dozing. Gerry went back to her own room and dressed.

"I don't remember dropping my clothes on the floor last night," she muttered, pulling white socks out from under the rocker. Only they weren't white socks.

She found herself holding the rag stuffing from Aunt Maggie's treasured antique cloth doll. "What on earth?" She got down on her knees and scrabbled in the dark corner under and behind the chair, pulling out bits of rag and other assorted objects.

From on her bed, Bob and Lightning watched. "Which of you?" she accused. Bob yawned, looked away and began grooming. "Aha!" She brought the assemblage over to her bed.

The doll had been gutted but could be repaired. Its head lolled on its shoulder and its deflated body made it look pathetic. Gerry put it and its erstwhile stuffing to one side. "Not a catnip mouse!" she admonished Bob, holding up her index finger and pointing from him to the doll.

Bob slowly sniffed the doll and sat back with a satisfied air.

"Cats have absolutely no consciences," mumbled Gerry, sorting through the other objects. Could they have been hidden in the doll? By a child? They were things a child might think were treasures: a lump of what looked like green glass, smooth and bumpy at the same time; a crow or raven feather, long and black; a heart-shaped piece of wood. A groan from the next room made her jump. She ran to assist Prudence.

Much, much later that morning, after Gerry had looked after the cats and checked on Prudence half a dozen times, she was having her breakfast when the phone rang.

"Hello?" she managed, swallowing a mouthful of toast practically unchewed. This set off a spasm of coughing.

"Hello? Hello?" she heard coming from the phone. She took a deep breath and sip of coffee.

"Hello, Father Lackey? Is that you?"

"Do you have a cold, Miss Coneybear?"

"No, no, just food going down the wrong way. How are you?"

"Fine. I'm fine. And I think I may know to whom your bones belong. Shall I tell you over the phone or will you come for a visit?"

"Much as I'd enjoy a visit, Father, I'm looking after a sick friend. Could you just tell me now?"

"Of course. Well, I worked my way back from the late 1800s, looking for a parishioner who had not been buried in St. Peter's graveyard."

"Yes?" Gerry was excited and sat back down at the table.

"I found several."

"Oh. That's disappointing."

"To be expected, I'm afraid. Then I looked for anyone with a connection to your family or property. I didn't find any." Gerry groaned. "Yes. But then I noticed Sheila McCormack, who'd sadly died at an early age — sixteen, I believe — and been buried at St. Pete's, and she'd worked for your forebear John Coneybear at The Maples."

A puzzled Gerry asked, "But if she's buried at St. Pete's?"

"She had a brother, indentured to Thomas Muxworthy." Gerry felt a thrill as she heard the name. "And I can find no record of his burial here."

"He might have moved away," Gerry suggested.

"As an indentured servant he couldn't have done that. And if his term of service was finished, the parish priest of that time would have noted it. I found several examples where he did so for others."

"What was his name?"

"Cormac McCormack. Cormac and Sheila McCormack from County Shannon, Ireland."

Gerry scribbled down the information. "You've been a great help, Father. Thank you so much." She hung up.

On the piece of paper where Cormac and Sheila were noted, she added John, Sybil and Thomas and drew a big circle around them all. Then she began drawing subsets, smaller circles that enclosed just two or more names.

Sybil and Thomas were easy — daughter and father. John and Sheila were circled — employer and servant. She circled Thomas and Cormac — a similar relation. When she had a multiplicity of circles, she put down her pencil.

All the people could be related one to another through their various relationships. If Cormac McCormack had been Thomas's servant, he would have known Sybil and would have frequently seen his employer's partner, John.

"If it was him, how did he wind up under the floor of the woodshed?" she asked Mother, who was stretched out on the hearth rug while the kittens played nearby. If Mother knew, she wasn't telling.

17

Gerry crept silently upstairs and paused outside Prudence's room. A steady snoring convinced her all was well. She went into her own room and tidied, putting the treasures from inside the doll on the mantel. Coughing from next door sent her rushing into the room.

Prudence lay back weakly. "It's just phlegm," she explained. Gerry emptied and rinsed the bowl, wrung out a clean washcloth and brought it to her friend.

"Here, let's give your face and hands a wipe. Could you drink some weak tea?" Prudence nodded. "Are the cats bothering you?" The Honour Guard — Blackie, Whitey, Mouse and Runt — all looked gravely at Gerry. The Honour Guard, so named by Gerry, as they had always slept with Aunt Maggie on this bed and kept up the habit even though she was dead. Prudence shook her head and closed her eyes. She was pale. "So much for moving your drawing table," she mumbled.

Gerry patted her arm. "You sleep for a bit and when you wake up, I'll bring you a nice cup of tea."

Downstairs, she noticed it was nearly noon. Though she'd rather be working on her cake-jumping cats, she turned her attention to updating her daily comic strip — *Mug the Bug*. To her horror, she saw she was only six days away from running out of strips. What if she caught Prudence's flu and was sick for a week?

Before she began, she opened the mail, which had been piling up on the mantelpiece. Another deadline, this one at the bank. She had a certificate due to mature. She'd have to get there soon and sort it out.

She worked hard for an hour, then put on the kettle. Christmas long gone for Mug — he was usually two weeks ahead of the real time of year — she decided to send him on a Caribbean vacation. She played around with how Mug, an infinitesimally small speck on the page, would deal with packing all his stuff in a full-size suitcase, how he would get a passport photo and passport, and how he'd deal with security at the airport. She'd got him to the point of being "frisked" by a baffled security guard (because of course Mug had set off the metal detector), when she made the tea and took two cups upstairs.

Prudence woke as she entered the room and Gerry helped her sit up in bed. "How do you feel?"

Prudence sipped the tea. "That tastes just wonderful. I feel weak."

"It's the house," Gerry stated. "Your house, I mean. And Christmas. And finding Betty Parsley. You were strong when I fell apart. And staying with Charlie and Rita." Gerry grinned. "Hopefully, staying here will prove more relaxing."

Prudence smiled faintly. "Hopefully."

Gerry chatted away. "So Father Lackey phoned. Wait till you hear what he had to tell me." She filled Prudence in about the McCormacks and about the box of papers pertaining to John Coneybear. "Oh, that reminds me." She put down her cup and retrieved one paper from the box in her room. "This puzzled me," she said, holding it out to Prudence. "Clay? At a jeweller's?"

"Don't they teach you French in Ontario?" Prudence queried. "The jeweller is French — Léonard Piché — so the receipt is in French. 'Clef d'or.' That's an 'f' not a 'y.' An old spelling of clé. A golden key."

"Oh. My. God. I missed the little 'd' and the apostrophe. And, yes," she sniffed, "they do teach French in Ontario, just not much or," she finished, lamely, "for long enough, I guess."

She ran downstairs and looked frantically amidst the odds and ends on the living room mantelpiece. Catnip mice, crumpled bills, a pine cone and cedar bough decoration that came apart in her hands when she lifted it. "Aha!" she exclaimed, holding up the little box that Andrew had given her at Christmas. She hardly noticed the finger bone nearby.

She ran back upstairs with the box. She opened it and was just about to say, "Look, Prudence!" as she entered the room. But Prudence had gone back to sleep.

It was hard not to be distracted, but Gerry spent the rest of the day organizing *Mug the Bug* and checking Prudence. Mid-afternoon she dashed out for some supplies — ginger ale and crackers for Prudence — and a quick visit to Lovering's antique shop, where the owner mostly made his money from decorative objects and the odd piece of furniture, but where Gerry knew he also had a tiny jewellery counter.

He verified the key was gold and old and wouldn't have been used for anything other than an ornament. "See the loop at this end? A chain could have been threaded through that, if the recipient wanted to wear it. Did you find a chain?" Gerry shook her head. "Pity. Sometimes an old gold chain is quite valuable. This is nice, but so small, it's not worth much." Gerry thanked him. By the time they were finished, the bank was closed. She went home.

She gave Prudence her snack, took care of the cats and put some leftovers in the oven for herself. Then she sat by the fire with the kitten Jay on her lap and thought.

Yesterday she'd found intertwining connections between a small group of long-dead people. She held them in her mind for a while. Thomas and Sybil. John. Cormac and Sheila. Then she let them go.

Next she thought about all the objects that seemed relevant: the bones, first and foremost; the key Andrew had given her; even the contents of the doll—a green stone, a black feather, a wooden heart.

The bones she associated with Cormac—at John Coneybear's house. The key came from John as well, had been passed down from Coneybear to Coneybear. She went to the phone and dialled. "Pick up. Pick up." She opened the oven door and was prodding her meat pie when Andrew answered. "Andrew!"

"Gerry. You sound excited."

"Well, you know. Leftovers for supper."

"Yum!" He sounded puzzled.

"About that key you gave me for Christmas—"

"Oh, don't you like it?"

"No. I like it. I like it fine. It's just—what exactly did Aunt Maggie say to you when she gave it to you?"

"Oh. Jeez. I was just a teenager, a moody teenager."

"Is there any other kind?" asked Gerry, thinking back to her miserable high school years.

He gave a short laugh. "She said it would unlock my heart's desire."

"And did it?"

"I guess it did," he said in a somewhat surprised voice. "I've reached a good place in my life. I know who I am. Yes, it did."

"And did she say anything about the key's origin?"

"I *think* she said it came from her father, Matthew."

Gerry, who was beginning to think she should just permanently carry around her family tree, or maybe have it tattooed upside down on her stomach, stretched the phone cord as far as the living room table and rummaged.

"Here it is. Sorry, Andrew. Just checking something. So Grampa Matthew was the grandson of John, the first Coneybear. That works."

"Does it? I'm glad."

"Listen, Andrew, I'm having a party this Saturday night. Are you free? Potluck, I think. Prudence has the flu but she should be better by then."

"Just the thing. Chase away the post-Christmas blues. What shall I bring?"

"Can I get back to you? I haven't done a menu yet."

"Sure. Look forward to it."

She put down the phone thoughtfully. Heart's desire. A wooden heart. A key. Just then the oven timer pinged. She ate her supper, finished the comic strips and phoned some of the people she wanted to invite to her party. Before she went upstairs to check Prudence, she did a tour of the house, visiting with the cats.

Ronald, a small white with a thin black moustache, was part of a heap that included the boys — Winnie, Frank and Joe — and Bob, all snoozing on the rug near Mother and the kittens. As Gerry knelt by the dying fire and used both hands to pet everybody goodnight, Bob detached himself from the group, stretched and gave his side a few quick licks.

"Going to accompany me, Bob?" He followed her down the hallway past the cupboards where the family's fine old china and crystal was stored. Gerry was struck by a thought and went back, opening the cupboards and handling the dishes. "We'll have a fancy sit-down dinner for a change, with candles and flowers." She walked through into the large dining room. Eight chairs stood around the massive table and eight sets of eyes followed her as she ranged from chair to chair, patting each one's occupant.

"Hello, Harley. Hello, Kitty-Cat, who should have been called Davidson." The two enormous cats — cow-cats as Gerry described them for their rectangular torsos and irregular black and white markings — were perhaps not quite as big as motorcycles, but each easily filled the padded chair it occupied.

"Hello, Max. Lightning. Hello, Jinx. Who's a good girl, Cocoon?" Gerry straightened and looked at the table. She'd remembered it being larger when she was a little girl. Leaves! It must have inserts to lengthen it. So I could fit another four, possibly six. She imagined laying a white cloth and using the silver salt and pepper shakers and candlesticks, and hugged herself with glee at the imagined picture she'd conjured up.

"Good night, Min-Min," she said to the white deaf cat, and "Good night, Monkey," to the grey tiger stripe, who was sister to the boys, but preferred the calmer company of other cats to the harum-scarumness of her brothers. "Good night, everybody," Gerry said in a soft tone, and switched off the light.

Wearily, she climbed the stairs and paused on the landing, looked out at the lake. Frozen now from shore to shore, it presented an unbroken white plane that began on the back lawn and finished at the pine forest far away across the lake.

She thought of her ancestors, bundled up in furs, walking on the frozen lake, possibly driving carts or carriages across. With a wave of nostalgia that caught in her throat, she thought, how wonderful to be alive, to have been alive as they had been, to walk and wonder, eat, work, enjoy. "We are the dead and they are us," she muttered. Now where had that come from?

Prudence was sleeping. An exhausted Gerry slid between her own covers, was dimly aware of her two cat companions, and dreamt of cats jumping over enormous boxes filled with family papers and family bones.

Next morning Gerry felt inspired. After bringing Prudence a cup of tea and a little bell to ring for assistance, she made a coffee and rushed to work on her book.

Max replied, "You know. Cakes on tables. Cats jump over them. Lots of fun. Woof! Woof!"

"But I've lived here for years," said Latooth, turning to the Queen, "and I've never seen any cats jumping over cakes on tables or anywhere else!"

"It's an old custom," replied Atholfass, "and one no longer much practised." Her eyes gleamed. "But in my day, the cats of Dibble were the most expert cake jumpers in all of Fasswassenbasset."

Lady Ponscomb timidly interjected, "What more can you tell us, Max?"

"Yes, tell us, Max."

All of them — Queen Atholfass, Latooth Élonga, Lady Ponscomb and Count Scarfnhatznmitz — turned to look at young Languida Fatiguée. This was the first she'd spoken in a very long time. They had become used to her silences punctuated only by sighs and to her slow perambulations through the rooms of Castle Dibble, a pre-adolescent apparition that would drift in whenever a fresh cake appeared, eat a slice or two, and drift out.

The friends stared, noting her ever so slightly brighter eyes, then everyone turned their attention to Max and waited for more information. Max eyed the glistening chocolate sponge, wondered about seconds, and absently told what he knew.

"They have this young cat in Crumpet, see? Name of Ernesto. Ernesto 'Crazylegs' Cucina. He's their best jumper. Supposed to be very fast, very high, very accurate. And so all the other cats of Crumpet, especially the young ones, are just crazy for cake jumping. They're all doing it. They have clubs and competitions. The ladies of Crumpet compete to see who can create the most fantastic

The phone rang. Gerry made a small sound of frustration, then jumped to answer it. A weak morning light illuminated her work on the living room table. And she'd just been about to consider the subject of the book's next drawing. Would it be Ernesto Cucina in mid-jump, high over a Gâteau Saint-Honoré, or no, even better, a *croquembouche*, a tower of creampuffs? Bob would be her model, of course. She foresaw a romance between Crazylegs and the Queen.

"Hello?" she said, without much interest, then focused as the word "police" made fantasies of cakes and cats disappear.

It was her contact from finding the bones. They had dated them roughly. Between 100 and 200 years old. They were male. Did she know any more about who they might have belonged to? She mentioned Cormac McCormack and Father Lackey. Did she want the bones? What was involved? They'd arrange to send them for cremation, which she would pay for, and then she could have the ashes.

Gerry felt responsible for the bones. She agreed and hung up. Next she called Father Lackey. "Father? Gerry Coneybear here." She explained what she wanted to do. The priest was amenable and said he'd make the arrangements. As she hung up the phone, she heard the little bell she'd given Prudence tinkling. Calling, "Coming!" she first plugged in the kettle, then visited the sick room.

Prudence was sitting up, her bed covered in old letters. At her insistence, Gerry had brought one of the boxes from the office and she was going through, reading, then meticulously describing the contents of each letter on a neat list. "You're so organized! Do you want lunch?"

Prudence smiled. "Maybe toast. And another cup of tea?"

"I'll eat up here with you and you can tell me what's in the box." Gerry prepared her favourite ham and cheese on a croissant, made toast and two mugs of tea. It all fit on one of Aunt Maggie's old metal trays, one with piecrust edges and stamped all over with a pattern of yellow roses. "Here we are."

The Honour Guard were elsewhere in the house on their own business and the women had the room to themselves. "Well, this is nice," commented Prudence. "It's almost worth being sick to be waited on like this."

"Don't get used to it," Gerry warned. "No. I'm kidding. Take it easy this week and go on your trip soon and you'll feel terrific again. What's in this box?"

Prudence finished the toast and carefully brushed crumbs off the front of her nightie onto the plate. "I took everything out and ordered it. And it's quite interesting. It seems to be mostly papers about the first Margaret Coneybear, Margie that was, but they end when she's widowed in —" Prudence consulted her list. "In 1897. Her husband, Jonas Petherbridge, fell through the ice during harvesting."

Gerry wrinkled her brow. "But how was there ice during harvest time?"

"They were harvesting ice. From the lake. It was a big business. They'd cut chunks of ice and bury them under straw or sawdust in warehouses, then sell them for iceboxes when the weather got hot."

"Oh. And Jonas fell through. Poor Margie."

"She had one son, also named Jonas."

"Wait. I'm going to get the tree. You'd think I'd know it by heart by now." Prudence smiled as Gerry's voice disappeared and she clattered downstairs. She sipped her tea until her return. "Now," Gerry said, breathlessly, "here's Aunt Margie. How many greats?" She counted back, using her finger. "Great, Great Aunt Margie. And her two Jonasas. Oh, look. Jonas the second was Uncle Geoff's father."

The women paused, painfully remembering Geoff Petherbridge, so recently deceased, and by his own hand.

Gerry was the first to recover. "So G.G.A. Margie is the other reason Uncle Geoff and Aunt Mary's children Margaret and Andrew are descended from both of John Coneybear's children. Fascinating."

"Yes. And even more fascinating is after her husband died, she started keeping a diary." Prudence handed Gerry an old volume with silky paper and a soft brown leather cover. "I haven't finished it yet. Read the first entry."

"'May 2nd, 1898. Mother's birthday. My mother was afraid to show me affection. I was ten and she was dead before I realized that she did sometimes, but only when my father was absent. Then she'd caress me and call me her little raven, her little crow. I suppose because of my dark looks.' Oh, that's so sad," Gerry commented.

"Read on," Prudence urged.

"'She said other things, too, which I didn't understand until she was dead and I found the letter which she'd hidden inside the doll.'" Gerry stopped. "But there wasn't a letter inside the doll. Just a few peculiar objects."

"What are you talking about?"

"I'll get them." Gerry fetched the ripped up doll and the treasures it had guarded from her room. She laid them on Prudence's lap.

"But this is your Aunt Maggie's doll."

"Maybe Margie gave it to her?"

"Maybe. Maggie never said. It was just an old doll, handed down in the family. And you say these were inside? What made you look for them?"

"I didn't. Bob thought the doll was a giant catnip mouse, I guess, and ripped it open a few nights ago. I woke up to find its stuffing and these on the floor."

Prudence picked up the green glassy lump. "Huh. I haven't seen a piece of this since I was a girl. We used to dig for it where the old glassworks had been. We thought we were archaeologists or something."

Gerry took the fist-sized lump. "So it's glass?"

"Slag. Leftovers."

"It's pretty." Gerry put the lump down. "Prudence, I have to go to the bank. Will you be all right?"

"I'll be in good hands," Prudence smiled, as the Honour Guard slunk in and, one by one, leapt onto her bed.

Gerry parked in front of the bank. As she walked to its entrance, she saw the old black pickup truck parked there as well. Her eyes widened as she saw, painted on the tailgate, a mass of tiny grey skulls.

After explaining her need, she waited in a little sitting area off to one side. A tall, redheaded man was talking to the cashier dealing with business accounts. As he leaned against the counter, chatting to the girl, Gerry felt her cheeks grow warm. Bea was right. She did feel something for Steve Parsley. She assumed he was on an errand for the Parsley Inn, using his brother's truck.

When he'd finished and was on his way out, he noticed her. He smiled. "Gerry! Sorry I haven't called. It's been so busy at the inn."

"That's okay," she replied in what she hoped was a calm voice. "How are Phil and the kids?"

He sobered immediately. "Still very shocked. The body hasn't been released so the funeral is on hold. It's very disturbing for them."

"I'll bet." She took a deep breath. "Steve, I should have asked you this before. What were you and Betty Parsley arguing about after church just before she was attacked?"

There was a second as he blinked, and then his face went blank. "I don't know what you mean. I never go to church. Unless it's for a wedding. Or a funeral."

She was taken aback and somewhat relieved. "Oh. Maybe it was Ralph. I don't know you well enough to tell you apart."

"I'll ask him," he replied smoothly, "but I doubt he was actually in the church." He laughed. "We were dragged there every

Sunday by our parents. We've both had enough church to last our lifetimes." He looked thoughtful. "But I'll certainly ask him. Yes, I'll do that. See you, lovely lady." And with a wave, he sauntered off.

Gerry concluded her banking. When she got home, she phoned the police. It might mean nothing — Steve and Ralph Parsley might be innocent of Betty's death — but it was time she shared what she'd seen.

18

When Gerry hung up the phone, she realized someone other than she had been active in the kitchen. Cake had been sliced and tea made. "I don't believe it! She's recuperated already?" She made her way upstairs and was surprised to hear another voice as well as Prudence's. She tapped at the partially closed door. "It's me."

"Come in," called Prudence. Lucy Hanlan sat on a chair by the bed.

"My brother had to go to the hardware store," Lucy explained. "He brought me. We're going on to a movie after. I thought Prudence might be up to it, but now I see her…"

"I'm feeling much better. But not washing, dressing and going out better." Prudence had tidied away the contents of Margie's box, except for the diary, which lay on the bed. "I hope you don't mind, Gerry, but I read little bits of Margie's diary to Lucy."

"Such a long life," Lucy commented.

Gerry said, "Remember when you were here before, Lucy? We were talking about the bones in the woodshed." Lucy nodded. "I didn't tell you this yet, Prudence. Father Lackey called me the first day you were ill. He thinks the name of our bones may be Cormac McCormack." Gerry concentrated on Lucy. "Ring any bells?"

Lucy shook her head. "No McCormacks in Lovering now. It's an interesting name, though."

Gerry cocked her head to one side. "You mean because of the repetition?"

"Oh, gosh, no. That's common, or used to be. Neil McNeil or Donald Macdonald. No, I mean its meaning. Cormac means raven. Raven, son of raven. He was probably a dark man, and son of a dark man."

"Prudence, are you all right?" Gerry half-rose. Prudence had paled and had one hand pressed to her chest.

"No, no. I'm — just — tired."

Lucy rose immediately. The doorbell rang. "That'll be my brother. Well, I hope you recover in time for your holiday. Take me with you, eh?" As Lucy preceded Gerry from the room, Prudence mouthed, "Come back quick."

Gerry saw Lucy out, then took the stairs two at a time. "What? Is it your heart?" Prudence, head bent, was flipping through the pages of G.G.A. Margie's diary.

"I've been reading ahead. But remember she starts by talking about her mother, how she calls Margie her little raven, her little crow?"

"Yes, yes. Oh."

"Now. Read this." Gerry read silently to herself:

One day, shortly before my brother Albert was born, and my mother subsequently died, she allowed me to play with her doll. Her mother had made it for her and she treasured it. Father was away on business.

After a while, Mother unbuttoned the back of the doll and took out a carved wooden heart, a lump of green glass and a black feather.

She'd been very ill during this, her most recent pregnancy, and sometimes I would find her holding the doll and weeping. She handed me the three objects and said, "These were given me by my very best friend in the world." I knew at once that it could not be my father who was her best friend, as my mother seemed to

*shrink inside herself whenever he came into a room or
approached her.*

*She continued, "He, he had to leave. This is a jewel
he found and gave me." My ten-year-old hand took hold of
the slag, my ten-year-old brain imagining it to be a huge
emerald. Next she handed me the wooden carving. "This is
his heart, he gave me before, before I married your father.
And this—" She caressed the black feather. "This is his
spirit, the spirit of Cormac."*

"She named him!" Gerry exclaimed. "She named Cormac!"
Prudence waved her hand. "Keep reading!"

*My mother let me handle the objects for a few more
minutes. I especially liked the green glass. Soon we replaced
the objects inside the doll and buttoned it back up. My
mother made me promise not to open the doll again until
I was a grown-up lady.*

*"How will I know I'm grown up?" I asked. "When you
get married," she smiled. "Then you can open the doll. But
you must never let your father see what's inside. Promise?"
I promised, and I kept my promise, except I didn't wait
until I got married.*

*My mother died of a fever, an infection, I guess, a
few days after Albert was born. I and the servants looked
after him. When I was sixteen I decided that wearing long
skirts and being a surrogate mother to a six-year-old boy,
as well as serving as my father's housekeeper, qualified me
as grown up. I opened the doll.*

*Sometime between our conversation and her death,
she'd sewn it closed. I carefully ripped out the stitches and
put my hand inside. I felt wood. I felt glass. I located the
feather. But there had been something added. My mother*

had written me a letter. I read it right away, read it again,
scarcely believing the contents, then fulfilled her request to
me in two ways. I burnt the letter. And I never discussed
any of what I'd learned with my father.

Gerry groaned. "Oh, Prudence. How terrible. She burnt it.
What do you suppose it said?"

"I don't know. Full disclosure? Telling her she was
Cormac's child?"

"Have you finished the diary?"

"No."

"Keep reading! I'm going to Cathy's for supper tonight.
I'll bring you some soup before I go. Try and finish the
diary tonight."

Later, walking to Cathy's, Gerry was fizzing with excitement.
They might learn everything tonight! One mystery might be
solved! As she went up the wide steps onto Cathy's house's
veranda, she remembered the second to last time she had been in
the house. She remembered Betty Parsley.

She knocked and the door opened almost immediately.
"Oh! Hello."

The woman who stood there was tall and thin and nicely
dressed in tight faded jeans and a pink cardigan over a matching
pullover. Little pearl earrings glowed softly. Her makeup was
discreet. The woman put out a hand. "I'm Markie, Cathy's sister.
You must be Gerry. Let me take your coat."

"Thank you. Cathy didn't tell me — I didn't know —"

"I had a few things to wrap up in Arizona, so had to let Cathy
return alone. It was good of you to look after her that first night.
What a dreadful experience for you, finding the body."

Gerry found herself seated on the sofa in the living room, a
gin and tonic in her hand and a bowl of macadamia nuts being
pushed towards her. With a sigh, she leant back and relaxed.

"You've got Cathy's way of making people feel at home. Does she need help?"

"Nope. It's all done. She's upstairs. I made her take a nice hot bath. And I'm going to have a whisky."

They heard the tentative kerplop, kerplop of Prince Charles descending the staircase. He landed at the bottom, paused, and then clicked his way into the living room over to Gerry.

"Hello, Charles, old man. Recovered from your flight?" Gerry gave him a nut. He took it to the hearth rug, where he lay and carefully nibbled. "So what is it you do in Arizona, Markie?"

"I'm a designer."

Gerry looked at the sophisticated woman across from her. "As in, interior designer?"

Markie laughed. "I design aircraft. I'm an engineer as well as a designer. And you? I've heard how you're a commercial artist with a successful comic strip. That's quite an accomplishment for someone so young."

Gerry mumbled something, feeling embarrassed. It was almost as if Cathy's sister was flirting with her!

Just then, Cathy entered the room: a calm, well-dressed, even well-coiffed Cathy. Gerry rose and hugged her friend. "Okay, now I know I'm underdressed."

"Nonsense." Cathy sat on the sofa and Markie brought her a glass of sherry. "I wanted to thank you for our Christmas presents: the little painting of the bluebells on my lawn in the spring, and Charles' jacket." Cathy kicked off a shoe and stroked Charles with her foot. "It makes him look very handsome." Charles grunted. Markie's eyebrows rose in amusement as she and Gerry exchanged looks. "How's Prudence?" Cathy asked.

"Coming along. Ate soup for supper. Sitting up and reading. I take it you had a good trip before you heard about Betty?"

"It was wonderful. We did the galleries and shops. We drove out into the desert. We ate in all kinds of restaurants. And when

Markie had to work, I just lazed in her garden. It's so interesting, Gerry. It's designed with stones and cacti and succulents, no lawn, but clumps of wild grasses. It never needs watering but it's beautiful all the same."

"Not like gardens here, eh, Sis?" Markie held up her glass. "Like another?"

"Yes, why not?" Gerry replied. "Thanks." She scooped up a handful of nuts.

Cathy jumped up. "Oh, Gerry, you're hungry! Well, you girls bring your drinks into the dining room and I'll serve supper."

Gerry and Markie sat at the beautifully appointed table.

"That reminds me," Gerry said as Cathy brought in the soup. "I'm having a potluck on Saturday night. I was hoping you might cook a bird, Cathy. You don't have any guests coming, do you?"

"No. January is slow and I planned to take a few weeks off after my vacation. I'd be happy to cook a bird. Chicken or turkey?"

"Well, at least a dozen are coming. A turkey, I think. I'm going to do a roast beef with garlic. And the dessert. This soup is lovely." Cathy had made a creamy butternut soup and swirled in a dollop of cilantro-infused yogurt.

The main course was a gorgeous chicken curry with a spiced rice side dish and several little chutneys and sauces. They finished with mango ice cream.

"I'm in heaven," Gerry sighed. "I hadn't realized how much I miss Indian food." This led to a discussion between Gerry and Markie about their favourite restaurants in Toronto, where it turned out Markie had lived many years previously. While they were still sitting at the table, Gerry remembered Prudence and rose from her seat. "I'm sorry to eat and read — I mean run — but I really should check on Prudence."

As they said their goodbyes at the door, Gerry kissed Markie on the cheek. Markie flushed and held her hands. "Very nice to meet you, Gerry," and Gerry thought she saw a pleading look in Markie's eyes.

When she got home, Prudence was asleep, the diary on her coverlet. Gerry hadn't the heart to wake her, nor did she take the diary to read herself. For once, she'd be patient. This was Prudence's project. There was no hurry. She went to bed.

She was just dozing off when a crash downstairs jerked her upright. Prudence hadn't woken, so Gerry went to investigate. "Dratted cats! Now what have you knocked over?" Drowsy innocent faces greeted her in the dining room. "Go back to sleep," she told Harley and Kitty-cat, patting their enormous heads.

"It must have come from in here," she muttered, moving to the living room and found the cause of the ruckus. Bob lay stretched to his considerable length on the mantelpiece. "Why, Bob, why?" She felt the mantelpiece; it was warm from the now extinguished fire. "Oh well, I guess that makes sense. But my plant!"

She knelt and collected bits of broken clay pot. "Lucky you didn't brain the kittens with this," she scolded. Bob yawned and went back to sleep.

She threw out the shattered pot, got an empty plastic yogurt container for the poinsettia. "Bruised but not broken," she murmured to it as she resettled its roots. The rest of the pot, dirt, and the now crisp cedar branch Christmas decoration she swept up and dumped into the garbage. Something small and white gleamed up at her.

She picked up the finger bone and put it in the pocket of her robe. "I know where I'm going to put you," she told it and went back to bed.

When she woke up again, it was morning and, on the way back from the bathroom, she smelled coffee, eggs and bacon. She clumped downstairs to find Prudence, dressed, serving breakfast. "Well?" she demanded.

"Well what?" Prudence loaded her own plate, leaving Gerry to serve herself.

"Well, did you finish the diary?"

"Huh. After you left, I fell asleep and I slept for close to fourteen hours. I read nothing. I feel fine, though. Thanks for asking." She gobbled her food.

Gerry felt queasy looking at Prudence's plateful of food and sipped her coffee. "Cathy made Indian food. And I met her sister, Markie."

"You mean her brother."

"No. She was definitely a woman. Markie."

Prudence opened and closed her mouth.

Gerry reacted with some alarm. "Prudence! I knew you shouldn't eat that rich food! Are you feeling ill again?"

"Mark Stribling. Was the boy. Who disappeared. Who I had a crush on. In high school."

"And you think? Oh." Gerry thought for a moment. "She's tall and thin."

"Like Cathy's father. Cathy takes after her mum. You read about it but you don't expect —"

"No. Well. I've invited them both to dinner on Saturday."

"It's good I'm prepared. Otherwise, I might have appeared startled and embarrassed myself." Prudence took her dishes into the kitchen and Gerry heard her running water.

"Prudence, I don't want you working today. If you can help me clean on Saturday that would be great, but till then…"

"I know," said Prudence, appearing in the doorway holding a dishrag, "until then, I'm the designated reader."

Gerry grinned sheepishly. "So much is happening. I'm going to spend the morning with my cats. I mean my imaginary cats. After I clean the litter of my real cats."

"Already done," Prudence said airily, and returned to giving the kitchen a thorough wipe down.

Gerry cursed under her breath and immersed herself in cake-jumping cats for a few hours. Now, where had she left off?

"The ladies of Crumpet compete to see who can create the most fantastic cakes for the cats to jump."

There was a pause as the others digested this news.

"We could do that."

The others jumped. Again it was Languida who had spoken.

"We could do that. I could be the assistant to the cats who jump, set up the cakes and measure heights and so on. And you," she turned to Latooth, "are such a good baker, I bet you could design some amazing cakes." Latooth blushed and sat up straighter. Her jewellery clanked.

"Max, you could show the young cats how it's done, at first. You're such a good jumper." Just to prove it, Max jumped over two chairs and Lady Ponscomb in quick succession, upsetting all three.

"And you, Your Majesty," here Languida curtsied prettily to Queen Atholfass, "would give your Royal Assent and Patronage to the whole affair."

"Never mind that," said the Queen snappishly, her full tail thrashing. "We must challenge Crumpet for the Championship!"

As she righted the last chair and shook herself free of dust, Tess, Lady Ponscomb, plaintively asked, "And I, Your Majesty, what am I to do?"

"Ponscomb, stop whining! You're in charge of publicity. And now, you may all leave me." With that, Queen Atholfass dismissed her court, curled up and had a ten-hour nap.

19

This is so much fun, Gerry thought. She drew a heavy line under the text. That was the end of the first bit. Now she needed an end-of-chapter sketch. She drew the Queen, nose tucked under her tail, asleep on a large cushion. Her crown reposed on a smaller cushion nearby. The other characters tiptoed out of the room through various doors and windows.

Regretfully, Gerry pushed the papers from her. Two days until her party. Two days until her party! She dragged the cake recipe book closer and flipped the pages furiously. "Fancy but not too difficult. Yum. I could do that." She made her grocery list, checked Prudence, who had gone back to bed, clothed, and dozed off lying on top of it. "Prudence, do you need anything in Lovering?" A grunt was her reply.

Gerry decided to do the shopping, then have lunch at the Two Sisters' Tearoom. It was with a happy sigh that an hour later she perused the little menu. Jane stood at her side. "I just made the egg salad. It's served with watercress."

Gerry beamed. "I'll have that then, though I was tempted by your curried chicken sandwich. But I had curry last night."

"So, egg?"

Gerry nodded. "And a coffee, please. Your coffee is so good."

A pleased Jane bustled away and Gerry sat back and let her mind drift. She loved Prudence and loved having her stay, but had to admit she'd grown used to being alone in her own house. Prudence must feel the same. No rush to get back. She let her mind roam over her guest list.

Cathy, Markie, Cece, Bea, Prudence and me. That's six. Mr. Parminter — I mean Blaise — Andrew, Doug and David. Ten.

Jean put down an appetizing-looking sandwich with potato chips on the side, then got the coffee, cream and sugar. "Enjoy," she said and disappeared into her kitchen.

Gerry was the only customer. It was true then, the people of Lovering really did hunker down at home in winter. And tourists were scarce. So why was Jane open?

The woman herself appeared with a tray of scones. Gerry could smell they were warm from the oven. She speeded up eating her excellent sandwich. "Jane, I thought you were going to be closed longer over the holidays."

Jane came over to Gerry's table. "Mind if I sit down? I've been up since before dawn, which, admittedly, in winter is only about eight o'clock. Betty Parsley's visitation is this afternoon. I'm preparing dozens of scones and sandwiches. Apparently, she was quite a fan. So I thought, as long as I'm here, I may as well open."

Gerry was surprised. "So the police have finished with the body." Suddenly, it felt wrong to be sitting here enjoying herself when Betty Parsley was about to receive her send-off. She pushed away the remains of her sandwich.

"You done with that? I'll bring you a nice hot scone — cranberry lemon." Gerry let Jane go. Should she go to the funeral home? No. She felt she'd be intruding. She was just a customer of the Parsley Inn, but then again, she was some kind of cousin to that branch of the Parsleys. She decided no to the visitation and maybe yes to the funeral.

"No, I can't go to either," she said aloud. "I've got to prepare for the party. Oh, I'll ask Prudence." She was enjoying her scone — it was very good — with a second coffee when Annette Bledsoe walked in.

Gerry invited·her to sit.

Annette's face was flushed. Self-importantly, she leaned forward and in hushed tones, said, "You'll never guess." What she had to say made Gerry alter her list of party guests.

Thoughtfully, she drove home, and was just in time to say hello, goodbye before Prudence left, picked up by her friend Lucy. "I'm going to see Mrs. Smith and then I'm going to Betty's visitation. They're my first cousins, Phil and Bill. I didn't think you'd want to come. It's between three and five and seven and nine, if you do."

Gerry unpacked the groceries and decided to get a head start on Saturday's dessert. She baked a sponge cake and made a custard — her first — and left them both to cool. Then she decided, the heck with it, she was a fast reader; she'd have a look at Margie Coneybear's diary herself.

She went upstairs to Prudence's room. Now where? The book could not be found. Mystified, Gerry went back downstairs. It wasn't anywhere she could see. She saw the poinsettia still in its yogurt container. "Right," she told Mother and the kittens. "We're having a party soon. Better spruce the place up." She put on her coat and went out to the woodshed, to the little area they called the potting shed.

She rummaged around for a likely pot and saucer. Then she walked through into where the firewood was stored. What am I missing? she asked herself as she stood and looked down into the hole. Wait a minute. If Cormac worked for Mr. Muxworthy, Sybil's father, why was he even at The Maples? Assuming he'd died there. It wasn't like he had freedom of movement. And his sister, who'd worked at The Maples, was already dead and buried at St. Pete's.

So had he sneaked away, possibly at night, to see Sybil? Had they been together? Was Margie his child? Had John Coneybear found them — Sybil and Cormac — together at The Maples? Or had John found only Cormac, loitering, hoping to catch a glimpse of Sybil?

Gerry felt the hair on her scalp prickle. She saw John Coneybear roll Cormac's body into the hole. Suddenly, Gerry felt sorry for John. Maybe the death had been accidental. A cold sensible voice in Gerry's brain asked, then why hide the body? Marks of violence on it, perhaps? Oh, Sybil didn't know. Of course. If he just threw it in the lake someone might see him, and the recovered body would scream "Murder!"

Gerry pictured John using a crowbar to raise two or three broad floorboards, hiding Cormac, then muffling a hammer as he repositioned the boards. Had the crowbar been the fatal weapon? Had John wiped it with trembling hands before returning it to its usual place in the shed?

She roused herself. All your imagination, she thought, and took her plant pot inside. She repotted the poinsettia and moved it to a window. "Poor thing," she said. "Not much light these days." She put away her cake and custard and made a pot of tea.

She was loath to go to the funeral home. She wouldn't be missed. She made up the fire and waited for Prudence.

Around five o'clock someone knocked at the front door. "That's funny; my friends know to come to the side," she muttered. A brown delivery van was awkwardly parked in the narrow circular front driveway. "I'm not expecting—" she began, then read the name of the sender, a local funeral home. She thanked the driver. "Another time, it's easier to park at the side, at least in winter." She held the box, listening as the driver reversed and pulled forward, reversed and pulled forward, until he could ease the van back on to Main Road.

She opened the box on the entrance hall table and placed the urn containing Cormac's newly cremated ashes there, directly under the painting of John Coneybear. She was ruminating in front of the living room fire when Prudence returned.

"How was it?"

Prudence disrobed, poured herself a cup of tea and sat in the rocker next to Gerry. She breathed in and exhaled deeply. "I may have overdone it," she finally said.

"Have an early night. But what did Mrs. Smith say?"

Prudence reached down into her old black purse and pulled out G.G.A. Margie's diary. "I brought this. I thought it might help Mrs. Smith."

"And did it?"

"We didn't get that far. Mrs. Smith asked if the spirit who'd previously communicated the names Coneybear and Muxworthy wanted to manifest and all hell broke loose." She closed her eyes. "Not at first. At first Mrs. Smith just asked the spirit what it wanted. 'To be with her,' was the answer. Mrs. Smith asked, 'Is she a Coneybear?' and a glass on her kitchen counter shattered. Then she asked, 'Is she a Muxworthy?' One of the chairs at the table rocked from side to side.

"I had written 'Cormac' and 'Sybil' on a piece of paper so Mrs. Smith asked, 'Are you Cormac?' and the chair rocked. Then she asked, 'Is "she" Sybil?' and the chair rocked again.

"I scribbled 'murder' on the paper and showed Mrs. Smith. She was very nervous at this point. 'Get ready,' she said and we clutched the table. 'Were you murdered, Cormac?'

"We both felt the energy in the room get very low, as though our lives were being drained out of us. Then everything in the room started moving. The chairs we weren't sitting in rose, hanging pictures strained away from the wall, the light fixtures twisted. When we felt the table begin to rise, Mrs. Smith shouted, 'Enough!' and it all stopped."

"Good God! What happened then?"

"He'd gone. Mother came through and reminded me to ask Lucy to make new curtains for my bedroom."

"Lucy wasn't there?"

"Lucy's a churchgoer. She doesn't approve of Mrs. Smith. She says, 'Leave the dead to God.' We've agreed to disagree. She waited in her car. I helped Mrs. Smith straighten up her place, then left."

"And then you went to the funeral home? No wonder you're tired."

"Poor Phil. He's lost weight and looks lost. His kids are stepping up, though. Betty trained them well, making them help out at the inn since they were little. They had that visitation organized and moving smoothly."

"How many of them are there?"

"Four. Two boys and two girls. The Two Sisters' did the food. It was terrific."

"I know. I ate there today." Gerry picked up the diary. "Did you finish this?"

Prudence got up and took the book from her. "Not quite. I'll say goodnight."

"It's only six-thirty!"

"Well, I have to sleep now. If I get hungry, I'll fix myself a snack later. Oh, Gerry."

"Yes?"

"The Parsley twins were there."

"Oh?"

"And they were arguing. One of them stomped out while the other stayed and made polite conversation, then he left too."

Gerry murmured, "Ralph and Steve."

Prudence added, "Or Steve and Ralph. I couldn't tell them apart."

After Prudence went upstairs, Gerry made up the fire, ate a sandwich and sat at the table. On one side lay her family papers: the genealogical chart; her notes and Prudence's, listing the contents of various boxes; and one of the as yet unsorted piles. On the other side of the table were the text and sketches for her cake-jumping cats.

Somehow, she wasn't in the mood for either. As her energy temporarily flagged, she decided she needed a break. From the two deaths, from her frenetic work schedule. A day trip somewhere.

She tidied the kitchen, then decided to assemble her dessert for Saturday night. She laid out her materials and began.

She cut the sponge cake into fingers, which she placed in a silver-rimmed cut glass bowl. She sprinkled sherry. She layered raspberry jam, custard, tinned peaches and more sherry-soaked cake — twice. She covered her creation with plastic wrap and put it in the fridge. That's done, she thought with satisfaction.

Now she was in the mood for a slice of Dibble.

Chapter Two
Preparations

Things got off to a slow start.

First to appear were a series of posters, attached by Tess (assisted by Max) to the bottoms of telephone poles and next to the steps at the entrances to Dibble's places of business — the fishmonger's, the butcher's, the pet store, the dog- and cat-grooming salon — where she felt sure they would be noticed by the village's population of perambulating felines.

The first poster simply said CAKE in giant letters, above a drawing of a table crowded with lavish cakes of various shapes and colours.

A few days later, a second poster replaced the first. Now the word JUMP was on the bottom of the poster and a cat was soaring over it.

The third poster, appearing nearly a week after the first, told most of the story. A cat was suspended in mid-jump over a pyramidal cake. A phone number — Castle Dibble's — piped in icing ran around the side of the cake.

So much for publicity, thought Ponscomb, regarding the third poster with satisfaction.

Here Gerry paused from scribbling to sketch the three posters being put up at three different locations. In one little picture, Max was licking the back of a poster, his saliva the glue, while Tess, holding the poster, shrank back in dismay, droplets of spit flying everywhere. In another, in front of the butcher's, Tess struggled with the poster alone while Max howled in front of the shop window where sausages and other delicacies hung out of reach. In the third — well, here Gerry's imagination temporarily failed her and she simply showed the dogs sitting either side of the poster as human legs passed in front of them. She returned to her text.

Meanwhile, Languida and Max (when he wasn't helping Lady Ponscomb) had been figuring out the logistics of jumping. They had to consult with Queen Atholfass, who referred them to the castle library, where they found ancient texts and diagrams, which helped a lot.

Then there was a great deal of quiet measuring and cutting (on the part of Languida) and hammering and yelping (on the part of Max) before the course was ready.

They gathered the others to view it. Max proudly galloped around a few times, to demonstrate, and then a few times more, for emphasis.

The course jumps consisted of planks of wood resting on barrels, old tables with chairs balanced on top, and, as the grand finale, a springboard. As Max boinged off the springboard one final time and landed squarely in a bed of geraniums, Languida said, rather desperately, "Of course, it will look much better with the cakes in place. And this is just the training course. We'll make a better one for the competition."

"Yee-es," said the Queen doubtfully.

Gerry sketched a full-page illustration of all the characters watching, horrified, as Max sailed through the air towards the flowers. Even the butler, Sneathe, peered superciliously from a castle window.

"And that's enough for tonight," Gerry said aloud. She left a note for Prudence, explaining about the next day and, after setting her alarm clock, fell into a deep sleep.

She heard the train whistle blow far down the track where it curved. She began to run, but the case containing all her papers opened with a snap and sheets of illustrations, her family tree and old letters fell out onto the road. She stopped to gather them up.

The whistle blew again and again she ran. She made it to the station platform when the case opened again, and again, all the papers fluttered out.

The conductor shook his head as she approached the steps of one of the cars, retracting them and closing the door.

As the train passed her, she saw her Grampa Matthew, his dead face immobile and pressed against a window.

Her hand slapped the alarm on the clock radio off. "Ugh," she said to Bob. It was so dark out, she almost changed her mind. "No. I need this," she encouraged herself.

She was still encouraging herself when, an instant coffee in her travel mug, she drove to Lovering's train station. But she was congratulating herself when, an hour later, the weak sun appearing ahead of the train, they pulled into Montreal.

After a leisurely breakfast at a patisserie, she visited the auction house where her Borduas was reposing, then waited for the Museum of Modern Art to open. She spent a fabulous day, wandering from gallery to gallery, making notes about technique and subject; ate a super lunch in the museum restaurant of poached salmon on lentils surrounded by a warm arugula salad, and finished with the best lemon meringue pie she'd ever tasted.

Then she walked around Montreal for a while before grabbing a coffee at the station for her ride home. When she came into the house, she knew right away Prudence had gone.

On the back of Gerry's note Prudence had written, "Cleaned house today. Gone to Charlie and Rita's. Construction tomorrow. Will return in time to make pudding for party."

Gerry wondered, pudding?

20

Saturday morning she woke up early after a restless night. A regular dripping noise outside drew her to the window. Water was running off her roof into the eavestroughs.

The day was grey, the frost on her window melting; thin chunks slid down the wet glass. She could see out! Across the road, Andrew's house was a clear black and white. "He's not up," she yawned. Lightning, as usual when Gerry awoke, avoided intimacy by jumping off the foot of the bed and exiting the room. Bob, however, rolled on his back, inviting a game. She rubbed his tummy with one hand while searching for a tissue in the pocket of her robe with the other. "Oh!" she exclaimed and drew out the finger bone. She put it on the mantelpiece next to the things that had been hidden inside the doll. The key was there, too.

"I don't have time for you today, Cormac. I'm sorry." The bone lay indifferently among Sybil's keepsakes. Bob's eyes gleamed as he spied his previous treasure, but he followed Gerry downstairs. After all, it was breakfast time.

Cats fed, litter freshened, coffee in hand, Gerry sat and plotted her day. She worked backwards from when she expected her guests to arrive to the present and found that, if she did her errands this morning, she'd be free until teatime.

The house was almost immaculate from Prudence's cleaning on Friday. A few cat hairs here and there weren't going to scare any of Gerry's friends. Then she thought of the elegant Markie Stribling. Maybe she should fit in a last-minute vacuum of the entranceway and dining room. Her thoughts turned to what she should wear. Rats! She hadn't stipulated dress-up or casual to her guests. It would probably be a mix. So I should dress somewhere in between so everyone feels comfortable, she decided.

This thought process entailed a visit upstairs to peruse her wardrobe. Black dress pants, a white blouse and red scoop-necked sweater were approved. "And I'll make an effort and wear nice shoes," she mumbled, unearthing a pair of pumps from her cupboard.

Somehow, what with getting in wood, playing chase-the-catnip-mouse-tied-to-a-string with the kittens and fretting over clothes, the morning had vanished. "Eeks!" she said when she saw the time. She rushed to Lovering and back, finished her trifle, prepared her beef for the oven and did a quick vacuum. She was just wondering if she should call Prudence to see if she needed a ride, when the woman herself arrived.

Dressed in her work clothes, Prudence had brought a small suitcase. "I'll change later, of course, but I just want to do a quick vacuum."

"It's done," a proud Gerry replied. "All that's left is to cook the beef and set the table. And, er, for you to make your pudding."

"Beef needs to go in now," said Prudence, putting on an apron.

"It's okay. It's prepped and the oven is hot. See?" Gerry proudly took the garlic-studded roast from the fridge to the stove.

"Humph," sniffed Prudence. "You seem to have everything under control. Have you washed and dried the plates and crystal? Polished the silver?" She couldn't keep a straight face when she saw Gerry's anxious one, and laughed. "Hah! Got you. I did it yesterday. Let's get cracking."

In the large dining room, they gently chivvied sleeping cats off of chairs, removing cat towels and relocating them elsewhere in the house. The towels, that is. Relocating cats proved impossible. There were no doors in the wide doorways leading into and out of the dining room. "Whatever are we to do?" wailed an increasingly frustrated Gerry, carefully detaching cat claws from upholstery. The boys had jumped onto the table and were staring up at the crystal chandelier as though they'd never seen it before.

"They'll settle down if we're persistent," calmed Prudence. "Remember, they're creatures of habit." She went into the kitchen and returned with a can of cat food. "Supper time!" The cats as one followed her back to the kitchen. "We'll feed them early, keep them in here for as long as it takes to set the table, then move them elsewhere."

Gerry helped her prepare all the cat dishes, then the women shut the kitchen door on the feeding army of felines. "Whew!" Gerry exclaimed.

They hurriedly spread a white tablecloth and laid the table. The fine china — white with a simple floral pattern in dark blue and orange — and shining crystal and cutlery looked fine. They added silver candlesticks and salt and pepper shakers and stepped back to admire their work.

Increasingly, they became aware of meows coming from the kitchen. The cats, unused to being shut in anywhere, were making their displeasure heard. "This is a nightmare," Gerry moaned. "I'm sweating."

"Come on." Prudence gave Gerry an armload of cat towels and took another herself. They dashed upstairs and spread towels on their beds. Then they each took a litter box, cleaned it, and put it in their bedrooms.

Looking at the little box in a corner of her room, and envisioning ten or so cats attempting to share it, Gerry shouted, "One isn't enough!" and joined Prudence on the stairs.

"I agree!" They repeated the process, then ran to the kitchen and opened the door. "Quick, we haven't much time," gasped Prudence, and, taking one for herself, handed Gerry an open can of tuna and a large dish. Even though they'd just eaten, the smell of the fish focused the cats wonderfully and they followed the women upstairs and into the bedrooms, where they each dumped a can out onto a dish.

With barely enough time to grab her clothes and shoes, Gerry slammed the door to her room. Prudence met her on the landing, laughing and holding a hand to her side. "We can let them out once the guests are seated," Prudence assured Gerry. "Then it's everyone for themselves."

They washed and dressed in their party clothes and met in the kitchen. Prudence had on her emerald green dress. She put a clean pretty apron over it and said, "Now for the pudding."

Gerry remonstrated. "But, Prudence, I made a custard for my dessert. Don't you think a pudding is unnecessary?"

Prudence opened the oven and extracted some of the fatty beef juice that had collected in the roasting pan. She squirted it into a buttered baking dish and put it back into the oven. "Watch and learn."

She beat a very few ingredients together and Gerry was watching and trying to learn when the doorbell rang. "They're here!" she exclaimed and went to greet her guests.

First were Cathy, Markie and Mr. Parminter. Cathy carried the large covered turkey pan into the dining room, Markie handed Gerry an enormous bouquet of flowers and then helped settle Mr. Parminter in a chair at the table. Gerry took a glass plate out of a nearby cupboard. The bell rang again. She gave the plate to Markie. "Could you arrange the cheese on that? Excuse me." She heard Mr. Parminter begin, "Last time we had a thaw like this, the ice —"

This time she admitted Cece, bearing another large covered dish, while a sack from the liquor store hung off his arm. Bea entered using a cane and was ensconced next to Mr. Parminter.

Now that Mr. Parminter had company, Gerry saw Markie continue to make herself useful, finding vases and arranging her flowers, some on the table and some in the entrance next to the urn. Then she opened a bottle of wine and started pouring.

Meanwhile, Gerry was at the door again. Andrew, with more wine, and Doug and David with a box of Christmas crackers, jostled in the entranceway, shedding their boots. "*Dahling*, you look *mahvellous*," drawled Andrew, kissing her cheek.

"Yes, you do," confirmed Doug, likewise saluting her.

"Hi, Aunt Gerry," murmured a shy David, following his father and handing her the box.

"Let me take your coat, David, and then why don't you go through with these—" She handed him back the crackers "—and put one in front of each place setting; it doesn't matter exactly where."

Gerry hung up people's coats on the rack and restored order among the boots strewn on the floor. Then, taking a deep breath, on the occasion of her first formal dinner party, she walked into the dining room.

It was all ready. Her roast was centre stage, flanked by Cathy's golden turkey, Bea's roasted rosemary root vegetables and all the little relishes, pickles, gravies and sauces necessary to the feast.

At that minute Prudence entered, bearing an enormous Yorkshire pudding and everyone at the table cheered. "To Gerry!" toasted Andrew. "To Gerry!" they echoed. Then each of the other cooks was toasted, more wine was poured and they set to. Crackers were pulled, inane jokes read out and paper hats perched on people's heads where they were swiftly forgotten by some and enjoyed by others.

It did Gerry's heart good to look around her table at family and friends, think what a difference the last year had made in her life. Last year's Christmas had been fun. She'd spent it with friends who had a rooftop deck. It had been a mild Toronto day and they'd barbequed their turkey breast and sat around afterwards eating chocolate and listening to their host's collection of jazz.

Now she was in Lovering. The temperature, usually, was sub-zero, but she had all these new people in her life and all these cats. The cats! She excused herself, went upstairs and quietly opened the doors of her and Prudence's rooms.

All was calm. Everyone had settled down. She left the doors open so they could mingle if they wished and returned to her guests.

She noted Cathy and Markie exchanging hats, so Markie's would match her mauve jacket. The yellow hat looked well on Cathy's dark hair. They were obviously having a ball.

Mr. Parminter's red hat slipped off and wafted to the floor where David quietly retrieved it and put it on the table. David was hatless, of course. At seventeen, one's dignity couldn't survive the wearing of a funny hat! Gerry smiled at him and he smiled back. He'd be all right, she hoped.

She looked at his father and wondered if she still felt anything for him. Doug caught her eye on him and toasted her silently, his lips curving slightly.

Gerry toasted him back, keeping her looks demure, but felt her stomach flip and her cheeks redden. Question answered.

She shifted her gaze down the table towards Andrew. He seemed fascinated by Markie, was watching her face and hands, laughing with her frequently. That would be nice, though Markie must be considerably older than Andrew. Like Doug is older than you, a mischievous inner voice reminded her.

"Dessert!" Gerry collected dirty plates and, to her surprise, David, after a nudge from his father, helped her bring them to the kitchen. She prepared coffee and tea and sent him back with the pots. Then, with trembling hands, she sprinkled sliced almonds and candied orange peel on the whipped cream atop her trifle and bore it triumphantly into the dining room.

The guests united in one "Ahhh!!!" Gerry was just digging in with a shining silver serving spoon when a knock at the door surprised them all — except Gerry. "I asked a couple of acquaintances to drop in for dessert," she explained. "Doug? Would you?" He went to the door.

Andrew produced a large box of chocolates and had just begun passing it around when a puzzled-looking Doug led Steve and Ralph Parsley through.

"Pull up a couple of chairs, Steve. Ralph. Trifle?" Gerry saw Prudence and Bea give her quizzical looks. "Ralph and Steve play on Doug's curling team. I met them when Doug was introducing me to the sport."

Ralph was enthusiastically wolfing down Gerry's trifle. "Say, you got booze in this?" He half rose from his seat. "I brought a two-four. It's in the truck. You want I should get it?"

"That's very nice of you, Ralph, but we're okay for now."

"All right. You just let me know. If you run out of wine."

Steve sat upright in his chair, eating the dessert and drinking a coffee. "Very nice, Gerry." His gaze travelled around the room. "Thank you for including us." His eyes rested on Markie. "I know everyone except this charming lady."

Gerry did the honours. "Markie Stribling, Steve Parsley."

Markie graciously made an effort. "Any relation to the Parsley Inn Parsleys? My sister tells me we must dine there before my holiday is over."

"It's closed," Ralph blurted, "until our cousin gets his act together. Meanwhile, us employees starve."

"We're not starving, Ralph," Steve said. "Phil's lost his wife. It's to be expected he'd take a break from work." He looked at Markie. "And yes, we are related to Phil, but the connection goes back a few generations."

Cathy interjected in a low voice, "I wonder if the police are any closer to finding who did it. It makes me anxious, knowing the person who killed Betty is still out there. As soon as I got home, I had the locks changed."

Gerry nodded. "You were wise to do that, Cathy." She lowered her voice. "I called the police this week. To tell them something I hadn't thought important enough. And they've been questioning someone who works at the inn. One of the waitresses."

Ralph sat up straight on hearing this bit of news. Steve just sipped his coffee. The other guests focused on what was happening. What *was* happening?

Gerry continued. "I called to tell them I'd seen Steve, or Ralph, arguing with Betty Parsley after church the Sunday she went missing. I told them I was sorry, but I couldn't tell the twins apart." There was a painful hush in the room. Ralph Parsley blinked furiously. Steve gently tapped the table with one finger. Prudence left the room.

"And then I met Annette Bledsoe, one of the Parsley Inn's waitresses, at the Two Sisters'. And she told me a bit about DNA — what the police told her. About how they'd found Phil Parsley's DNA on Betty. But only where you'd expect. Apparently, he kissed her cheek." Here, Gerry's voice caught, as the reality of Phil's loss and Betty's loss of life, took her over.

"But the police found other DNA on Betty's face and head. She'd been beaten, you see." Gerry was sorry to see Mr. Parminter shading his eyes with one hand, but heartened when David put one arm around the old man's shoulders. She smiled briefly at the boy and he nodded.

"That was the cause of the delay in the investigation — the other DNA was so similar to Phil's. It had to belong to a Parsley." Ralph Parsley caught his breath and looked wildly around the room. His brother laid a hand on his wrist to calm him.

"Lots of Parsleys and Parsley relatives in Lovering," Steve said smoothly, "And in this room." He looked at Prudence, who'd just slipped back into her seat.

"I know," said Gerry. "That's why they were so pleased when I phoned. It narrowed the field. So they started interviewing the staff at the Parsley, discreetly."

"Didn't interview me!" Ralph interjected violently. "They interview you, Steve?" Steve shook his head.

Gerry focused on Ralph. "She saw you, Ralph."

His mouth hung open. "Who?"

"The waitress I said was helping the police. Saw you bringing boxes of liquor up from the inn's basement during the party."

"Annette? Well, she told me to. Told me Betty wanted this and that, so I brought the stuff up. Didn't I, Steve?" Steve nodded.

Gerry turned her gaze to him. "Oh, were you at the party, Steve? I'd have remembered seeing you, I think."

Steve answered quietly, "Helping out behind the scene. Like Ralph."

"Huh. I'll bet." Gerry appeared to think. "I'll bet it'll turn out you, Steve, and possibly you, Ralph, were fiddling either the books or the liquor orders, or both, and Betty suspected you and accused you. 'Cause you weren't in love with her, were you? Remember when you said how sorry you were I found the body?" All eyes shifted to Steve, who remained impassive. Gerry continued. "That got me thinking. What a weird thing to say." She shivered. "And cold. So if it wasn't for love, it must have been for money. I'll bet you told her some story about the missing liquor being 'temporarily' stored in Cathy's basement and got her there the night of the party, ostensibly to show it to her, even return it. I wonder if you, Steve, tried to blame Ralph and protest your own innocence and she didn't buy it."

Ralph blustered. "Steve wouldn't rat on me, would you, Steve?"

His brother merely laid a restraining hand on his twin's arm and looked warily at Gerry.

She continued. "Anyway, back to DNA. Annette helped with that, too."

Steve narrowed his eyes. "Oh, yes?"

"You two were giving Phil a hand with inventory a few days ago. And she brought you cans of pop when you got thirsty."

"Yeah," Ralph said indignantly. "She gave Steve the last cola and me a ginger ale, when she knows we both always drink cola." There was a pause and Ralph added a deflated, "Oh."

"We're identical, I'd just like to point out," Steve stated calmly. "And, as far as I know, our DNA is, too. Come on, Ralph. I think we've provided enough entertainment for these ladies and gentlemen tonight."

Gerry, her heart pounding, watched them stand and turn to leave. "Oh, you are identical, Steve, but there's a newish test that can differentiate between twins. Didn't you know?" Steve stood still to listen, his back to the room. Ralph turned, his mouth agape.

"It's called melting curve analysis. I think." Gerry's voice faltered. "I googled it," she added defensively. "Identical twins' DNA is identical, but as they age, their lifestyle choices change their DNA, as they change all of our DNA. For example, Ralph, here, smokes. I've never seen Steve with a cigarette." As Steve slowly turned to face her, the brothers exchanged a look. Gerry gave another example. "And while I know Steve drinks — remember slipping that dose of whisky into my coffee, Steve?" Doug's eyes narrowed and he stood up suddenly, his chair falling over backwards. Prudence laid a cautionary hand on his arm.

Steve flicked them a contemptuous smile and nodded. "I remember."

"While Steve likes a drink, I think it's Ralph who's the alcoholic."

Ralph snarled, "I can quit anytime. I just like the taste of beer, that's all."

Gerry repressed a startled reaction as a cat's body pressed around her ankles. "So the police are quite confident that they'll soon identify whose DNA is at the murder scene and on Betty Parsley's body." The cat, Bob, jumped onto Gerry's lap. She stroked him, feeling her sweaty palm on his fur. She looked right at Ralph Parsley. "Who does it belong to, do you think? Ralph?"

With a cry of terror, Ralph took a step back, jostling Steve, and Doug moved to do something — Gerry later wondered what — smack Steve in the nose? Markie also made as if to rise.

But Bob beat them all. He used the short hop from Gerry's lap onto the table to launch himself over the trifle straight at the twins.

21

Mr. Parminter slumped suddenly in his seat and all eyes shifted to his frail form. Almost all eyes. David and Markie moved. David pulled Mr. Parminter out of harm's way while Markie reached Ralph and punched him so hard in the jaw he fell onto the floor.

Gerry shouted, "Call 911! Call an ambulance! Oh, my God!" She moved to the end of the room, where David was supporting a suddenly revived Mr. Parminter, who was taking in the action with sparkling eyes. "He's all right?" a dazed Gerry asked.

Meanwhile, Bob, after raking Steve's face, had ricocheted back onto the table, where he sniffed the remains of the trifle, recoiled at the smell of sherry, and settled for lapping cream out of a jug. Doug grappled with Steve.

Ralph moaned, "You said she fell, Steve. You said she fell."

Steve, hearing his brother incriminate him, made an extra effort and freed himself from Doug. He made for the front door. Flashing blue lights on arriving police cars caused him to turn. He raced out the back door onto the porch. Those still in the dining room saw his blurred outline for a moment as he dashed past the windows. Then he was gone. Doug rushed out after him.

Suddenly, the dining room was silent. Everyone started talking at once.

"Are you sure you're all right, Mr. Parminter?"

"You're never going to call me Blaise, are you, Gerry?"

"Blaise, are you all right?"

"We created a diversion, didn't we, David?"

David positively grinned.

Cathy patted her sister's hand with a water-moistened napkin. "Oh, sweetie, I wish you'd remembered to take off your rings."

"It's not too bad," Markie replied gruffly. "Don't make a fuss."

"Well, I think you're very brave," commented Bea.

Ralph, being watched over by Andrew, wailed from the floor, "No chick packs a punch like that! That ain't no chick!"

"She is if she wants to be," Andrew replied, giving Markie an admiring glance.

Calmly, Prudence and Cece cleared the table of the dessert plates. When Gerry followed them into the kitchen, she found them washing up. "You called the police, didn't you, Prudence?"

Prudence nodded.

"Sensible woman," Cece commented.

Gerry continued, "Aren't you curious about what's happening outside?"

"Go and look," suggested Prudence. Gerry put on her coat and boots and let herself out the side porch door.

She breathed the unusually soft air. Almost like spring, she thought. A fine mist fell from above and the land exhaled a thin vapour. She turned her attention to the frozen lake, where a few lights bobbing along the shoreline informed her of the presence of the police. But where was Steve? And Doug? She walked down the backyard's incline to the edge of the lake.

Far out, she spied first one, then two dark figures running. Steve must be trying to cross to get to the deep dark pine woods on the other side. The figure closest to her was gaining on the other. Doug must be so pissed off, she thought.

Steve looked over his shoulder, put on a burst of speed, lurched and dropped from view. He'd gone through the ice.

Doug braked, then, to Gerry's horror, got down on his stomach and began slowly crawling toward the hole in the ice. "Hey! Hey!" Gerry yelled, jumping up and down and attracting the attention of the police. "Man in the lake!" she cried. Two of the officers dashed onto the ice while the other two rushed toward her.

"Do you have a long ladder, a rope?" one shouted.

"Yes! Yes! Both! In here!" she struggled up the slope to the shed. Locked. Banging open the kitchen door, she clawed for the key on the rack, handed it to one of the police, then shouted at the startled Prudence and Cece, "Steve's gone through and Doug's going after him."

"Good God!" she heard Prudence exclaim as she dashed back outside to the shed.

"No! No! We can't go in that door!!" She led them to the front of the shed. Focus, Gerry, a voice told her.

They located the ladder, the one last used by Doug to clear the eavestroughs of autumn's leaves, and the rope. Gerry realized there was no way they could turn the ladder to fit out the small door they'd just entered by. "Break a window!" she said.

They heaved a piece of wood through the glass and pushed the ladder out. By now most of the occupants of the house were outside. Cece and David ran with the police and equipment onto the ice. "I'm going, too," said Gerry.

"No, you're not," Prudence replied firmly, holding her by the arm. "Unless you want me out there with you."

Andrew, supporting the sagging Ralph, joined the group. "Certainly not, Gerry. Let the professionals do their job."

And indeed, once near the break in the ice, the police motioned Cece and David to stay back and went into action.

Gerry counted bodies. "One, two, three, four. How many police were there? Where's Doug?" A gasp went up from the group assembled in the backyard as the police pulled one body out of the freezing cold water.

"Oh God, oh God, oh God," moaned Gerry, jumping up and down. Then a cheer broke out from her guests as David stumbled toward the rescued man, clasping him; he and Cece leading him back towards the house.

"Steve!" The force of Ralph's scream ripped through their hearts. He broke free of Andrew and stumbled through the snow and onto the ice. Cece and David had their hands full with Doug and ignored Ralph as he raced past them. The watchers saw one of the officers catch him and handcuff him and turned their attention to Doug, who could hardly walk.

"*Not* brandy," said Cece. "Hot tea with sugar. A heating pad, hot water bottle, wool. Anything to warm him up." They all ran toward the house.

Doug's white face with blue lips scared Gerry but galvanized Prudence. "Bring him by the fire. Move the cat's box, Gerry. Wool blankets on the back bedroom's bed, David. You know where it is. And there's a heating pad under the covers. Hot water bottle in the upstairs toilet. Better bring some towels, too. Cathy, make tea. Markie, go tell Bea and Blaise what's happened. Gerry, go get your robe and slippers."

They dispersed on their errands. By the time Gerry returned, Doug had been stripped of his wet clothes and wrapped in Cece's coat, his bare feet outstretched toward the newly blazing fire. He was shivering violently.

David appeared, his arms full. Prudence took a blanket, held it as a screen while Cece rubbed Doug down with a towel. "Gerry, your robe," Prudence commanded. Gerry handed it over along with her slippers. So focused were they all that the arrival of a fire truck and ambulance barely registered.

Gerry could hear Doug's teeth chattering. Prudence wrapped a woollen blanket around Doug's upper body, including his head, then used another to enclose his lower half. "You'll do," she said, pushing him back down into a rocking chair.

"Tea!" Cathy said. "We made enough for everybody." People brought chairs in from the dining room. Bea and Blaise were helped into the now warm living room. Everyone sipped their tea. Prudence held Doug's mug to his lips.

"W-W-W-Winnie-the-Pooh?" whispered the shivering form huddled by the fire. It stuck one foot out from under its blanket wrapping. "Sp-SpongeBob s-s-slippers?" There was a startled silence followed by a roar of laughter as they realized Doug was critiquing Gerry's wardrobe selection.

"I draw comics, okay?" She grinned defensively. "Those guys are my heroes." This seemed to strike everyone as even funnier and they roared the louder.

Prudence kept to the protocol and removed one slipper. "His toes are all right," she commented. "Let's see your fingers."

"No Scooby-Doo mittens?" joked Doug in a steadier voice and poked his hands out for inspection.

"They're pink," Prudence announced calmly. "Let's see your face." She bent over and peered under the hooded blanket. "No more blue lips. You'll live."

"Thank God it wasn't twenty below," said Bea.

"If it had been, the ice in the middle of the lake wouldn't have thawed and no one would have fallen in," Cece replied soberly. This reminded them that someone else had gone in the water and their faces became serious.

Doug shook the blanket off his head. "Can I come out now, Prudence?" he requested meekly. "I'm sweating." She felt his brow and nodded. Doug slowly emerged. "I'm stiff," he said. "Not used to running. What's happening out there?"

Markie and Andrew were nearest the window. Markie spoke. "The police are standing around. With firefighters, too. And they have a stretcher. There was a pause. "They're coming this way, but they're not hurrying." The implications of this sunk in.

"Poor Ralph," Gerry said softly.

Only the meowing of hungry cats got Gerry out of bed the next day. That, and the sound of the bell at St. Anne's church, alerting her that it must be almost ten o'clock.

"Cats must eat," she grumbled, as she sat on the edge of her bed. Where were her robe and slippers? The events of the previous night came rushing back. "You knew, eh, Bob?" She tickled his tummy, and his paws, claws sheathed, clutched her hand. She felt an uncharitable spurt of pleasure at the thought that maybe Bob had inflicted on Steve Parsley a fraction of the pain he'd caused Betty.

The meows downstairs grew more insistent. Slipping on a pair of socks, she padded downstairs in her pajamas, eyes half shut. She fed the cats and prepared coffee.

In the living room, she found her robe and slippers in front of the dead fire. One of the kittens was curled up inside one of the slippers. Shifting the little beast back into the banana box, she yawned and put on her robe.

It smelled of Doug. Her senses tingled and suddenly, she was awake. She was just enjoying a second sniff when she heard Prudence's shuffle behind her. Hastily, Gerry bent over and slipped on her slippers.

"Going to sniff them, too?"

Gerry scowled at Prudence's back as the housekeeper entered the kitchen in search of her own coffee. She decided dignity demanded she ignore the remark.

"You were very efficient last night, Prudence." Gerry's voice sounded stiff and formal in her own ears. It warmed as she added, "You were great."

Prudence took possession of the other rocker with a sigh. "You were pretty great yourself, getting the ladder and rope out so quickly. The story might have had a different ending if you hadn't." They were silent, mulling over that possibility.

Gerry spoke first. "I think everyone was splendid. Imagine Blaise faking a heart attack to distract Steve and Ralph."

"And Markie," added Prudence.

"I know, right?" There was another pause. "She and Andrew seemed to hit it off. You all right with that?"

Prudence nodded. "I have to be, don't I?" Both stared at the cold fireplace.

"So," Gerry queried, "breakfast? There's leftover trifle."

Prudence smiled her thin-lipped smile. "You go ahead. I'll just have toast."

After they'd eaten and dressed and tidied up the remaining mess from the party, it was lunchtime. Left-over roast beef and turkey made wonderful sandwiches. Just as they were wondering what to do with themselves, Father Lackey phoned.

"Would this afternoon suit you? It only takes about twenty minutes."

Gerry agreed, hung up and inquired of Prudence, "You coming?"

"Of course. He contacted me, after all."

They drove to St. Pete's. Father Lackey came out onto his porch as they parked. "Sunday is, of course, my busiest day, but I wanted to get this done as soon as possible. There he is. Good."

If he noticed the seal on Cormac McCormack's funerary urn was broken, he chose to say nothing, and led them to a freshly dug little hole in the cemetery. "We think this is where the paupers were buried long ago; people who couldn't afford a grave marker. So, presumably, his sister Sheila is close by." He said a few prayers; Gerry put the urn in the ground, a lump in her throat; a few more prayers and it was done. Both women sighed.

"Thank you very much, Father." Gerry shook his hand. Prudence did likewise and they walked away. "Did you —" Gerry asked Prudence.

"Shush. Tell you later."

Once home, their energy flagged. They relaxed. Gerry made tea. "Why did you open the urn?"

Prudence produced G.G.A. Margie's diary. "Because of this."
"You finished it?"
Prudence nodded. "Read this bit. Towards the end."
Gerry read:

*Feb. 14, 1945. Now that I've outlived both my husband
and my son, I see no reason to keep hidden the thoughts
and revelations that have occurred to me during a long
long life.*

*I'm ninety years old and can't live much longer. My
sister-in-law Elizabeth, though elderly herself, is more
vigorous than I. I feel sure she will outlive me. But in
case she doesn't, I wish to leave a correct account of my
parentage, so no wrongful inheritance ensues.*

*When I was ten, my mother died, and when I was
sixteen, noticing a doll she had cherished was becoming
frayed by my brother Albert's handling of it, I examined it
with a view to repairs.*

Gerry looked up. "But earlier, she wrote that she decided to
look inside the doll because she felt grown up."
Prudence shrugged. "The memory plays tricks. Both may
have been true. She saw the doll was frayed and remembered her
mother's words."
Gerry continued:

*As I poked at the stitches, something crackled inside
the doll, so I opened her up. Inside were the feather, the green
glass lump and the wooden heart, all as I remembered.
And, somewhat crumpled, was an envelope with my name
on it, written in my mother's hand.*

*As I took out the letter, a small golden key fell onto
my lap. I set it aside and read.*

Gerry looked up again. "It's like peeling an onion. Layer upon layer."

"Be careful you don't cry," Prudence admonished dryly.

I will paraphrase from my mother's letter. All those years ago, I was aware only of shame and revulsion and though I destroyed it after I read it, terrified my father or Albert might one day read it and discover — but I'm getting ahead of myself.

My mother told of her happy childhood in Lovering and of how, when she was about ten, her father indentured a servant, a little Irish boy named Cormac McCormack, who, with his sister Sheila, had immigrated to Canada.

Her father had no use for Sheila and she became a servant elsewhere and eventually in the house of John Coneybear. My mother, Sybil, grew up an only child and so was attracted to Cormac, first as a playmate, and then, as the two became young adults, as more than playmates. They became lovers and my mother became pregnant, though she said she didn't know she was.

She'd long been affianced to John Coneybear by her parents, but, as Cormac's period of indenture was almost up, planned to marry him. In a piece of bad business, her father claimed the accumulated time Cormac had been ill over the years was to be added on to his period of servitude and refused to free him at the previously appointed time.

Terrified of running away and fearing to lose her parents' approval, my mother acquiesced and married John. Weddings were different in those days; quiet, the way Christmas used to be. A quick ceremony, a breakfast with her family, and Sybil was led away to her husband's house. And, eight months later, I was born.

I used to wonder why my father would sometimes fix me with a look, especially when I was chattering or laughing, a look in which his curled lip and narrowed eye spoke of contempt. I don't remember if he looked at my mother the same way.

I only know that by the time I was aware of her as a person she had wilted and died. And, shortly after I was born, Cormac McCormack was also gone.

My mother wrote that one morning her husband brought her the little gold key he'd given her before they were married. He had a strange look on his face. He asked her if she'd lost it and she had to say yes. Of course, she'd foolishly given it to Cormac after her marriage, in an attempt to assure him of her continued love. Soon she learned from her mother that McCormack had "run off." And she believed he had until just before her death.

Painfully, I read how my father (Perhaps I should refer to him as Coneybear, as he was not my father, though he supported me until I married.) pressed himself for years on my unwilling mother, and how she bore him child after child, only to see them sicken and die. How, while she was pregnant with my brother Albert, he told her what had happened to Cormac ten years earlier.

How, made sleepless one night by my infant crying, Coneybear had gone outside. How he'd surprised Cormac lurking behind the shed. How Cormac had reviled him and declared his love for Sybil. How Coneybear, angered, had seized a rock, rushed at the much younger man, who'd tripped. How, while Cormac had lain there, stunned, the other hit him once in the head. How once had been enough. How he'd slid the great doors of the shed open, praying no one would hear. How he'd pried up the floor of the shed, dragged and dropped the body, *replaced the floorboards, and returned to his house. How he'd found the key on a cord around Cormac's neck and taken it. How he'd later brandished it in front of my mother's sorrowing face.*

It's no wonder my mother died shortly thereafter. I believe she simply turned her face to the wall and let go. I helped the servants care for Albert until he turned twenty-one, at which point I married Jonas Petherbridge, a good man, taken from me too early.

"That's enough," said Prudence, handing Gerry a tissue. "The rest is about her marriage and her son, with a little about your Uncle Geoff at the end."

"And now they're all gone," Gerry said, wiping her eyes. "Well, we suspected murder, but it's terrible to have it confirmed."

Prudence produced a small Mason jar half full of pale grey ash. "It's obvious Cormac wants to be with Sybil. You know it's her over in the crypt?"

"I never got over there to check," said Gerry. "And John?"

"In the graveyard with Albert and Margie. I thought we could take this over to the crypt and sprinkle it around. It's as close as we can get him to where she's buried."

Gerry spoke thoughtfully. "Why have a crypt, anyway? I know St. Anne's wasn't built yet when Sybil died, but there were other churchyards."

Prudence shrugged. "Too far? People liked to keep their dead nearby, the way you buried Marigold under her favourite hydrangea bush. We guess where spirits need to be to rest."

"Let's do it now," Gerry said impulsively, jumping up.

They crossed the road to the bit of land where the Coneybear family crypt squatted in the twilight. Gerry carried a pointed spade. They eased through the hedge and stood in damp melting snow, looking at the plaque. "Sybil and her babies." Gerry shivered.

The crypt had been sealed with mortar and stone long ago. Gerry dug a small shallow trench below which the earth was frozen. "That's good," said Prudence, who crouched and gently shook the ashes out of the jar, then covered them.

"Should we say anything?" Gerry whispered.

"No need," Prudence replied in a low voice.

Arm in arm, the two women returned home.

*T*he black cat crouched in the hole, his white-tipped tail twitching. Once again, without her seeing, he'd followed the girl into the shed that smelt deliciously of mice, and once again, after she'd taken her many loads of wood into the house, she'd unknowingly locked him in.

It was early evening. He could, if he wanted to, jump out of the hole, onto the woodpile and through the newly broken window into the soft cold snow outside. He could make his way to one of the many doors or windows of the house and meow, make himself known to the two inside.

But he'd had his supper and was content to stay in the hole, listening for the sound of a mouse moving in the walls of the shed.

And he had his toy.

The wispy man who didn't speak had woken him from a nap on the girl's bed that afternoon, had pointed to the bone on the mantelpiece.

The cat had jumped from bed to floor to chair, from chair to mantel, and retrieved it. The wisp had beckoned him downstairs where they'd waited quietly for the moment when the girl opened the kitchen door and then the door to outside.

The cat nudged the bone and waited. He cocked his head, then turned it. The wisp disappeared through the cat-sized tunnel under the road. Picking up the bone, the cat trotted after him.

Deep enough to stay unfrozen, the tunnel smelt of fresh earth. The cat paused and his ears flattened as a vehicle drove over the road, making the earth vibrate. Once on the far side of the road, the cat turned to follow his usual path to the basement where all the fuss about a strange woman's body had occurred.

But the wispy man had gone a different way, a way the cat had always avoided because it was too wet. And because of the *unseasonal thaw, the little underground stream that had made the alternate path was moving.*

The cat made a growling noise. But the wisp was beckoning. Making a second small complaining noise, the cat followed.

Ordinarily, he was not a cat who minded getting his white boots wet. But this was cold. The little waterway had carved out a tunnel, now half-filled with water, and the cat became soaked to his belly.

The tunnel sloped upward. The cat followed the wisp and climbed out of the tunnel into a little stone room. Inside were a large long box and four little boxes. The wisp was swirling in one corner of the room.

The cat dropped the bone on the floor and sat.

It took a few seconds, but soon the largest box began to leak another, different smoky wisp. The cat watched the two comingle and become one. They seeped back into the box and the room became still.

Regretfully, the cat left its toy on the floor and turned to leave. He hesitated. He could go ahead to the warm basement or back to the cold shed. Either way, he wasn't worried. Somebody would let him in.

A NOTE ABOUT BLAISE'S POEMS

Sadly, *Elegies in Elysian Fields* is long out of print, though one of the poems — "The fields begin to sheathe themselves'" — recently appeared online in *JONAH Magazine,* and another — "This cold winter" — was published in *The Nashwaak Review* not too long ago.

GERRY'S VERSION OF
"THE TWELVE DAYS OF CHRISTMAS"

On the first day of Christmas, someone gave to me,
my car crushed under a tree.
On the second day of Christmas, someone gave to me,
two ham and cheese.
On the third day of Christmas, someone gave to me,
three of Jane's scones.
On the fourth day of Christmas, someone gave to me,
four loads of firewood.
On the fifth day of Christmas, someone gave to me,
five golden onion rings.
On the sixth day of Christmas, someone gave to me,
six litter boxes.
On the seventh day of Christmas, someone gave to me,
seven marshmallow squares.
On the eighth day of Christmas, someone gave to me,
eight lovers' letters.
On the ninth day of Christmas, someone gave to me,
nine red herrings falling.
On the tenth day of Christmas, someone gave to me,
ten catnip mice.
On the eleventh day of Christmas, someone gave to me,
eleven cats a'leaping.
On the twelfth day of Christmas, someone gave to me,
twelve Austin Minis.

A NOTE ABOUT THE AUTHOR

Born in Montreal and raised in Hudson, Quebec, Louise Carson studied music in Montreal and Toronto, played jazz piano and sang in the chorus of the Canadian Opera Company. Carson has published six other books: *Rope*, a blend of poetry and prose; *Mermaid Road*, a lyrical novella; *A Clearing*, a collection of poetry; *Executor*, a mystery set in China and Toronto; *In Which: Book One of The Chronicles of Deasil Widdy*, historical fiction set in eighteenth-century Scotland (book two, *Measured*, and book three, *Third Circle,* are scheduled for publication in 2018 and 2019); and *The Cat Among Us*, the first Maples Mystery. Her poems appear in literary magazines, chapbooks and anthologies from coast to coast, including *The Best Canadian Poetry 2013*. She's been short-listed in *FreeFall* magazine's annual contest three times, and won a Manitoba Magazine Award. She has presented her work in many public forums, including Hudson's Storyfest 2015, and in Montreal, Ottawa, Toronto, Saskatoon, Kingston and New York City.

She lives in St-Lazare, Quebec, where she writes, teaches music and gardens.